Cruise

BOOK #6 IN THE MOONSHINE TASK FORCE SERIES

LARAMIE BRISCOE

Edited by: Elfwerks Editing
Cover Art by: RedBird Designs
Proofread by: Dawn Bourgeois & Danielle Wentworth
Beta Read by: Keyla Handley, Danielle Wentworth, Ash Luna
Cover Photography: Wandar Aguiar
Model: Forrest

ALSO BY LARAMIE BRISCOE

Heaven Hill Series
Meant To Be
Out of Darkness
Losing Control
Worth The Battle
Dirty Little Secret
Second Chance Love
Rough Patch
Beginning of Forever
Home Free
Shield My Heart
A Heaven Hill Christmas

Heaven Hill Generations (Spin-off Series)
Hurricane

Rockin' Country Series
Only The Beginning
One Day at a Time
The Price of Love
Full Circle
Reaper's Girl

The Red Bird Trail Trilogy
Flagger
Collision
In-Tune

Stand Alone
Sketch
Sass
Trick

Moonshine Task Force Series
Renegade
Tank
Havoc
Ace
Menace
Cruise

SIGN UP FOR NEW RELEASE ALERTS
www.subscribepage.com/LBML

JOIN MY READERS GROUP
http://fbl.ink/LaramiesLounge

DEDICATION

To women like my friend, Keyla who love the men that keep the streets safe. Who stay at home at night with their children while their loved ones take care of everyone else. To the spouses and significant other's whose hearts skip a beat as they wait to hear them come home at the end of every shift.

To men like her husband, KC who risk their lives every day they go to work. Many times they aren't sure if they'll make it home, but they are the first people we call when we need help. They selflessly give every piece of themselves, even when others may not appreciate it. Thank you for your commitment and sacrifice.

To everyone who loved the series enough to read it through the end. Thank you for loving these characters, for embracing them, and letting me show another side to what everyone assumes they know. Thank you for letting me show these men as friends, husbands, sons, fathers, and brothers.

What started as a little pew pew turned into a life-changing experience for me. The town of Laurel Springs will always have a special place in my heart!

Thank you for loving the MTF and thank you for reading!

The kid is now a man, and he's got something to prove…..

Summary:

Caleb "Cruise" Harrison

"A dad is a son's first hero…"

All my life I've looked up to my dad, there's nothing I ever wanted to do more than be a member of the Moonshine Task Force right next to him. I said no to playing football professionally to stay in Laurel Springs and fulfill my dream.

I'm biding my time, paying my dues, and learning from the elder MTF members. To most of them I'm the kid they watched grow up, and while they're proud of me, they don't take me seriously.

Life is status quo until the morning all hell breaks loose in our small town threatening everyone I know and love – including the one woman I can't get out of my head.

Ruby Carson

"My favorite place? In his arms…"

Caleb saved me from the worst date of my life, swooping in like the fixer he is. Smiling his panty-melting grin, he grabbed my hand and extricated me from the longest ninety minutes known in the history of the world. After saving me, he took me on the best date I've ever had. We've been inseparable since that crazy night.

It hasn't been picture-perfect. His job is dangerous; it worries me, even when he tells me not to. One gorgeous summer day, it all comes crashing down on us.

The man who has my heart is in the middle of a FUBAR situation that has no good ending. My hope is when the smoke clears Caleb will be walking toward me, arms outstretched, with that grin on his face, before he envelopes my body into the hug only he can give.

That's what would happen in a perfect world – but I've never known a perfect world – not even with Caleb…

AUTHOR'S NOTE

While the series is called The Moonshine Task Force Series, please be aware the task force is what bought most of these men together. It's the catalyst (if you will) that has made the friendship of the five men you'll meet in the series.

Like most of my recent books, these are character-driven. The action, as it is, advances the storyline or sets up the storyline for subsequent books. There won't be manufactured drama or manufactured storyline. These are very much what you see, is what you get. Each book follows one member, and you'll get to see how they change and grow through-out the course of the series.

I hope you'll love the final story featuring Ruby and Caleb!

Enjoy!
Laramie

Cruise

PROLOGUE

Cruise

"DISPATCH, BE ADVISED I'm stuck on the railroad tracks." I bang my head against the steering wheel as I hear the snickering answering my admission.

I can literally hear every single one of the MTF members laughing – my damn dad being the loudest. His loud chuckle could be heard in a group of hyenas.

Dispatch manages to hold it together, as she speaks to me. "Do you need a wrecker…" She trails off, and then I hear it. "Newbie?"

Pushing my fingers through my hair, I lean against the hand holding the radio. I groan before I press the button. "Yes, I'd rather not get my squad car crushed by a train."

"Help is headed your way," she answers, and again I can hear the laughter in her voice.

It's not long that I have to wait until another squad car pulls up. It parks a safe distance away, and as the two get out, I let out a short breath. "Fuck my life."

Not one to back down from anything, not anymore, I get out, facing the proverbial firing squad.

"Caleb." Havoc runs his hand over his chin. "What the fuck did you do?" He laughs as he observes the way my car sits across the tracks, the tires in such a way I can't get out.

"Don't even ask." I put my hands on my hips as I shake my head. "Renegade got the guy, and that's all that matters."

I shoot my dad a look. "You wanna say something?"

He saunters over to me, clapping his hand against my shoulder, squeezing tightly. "Welcome to the team, Rookie."

The twitching of his mouth at the corners causes me to lose control, and I let go with a loud laugh, not able to catch my breath as I bend at the waist. When I finally get it under control, I give them a smirk. "Fifth day on the job, and I'm already a fucking legend."

CHAPTER ONE

Cruise

Five Years Later
September

I T'S A RAINY night in Laurel Springs as I pull my Rubicon into one of the only empty spots in front of The Café. For just a moment, I turn off the ignition and sit, still amazed at how many people can fit inside. My rookie year on the MTF, Ernie passed away and Leighton had used her business smarts and degree, purchasing the place that meant so much to all of us. Ernie had no family, and her stepping in to keep an important part of the community alive had brought us all closer together.

We'd had an old-fashioned type of barn raising. People from two counties over in each direction came to help us remodel and expand The Café. It's now doubled in size, with updated everything, and I knew from talking to Havoc that Leighton was doing very well for herself. So well, in fact, she'd brought Brooks into the business two years ago, and they have become a formidable team. Once their family name was known for moonshine. Now? The Strathers are known throughout the six-county area for having the best food, desserts, and the most hospitality anyone could ask for. The establishment is alcohol free and caters to anyone who wants to have fun without being impaired.

Truth be told, it's where I eat most of my meals these days.

Today has been a long fucking day, and there's not going to be any break in this weather for at least the next two. Reaching over, I grab my hoodie, shrugging it over my head, making sure I'm covered before I duck out of the safety of the vehicle and make a run for it. My combat boots beat against the stone of the sidewalk, splashing water against the back of my legs, but at least they're covered by my tactical pants. As I get to the door, I hold it open for an elderly couple making their way as quickly up the sidewalk as they can.

"Thank you." The woman gives me a wide smile, while the man pats me on the side.

"No problem, I hope y'all have a good night." I let the door shut behind me and shake the droplets off my hoodie as I look around for my food partner tonight.

Morgan Santana is my food partner almost every night, if I'm honest. He joined the EMT squad right around the time I joined the MTF, we're the same age, and we share a lot of the same interests. I'd never had a best friend besides my dad before I met him, but I can honestly say Morgan is the closest friend I've ever had. I'd been close with my college roommate, Slater, but our friendship revolved around homesickness and college sports. Morgan and I talk about everything.

"Over here." He waves through the crowd. Looks as if he's secured us a booth away from a lot of the families and amongst older couples and younger ones on date nights. Fuck my life; it gets old being a single guy all the time.

"Thanks for putting us over here in loved-up central," I say as I take a look around, sliding into the booth across from him.

"Cut me a break, Harrison, it was the only seat that didn't have babies around it." He glances over the top of his menu.

"I don't know why you're even looking." I toss my menu

aside. "It's fried chicken night, and that's what both of us always get."

"Maybe I'm watching my weight." He pats his stomach, which is probably tighter than mine.

"Yeah," I chuckle. "Okay, sounds about right."

"Hey, guys." Leighton smiles as she strolls up to our table. "What's going on tonight?"

I put my arm out, pulling her to my side. "Oh, you know, arresting bad guys, writing tickets, fucking shit up. Normal stuff."

"Maybe for him." Morgan throws me a glare. "I got puked on today, by a baby. That was so not normal stuff for me." Which explains why he didn't want to sit next to any tonight.

"Ewwww." She curls her lip up in disgust. "I don't miss those days. Thank God Ransom and Cutter are out of that stage," she mentions her and Havoc's two boys.

"Where are they at?" I look around the building for them. Typically, when she works nights, they're with her.

"Ransom had football practice earlier today, so Holden took them out for pizza. Y'all ready to order?"

Their son is huge. He'll be playing college ball before we all know it. "I'd much rather have the fried chicken and mashed potatoes with gravy," I tell her as she writes down my order.

"Brown gravy?"

"Hell yes, and some water too, please."

Nodding she turns to Morgan. "What do you want tonight?"

"Give me a vegetable plate with grilled chicken and a water. Some of us are watching what we eat."

I shake my head as he tries to guilt me. "I weigh ten pounds more than I did when I played college football, and five of those pounds are probably muscle. You're not getting me to admit I shouldn't be eating this. Do you know how many years of my life I spent making sure I was within my macros? I try not to worry about it so much now."

"Gotcha." She leans in and says in a lowered voice, "Can you all watch the table beside you? The guy is giving me some creeptastic vibes and the girl is eating that appetizer like she hasn't eaten in the last six years."

Leighton turns away and immediately my attention goes to the couple at the table beside us. I can't see the woman's face, but one of my strengths is reading body language. Hers says she's highly tense, uncomfortable, and possibly scared, given the way her foot taps against the floor. Her back is ramrod straight, one hand is gripping the table, and there's an iciness in the way she's holding herself.

Quietly I watch as she all but shovels a potato skin in her mouth, then grabs for the last one on the plate. Any person with eyes can see either she's starving or trying to get this night over with. Given the vibes this guy is throwing off, I'm assuming it's the latter.

"Well, at least I know you like to swallow." He gives her a lecherous smile, licking his lips.

The move is creepy enough that it even makes my skin crawl. I shift around so I can see her profile; she looks young and way too innocent to be messing with this guy.

"Not typically." Her dry answer makes me grin.

"I woulda found out in a few hours anyway." He gives her a wink.

"Don't flatter yourself. I hadn't even planned on inviting you in, and given the way you've acted so far during this date, I'm not inclined to do so."

I love the way she's affected an ice princess tone. Very quickly, she's setting boundaries, and my cop senses totally approve of what's going on.

"Sweetheart." He tilts his head toward her, the grin now gone from her face. "You forget I picked you up? I know where you live. I can get in anytime I want."

The fork she'd been using to cut her potato skin falls to the plate with a loud bang, and that's when I get pissed enough to get up. "Be back." I tap the table at Morgan.

There's four chairs at the table they're occupying. I grab one, turn it around and straddle it.

"Hey fuck face, who do you think you are?" the guy asks, irritation in his voice.

Reaching into the hoodie, I pull the badge on a chain around my neck off and slam it down on the Formica. "Hey fuck face, I'm the police, and I think I just heard you threaten this young lady. Who do you think *you* are is the appropriate question here."

Ruby

"HEY FUCK FACE, I'm the police and I think I just heard you threaten this young lady. Who the fuck do you think you are is the appropriate question here."

I hear the scrape of the chair as the man who just spoke the words yanks it out from under the table and has a seat. Thank God he's showed up; the last line of conversation scared me more than I'd even like to admit to myself.

As my eyes take in the badge that's been slammed on the surface of the table, I want to kiss this man who's interrupted the date from hell. However, I can't seem to make my eyes move from the badge, I'm somewhat shaking as I hear what's being said between the two of them.

"I didn't mean anything by it." My date is stumbling over his words, fidgeting, sweat sprinkling his forehead. Besides being a cop, this officer is an intimidating figure all his own.

"No, I'm pretty sure you told her if she didn't perform oral sex on you, you were going to break into her house and get it. I could charge you with a pretty good amount of shit right now. Give me your ID."

The smooth voice, laced with power and authority, washes over me. This man, this officer, doesn't have as strong an accent as most people around here, and I wonder if he's born and bred.

My date fumbles with his wallet, finally producing an ID, handing it over with shaking hands. Finally, I allow myself to look up at the man who's saved me from who knows what. He's gorgeous. His features are strong, a close-cropped beard covers his face, and soulful brown eyes glance my way as he looks between the two of us. Pushing the sleeves of the hoodie he wears up, I see ink on his forearm, but the way he's moving it, doesn't allow me to get a good look. So badly, I want to reach over, still the movement, and feast on whatever it is he cared enough about to permanently mark himself.

"Seth Donovan," he rolls the name of my date around on his tongue, almost as if he's trying it on for size. "Is this address correct?" He pulls his cell phone from his pocket, tapping in a few numbers.

"Ye....ye.....yes," he finally answers, nodding excessively.

My knight in shining armor is talking to someone on the other end of the line, and I realize he's running Seth's name. For what, I'm not sure, but I've seen enough cop reality shows that I'm figuring it's for warrants.

"Is that right?" Those brown eyes land on the other man at the table, and the full lips, spread in a tight line. "Send a uniform, I'm off-duty. We're at The Café."

He disconnects the call, sets the phone down, stands up, and motions for Seth to do the same. "You my friend, have a warrant. Stand up, a uniform is on the way to get you."

"You're full of shit!"

My savior leans in close, whispering, but it's loud enough for me to hear it. "This is a family establishment, and you'll respect the people who work hard. Unlike you, who seems to like breaking and entering and stealing things that aren't yours. Put your hands behind your back or I'll do it for you."

This officer has at least twenty-five pounds of pure muscle on Seth, and for about thirty seconds, it looks like this disaster is going to get even worse. I get the feeling in the pit of my stomach that Seth will run, and he'll make a spectacle of himself when he does. Instead, he puts his hands behind his back, his head hanging low.

It's all a blur as he's read his rights, cuffed, and hauled out front. I'm fully aware of everyone's eyes on me, which is embarrassing, but I also worry about my job. I'll have to do damage control on Monday. Right now though, I just want to get out of here, which is going to prove difficult because Seth was my ride. Not long after they've walked outside, I see the flash of blue lights through the plate glass window. And a few minutes later, the man who did his civic duty is strutting back over to my table.

Oh this officer, whoever he is, doesn't walk like mere mortals, no. He struts. Every eye in the room is glued to him, and I'm impressed with the easy way he handles the attention. The soft roll of his hips. It's obvious that the women in the room wonder what it's like to be me, the men in the room wonder what it's like to be him. He stops in front of me, and I get a look at how tall he is, how powerful the body under his clothes must be. He sits back down in the chair he vacated.

"You alright, ma'am?"

There's a boyish quality to the way he's asked the question, along with the easy smile that's spread across his face. It sends butterflies from the pit of my stomach up my throat. I have to focus on my words as I say them. "I am. Thank you so much for coming to my rescue. My name is Ruby."

"No problem. Where the hell did you find that piece of work?"

"A friend from work." I think back to the librarian, Trinity, telling me what a nice guy she thought Seth was. I guess the two of us have totally different definitions of nice guys.

He runs a hand through thick, dark hair, and gives me a grin. "Not much of a friend, huh?" Tapping his knuckles on the table, he motions over to the booth he left, to the man sitting there by himself, watching this all play out. "My friend and I were getting some dinner, and since you're kind of stuck here, would it be okay if we ate with you? I'll take you home when we're done."

I want to say yes, but after what's just happened to me, I'm hesitant. Right then, Leighton, comes over, carrying three plates. "Trust me, honey. He's a good one, I've known Caleb since he was a teenager. He'll get ya home safe, or I can call Holden and have him take you. But Caleb works with Holden as part of the Moonshine Task Force; you're in good hands."

The Moonshine Task Force. I've heard of them, one of the fellow teachers I work with has a husband who's a member. I know they're trustworthy, and for the first time this night, I relax.

CHAPTER TWO

Ruby

"THIS IS ME." I point to the duplex I'm renting while trying to figure out how to live on a first-year teacher's salary. It's not as easy as I assumed it would be back when I was still in the dorms taking classes.

He chuckles as he pulls his Jeep into the gravel lot. This Jeep is the manliest thing I've seen. Completely blacked out with all the bells and whistles anyone could ask for. The glow of the dashboard is blue, and the contrast between the light, his coloring, and those soulful brown eyes of his is almost my undoing as we sit here in the dark, alone.

"Why the laugh? I know it's not much." I'm slightly offended by the way he's reacting to where I live. And really disappointed.

"I'm not laughing at you, Ruby." He grips the steering wheel with those long fingers of his, causing his forearms to flex tight. "It's just that back in the day, a couple of my co-workers lived in this duplex before they fell in love and got married."

"They allow women on the Moonshine Task Force?" I've never heard of it before, but it doesn't mean that it isn't true.

"No." He laughs again. "When I was a teenager I worked at The Café, and there was a waitress who worked there too. She had a bad experience with her husband, and Ace, now my co-worker with the MTF helped her out of it. They ended up living here next to each other, and when her divorce was final, they admitted their feelings for one another and got married."

The sigh that comes from deep within me is light. I'm a helpless romantic, and while that's sometimes played against me, I do love when two people come together in the face of adversity. "That's a sweet story."

"They're a sweet couple." He runs a hand over his chin. "Do you want me to come in and make sure everything's okay? Given the way Seth threatened you tonight, I asked the arresting officer to fill out a temporary protection order, especially since he's wanted for breaking and entering. He won't be getting out of jail tonight, and I have no idea what's going to happen when he goes before the judge. If you give me your phone number, I can text you and let you know. Chances are he'll be given bail, but if he can't make the amount, he'll be sitting in lockup until he's arraigned. I don't think you have anything to worry about." He shrugs. "But I'm also not God, so if you feel that something's off, please give us a call."

"Or I can text you?" I raise an eyebrow because I don't really want this whole town to know my embarrassment at being caught in this situation.

"Absolutely."

Within a few minutes, we have each other's numbers and he's walking me to my front door. "Thank you again." I turn, looking up at him. He's taller, so much taller than me that he dwarfs my body. If he wanted to surround me, it wouldn't be that hard, and I'd probably let him. I'm a sucker for a man who can take control of a situation and not back down. That's the epitome of what Caleb has done for me tonight.

"Just doin' my job." He puts his hands in his hoodie, rocking back and forth on his heels.

I don't know why, but those words hurt slightly. A part of me hoped he'd come to my rescue because he'd actually wanted to, not because he felt like he had to. The last thing I want to be is someone's job.

"I'm sorry to have ruined your night," I try to keep the emotion out of my voice. This has been the weirdest few hours of my life and telling myself the reaction I'm having is emotional isn't helping the lump I feel in my throat.

"You didn't." He pulls one of those hands out of his hoodie, bracing it against the door. "It was my pleasure to rescue you, Ruby. I'm glad you're okay, I'm beyond glad that asshole didn't hurt you, and what I'd really like to see again is that smile on your face you gave me a few times tonight."

My heart pounds in my chest, my throat dry as I try to swallow, and my stomach has those butterflies again. The smile he's asking about spreads across my face without me even thinking about it. "I'm lucky you rescued me; today could have ended pretty shitty for me," I admit, pulling my gaze away from his intense brown stare.

"It could have." His voice is sober. "But it didn't. I know this is crazy, but I had a good time with you tonight, even if it did start off kind of weird. Could I see you again? Maybe show you what a real man does to woo a woman?"

That heart of mine speeds up to double-time. My palms get slightly sweaty and I'm embarrassed to say my knees knock just a little. "I'd like that," I manage not to sound like an idiot.

"I work nights all weekend." His tone is apologetic. "But I'm available for breakfast in about ten hours, if that's not too soon." The look on his face is so hopeful that I can't help but be impressed.

A laugh bubbles up from my stomach, and I throw my head back with the force of it. "Breakfast it is."

"I know a place, over in Calvert City," he mentions a town about an hour away. "They have one of the best breakfasts around, and there's a nice little section of downtown we can explore, before I have to come back and take a nap before work. Is that okay?"

"Sounds great." I nod, thinking that I'll like the chance to spend some time with him. Even though maybe I should be apprehensive after what happened to me tonight, I inherently trust the man standing in front of me. Something tells me to trust my gut with this one, and my gut is giving me nothing but signals to go along with whatever this man is asking of me.

"I'll pick you up around eight? We should get there in enough time that we get breakfast but most of the rush is gone."

"I'll see you then." I lean in, kissing him on the cheek, before turning around, unlocking my door, and walking inside.

"Be sure and lock it, Ruby. Be safe."

"You too, Officer." I give him a little wave before doing exactly what he asked me to do.

Cruise

JOGGING BACK TO my Jeep, I get in and execute a three-point turn to get out of the drive, before I allow the smile to spread all the way across my face. I do a little dance in my seat and gleefully beat a hand against the steering wheel.

There are lots of things that have happened in my life that I can't explain. Why my mom left me at such a young age, why I was blessed to get another one in the form of Kari, why my little sister is nine and I'm twenty-eight, how my dad and I have such a great relationship even though we're only sixteen years apart in age. I've had tough times, and I've had great times, but there's always been parts I've never been able to explain. Much like what just happened.

From the moment I sat down at the table in The Café, I felt something drawing me to Ruby. I wanted to protect her, to make sure she got home safe, to be sure this dumbass she'd been set up with didn't try something he shouldn't have. The feeling increased as she had dinner with me and Morgan. We laughed, we joked, a meal that should have lasted an hour extended to almost two, and I could tell that none of us wanted to leave when we got our checks. There's been few times in my life when I had such a great meal with someone of the opposite sex who wasn't obviously trying to get into my pants. The invitation to breakfast tomorrow was spur of the moment, but now that I've extended it, I can't get it off my mind.

Turning the radio up, I sing along to the country song, tinged with a little bit of rock. If anyone had to ask me to describe myself, that's probably the best way. I love the simple things in life, they're my favorite. I don't like to make anything complicated, but at the same time I like to ride the edge – more sexual than anything – but I have a past, and sometimes I just gotta let it out.

The song is interrupted as a call comes through my Bluetooth. Mason Harrison. Probably checking up on his son. I allow the call through. "Hey, Dad!"

"You arrested someone at The Café tonight?" He goes right into the reason he called without even offering pleasantries.

I roll my eyes. Should have known he'd hear about it first thing in this small town. "No, I didn't arrest them, but Renegade did. I was sitting there having dinner with Morgan when I heard the guy she was on a date with threaten her. It was a fuckin' shitty move and I couldn't sit there and listen to it. She was obviously uncomfortable."

"He threatened her?"

I relate back the story, and my dad whistles through his teeth. "What a douche."

"Yeah, so when I called in his name, he had warrants for breaking and entering. I actually just took her home because she was stranded."

I leave out the detail that I'm seeing her tomorrow. Since Jess, who I dated during my senior year in high school, I don't introduce women to my parents unless I know they're going to stick around. In ten years, they've met one other woman, and that had been a huge mistake. I'd let her meet my family, and when we agreed to go our separate ways, it was sad for everyone involved. Unfortunately, she and I just weren't meant to be. There were no hard feelings, still isn't, it just wasn't right for either of us.

"Yeah, so that's my night in a nutshell. How's the fam?" I turn his attention away from me, onto the women in our lives.

"Good, Rina is already in bed and so is Kels, but I was still up because I worked a little over and wanted to check in with you after I heard what happened. I'm hitting the hay here soon." He yawns loudly in my ear. "You know you don't have to eat with Morgan all the time, you can come have dinner here."

"I have dinner there plenty," I argue. "At least three times a week."

"I'm just saying, it doesn't matter how many times a week you're here. We love to see you whenever that is."

"I know, and Morgan knows he's invited too, but sometimes we just want to be dudes."

"I get it," Dad laughs. "Your mom wanted me to tell you, in case you didn't know."

The transition from calling my stepmother Karina to Mom had happened slowly. It wasn't something that one day I woke up and just blurted out. It was a decision I made and then had to put into execution. But as Kelsea had gotten older, I was afraid she'd ask questions – why did she call her Mom and I called her Kari? The reality of the situation would be way too much for a little kid to comprehend, much less handle, and I'd made the decision on my own to take it out of the equation.

Never having called anyone Mom before, I had to try to the word out on my tongue. I had to practice saying it, really let the motion of moving my lips to form the word become second nature. I'd called her Mom in my head for months before I'd actually tried the word out in person. The day I had, she'd stopped what she was doing, turned to me, and cried like the emotional woman she is. She'd hugged me, clung to me, and thanked me for letting her be a part of my life. It's tough to admit, but even I cried that day, and a huge burden had been lifted off my shoulders. Karina Harrison is my mom, no matter if she gave birth to me or not. She's always loved me more than the actual woman who gave birth to me did.

"Tell her I'm fine." I pull into the apartment complex I'm living at for the moment and park my Jeep in my designated space. "I'm home, so I'm gonna go. I have to work night shift tomorrow," I groan.

"Good luck getting your sleep in."

The one good thing about having a parent with the same job as you? They get your sleep habits. "Will do, Dad. Love you."

"Love you too. Be safe, kiddo."

CHAPTER THREE

Ruby

L ISTENING TO THE rain beat against the roof has always been one of my favorite pastimes. And now that I live on my own, not at my parents' house and not at a dorm full of loud roommates, I can be lazy and listen to it whenever I want to.

On mornings like this, I think. And since I'm thinking, I'm rehashing everything that happened last night in my mind. To me, life has never been lived in hours. It's been lived in moments, goals, achievements, and special occasions. Hours though, hours mean a lot too. Take roughly ten hours ago.

If Caleb hadn't been there to save me last night, who knows where I'd be at this hour. I could be lying in this bed hurting, contemplating an entirely different trip today. It might be one to the ER, instead of a few counties over. It could be spent making police reports, rather than trying to decide what I want to wear. Last night I was taught a valuable lesson. I'll never take hours for granted again.

Throwing my covers off, I shiver at the chill in the room. This fall has been colder than most, and if I remember correctly, it's not supposed to get above fifty today. Perfect book weather, if you were to ask me. Getting up and doing my daily business is exciting because I know I'm going to get to spend at least part of my day with Caleb. As I'm brushing my teeth, I hear my phone go off on my night stand.

When I'm done, I rush over, wondering which of my friends is texting me on a Saturday morning. When I see that it's Caleb's number, I get both excited and worried. What if he's canceling on me?

> **C:** *Just wanted to make sure we're still on for today and give you an update. They denied bail because Seth had warrants in three other counties. He's actually going to be extradited. You dodged a bullet, Ruby.*

I feel how lucky I am, know how fortunate I was that people were watching out for me last night, and grateful to live in the small town I do.

> **R:** *Thanks for letting me know. Kinda makes me feel better, knowing he's not around anymore. And of course we're still on!*

> **C:** *Understandable. I'll be by to pick you up in about thirty minutes. I just have to drop my little sister off at a friend's house. She's having a sleepover tonight.*

Caleb has a little sister? Immediately I'm wondering how much younger she is than him, and I decide since he appears at least a few years older than me, she's probably a teenager.

Thirty minutes doesn't give me much time, but I spring into action, doing the best I can with what I have. Putting on a little bit of makeup, I run my fingers through my naturally curly hair. Because it's raining, it goes every which way, and I know the only way I'm going to be able to tame it is by putting it in a braid. Which makes me look all of ten years old.

It can't be helped; I think I'll always look young for my age. Even now, having my own classroom, people assume I'm a student and not a teacher. Swiping a little mascara on my lashes,

I put my pearl studs in my ears, and opt for a deep plum lip stain. At least maybe he'll be drawn to my lips for most of the day. With my golden blonde hair, it makes a striking contrast. Besides full lips and big eyes, about the only thing I have to work is my ample chest, which nobody will be able to see underneath my rain coat today, but that's okay. I'll tuck it away for a surprise, in case we go out on another date. Glancing out the window as I go for my rain boots, I see him.

The Rubicon, which I'd found so sexy the night before, pulls up into my drive. He doesn't turn it off, but he bails out, running to my front porch. And the brief glimpse I get of him is enough to send my pulse racing. Caleb wears a very worn pair of jeans, a t-shirt with a flannel unbuttoned over it, rolled up those forearms of his, with a hat pulled low over his eyes.

The knock that announces he's here is enough to set me on edge.

Calming myself, I open the door, as I'm slipping my rain jacket on. "Hey," I greet him, not able to wipe the smile off my face at seeing him again. It's crazy, we met last night, but I've never had a connection with someone the way I have a connection with him.

"Hey." He grins back. "Sorry about the weather. I ordered sunshine with a high of seventy. Instead I got this." He shrugs. "We can make the best of it, right?"

"How dare mother nature not listen to you?" I grab my cross-body bag, slinging it over my chest.

"That's what I'm saying." He plays along, his voice playful. "I mean doesn't she know I'm trying to impress you?"

He takes my elbow as we descend the porch, then he walks me over to the passenger side of the Jeep where he helps me in, before he jogs around the front. The inside is nice and warm, a familiar rock song plays on the radio, and the gentle thump of the windshield wipers cocoon me in a feeling of rightness like I've never had before.

"You don't have to try, Caleb, you're already impressing me pretty hardcore." I buckle up as he checks his blind spot and then begins backing out. "The guy last night honked the horn. He didn't even come to my door."

"Fuck that," he says the words like they taste bad. "My dad would have my ass if I didn't go get a woman at her door. He's chivalrous like that. Any kid who ever wants to date my sister will have to go through both of us," he preaches as he turns toward Calvert City.

"She's lucky to have a brother like you." I think of my own brother.

Cruise

"NAH, I'M LUCKY to have a little sister like her. I waited a long time for one," I admit as I turn onto the county highway that will take us to Calvert City.

I'm usually not a talker. Typically I have to get to know someone before I start belting out my life story, but there's something about this girl. Since I saw her sitting there last night, so stoic, so unsure of the situation she was in, I've wanted to talk to her. I've wanted to tell her everything will be okay and explain to her that even though things might seem a little scary now, they won't always.

"You ever been out here?" I change the subject from my family. For people who don't know where I come from, it's a little difficult to explain.

"I'm assuming we're going to The Hen Lays The Egg?" She mentions the name of the most popular breakfast joint in these parts.

"Is there any other place to go?" I question.

"The Café." She giggles as she slides her gaze over at me.

"Oh, you got jokes? I see how it is." I adjust my seat to make it a little more comfortable with my long legs and then sit back to enjoy the ride. "I go there all the time."

"I do too, I can't believe I've never seen you there before." She looks like she might be trying to place me. "But I do feel like maybe I have seen you before last night."

As a cop, especially as a member of the MTF, I'm recognized a lot. We're required to be at many functions, some of them are attended by the whole town, some by a certain population. Either way, we're seen a lot. "Probably in one of my official capacities."

"I don't think so." She shakes her head, her lips pursed, eyebrows together. "I've been trying to put my finger on it since I saw you last night. You're a member of the Moonshine Task Force, right?"

"Yup." No one will ever know how proud I am to carry on the tradition my dad started. When I'd been offered a contract in the draft to play pro ball, he'd argued with me for days about what I was giving up. The truth is, I've never wanted to do anything other than follow in his footsteps. The things I've aspired to do are to make a difference in my community, get alcohol off the streets, and not to let kids be in the same position I was in as a teenager. All of those things mean something to me. They mean something ball never did. Football gave me opportunities, but it wasn't my one true love.

"My co-worker has a husband who's on the Moonshine Task Force. You'd probably know him."

"Considering there's six of us? I'm almost positive I do." I chuckle as I think about who she could possibly know. We never discussed her job last night.

"Karina Harrison is a teacher at the same school as me."

I laugh as I look across the console into the passenger's seat. "No shit, huh?" I can't stop the laugh. Reaching into the cup holder, I grab my phone and show her my lock screen.

"She's your sister-in-law? That's awesome, she's such a nice lady. She's helped me so much in figuring out what I need to do."

I've never known anyone who truly knew Kari, so this should be interesting when I drop this bomb on her. "No, she's not my sister-in-law. She's married to my dad, but I call her Mom."

Ruby's mouth slams shut. She looks at me, looks at the road, looks at me again, opens her mouth, and then closes it. Her eyebrows come together in confusion, she opens her mouth, shuts it, then reaches into the cup holder, grabs the phone and looks at the lock screen again. "No way." She shakes her head. Looks at it again, and then shakes it again. "No way."

"It's true." I make a cross motion over my chest.

"There's no way that's your dad." She glances at the picture again. "Brother maybe, but not dad."

"I swear to God," I say with a laugh. She's cute in her confusion. "You wanna see my birth certificate? He's my dad."

"Did he have you at like fourteen?"

"Sixteen," I correct her. "Dad had me at sixteen and raised me by himself after my biological mom left. Kari and Dad got married almost eleven years ago. She got pregnant with my sister within a month of them getting married, while I was in my freshman year of college."

"Shut the front door. Are you shitting me?"

"I'm totally not, you can ask Kari next time you see her at work. In fact, it's probably where you've seen me. Sometimes I pick Kelsea up and take her to the school so Mom doesn't have to make more than one trip," I explain as I pass a slower moving car once we come to a passing spot in the road.

"You call her Mom?"

"I call her Kari sometimes, but mostly Mom. I used to not, but then Kelsea got old enough to where I was afraid she'd question it. And to be honest with you, Kari did more for me than my real mom ever did. If there was a woman who earned the title, it's her."

"I can see that." She glances out the window, gazing at the scenery as it passes by. "She does have a way about her. She makes everyone want to be her friend, everyone tells her their secrets, and if you ever need a shoulder to cry on or someone to tell you all the good things about yourself, she's the person to go to."

"Yes, exactly. Her and my dad, they have the type of marriage I want one day."

"I've seen them together." Her smile is huge, almost as if she's relieving a memory. "He came to work not long ago to bring her a coffee after school had let out. We were doing parent/teacher conferences and it was a really long night. He brought me one too, because I work in the same module as her. When he walked into the room, she lit up. I've never seen a couple so freaking happy to see one another before."

"That's them." I shake my head. "Kind of so sweet it's sickening. Back when I was in college, it used to embarrass me, but as I've gotten older, I realize how lucky they are to have it. My dad didn't have anything for a lot of years, and he hit the lottery with her. Hell, I did too."

"She told me once, when she was talking about her family, that she not only fell in love with her husband, but with her husband's son too. I thought she was talking about some little kid." She giggles.

"Nope, totally me." If I could strut, I would. I like when she says good things about me, and it makes it even better that it hopefully impressed Ruby. Kari and I, we have a special relationship. "I had the flu and she took care of me. From that point on, I never had to wonder if anyone besides my dad cared about me."

"That's a sweet story, Caleb. You're blessed to be able to call her Mom."

As we enter Calvert City proper, I reflect on her words. I know she's right. But I'm also blessed that this woman was somehow dropped into my life. Call it a sixth sense, maybe obsession, or a premonition. Call it anything you want, but I know this day is going to be the start of something good, and if I can stay the course, maybe I will have a relationship like my parents. Maybe I won't be the one member of the MTF who seems to be cursed when it comes to the women in his life.

"Looks like we'll have to park along the side streets and walk down. That okay with you?" The rain hasn't let up, and I worry for a second that she's a girlie girl who can't stand for her hair to get wet, who's worried about her makeup running, and her clothes getting damp.

"Nope, I figured we might, that's why I dressed the way I did. You don't have to worry about me, Caleb. I'm not gonna melt because I got a little wet."

Immediately those words go to a place they probably shouldn't, but I'm a guy and it's been awhile since I got laid. I tell my dick that she didn't mean it the way it sounded, but as she turns to get out of the Jeep and her ass is framed by a tight pair of jeans, I take a minute to thank my own lucky stars that this woman came with me today. After her scare last night, she could have told me to fuck off, but she didn't, and if I'm smart, I'll keep my body under control and my thoughts in safe places.

As I get out, I adjust my package, and pray nobody can tell just how much I want this woman.

CHAPTER FOUR

Cruise

"DO YOU LIKE teaching?"

We've gotten our drinks, ordered our food, and now we're just waiting for everything to be delivered. I'm going to use my time wisely and ask her about anything that comes to mind. Anything that will let me learn more about this woman who's intrigued me.

"I love it," she answers, happiness shining from her eyes. "It's hard being a high school teacher at my age though," she sighs. "At twenty-four, I'm not much older than they are, and I look younger than I am."

"You do," I agree. "But there's something about those blue eyes of yours that kind of drag me in. With a look, they tell anyone that you're old enough to know what you like."

I've caught her looking at me like that a few times. Like she wants to know all my secrets and what I look like without a shirt on. Can't say I don't want to know all of that about her too.

"You think so? This is my first year, but last year when I was a student teacher, it was a struggle to ask them to call me Ms. Carson, and that was my thing not theirs, but it's not gotten any easier yet."

"You get hit on?" I throw that in there. If she were my teacher, I'd totally hit on her.

She averts her eyes. "Yes, typically by guys who are young enough to send me to jail, which was why I was out on that date last night."

"Whoever your friend was that set you up should have known better." I take a drink of my coffee that's been brought to the table. "You should tell her she needs better friends."

"I'll definitely be speaking to Trinity on Monday morning." She takes an answering drink from her glass. "It's just so hard to date." She shrugs, sighing with what sounds like frustration. "I grew up in Laurel Springs, actually saw you play in a few football games, but I didn't recognize you at The Café. Even though I grew up here though, I didn't have a high school boyfriend, and college was fun, but I didn't find anyone there to spend the rest of my life with, ya know? My friends are in two groups. Single and ready to party it up or married and having their first kid. I'm single, but I want to be committed," she explains. "Probably just scared you off with that admission," she laughs nervously.

"No." I shake my head. Little does she know I've wanted this a long time, and I've been looking too. "You didn't scare me off. Kinda said some of the things I've been thinking about myself lately. I didn't grow up in Laurel Springs, but when we moved here, it was home. At my age, everybody is basically a bachelor for life, or they're on child number two. I didn't want to follow in my dad's footsteps – having me so young. So I think I've kinda stunted my own relationship growth, if that makes sense."

"It does." She nods vigorously. "When you have a goal you're concentrating on, you don't want anything to get in the way. Then when you reach that goal, you realize everyone passed you by."

"You get it."

"I do." She smiles over her cup at me. "Thank you for saving me last night."

I smile back at her. "Thank you for needing saving."

Ruby

I LEAN BACK in the seat I've occupied for the last hour, managing to stuff one last bite of apple streusel in my mouth, before I moan and push the plate away from me.

"Where the hell do you put it all?" I ask Caleb as he reaches over and grabs what was left on my plate, demolishing it in one bite.

"I work out," he defends himself. "Less than I should, but I run at least five miles every other day."

"So you're a distance runner?" I take a drink of my iced coffee. "Lots of stamina."

"I got all the stamina you need." He licks the fork he'd used to cut the sweet pastry, before he laughs at himself. I eye his tongue, hoping he doesn't notice, thinking about what it would feel like against my skin. "That was a really bad joke."

"Effective though." I give him a wink. "Do you just run or do you lift weights too?"

"I'm not a huge fan of lifting, like I used to be. Back when I was in college and in high school that was my thing. Bulk up, and cut, bulk up and cut. These days," – he pats his stomach – "I prefer to be lean. It's easier on my body, healthier for my mind. I indulge when I want, within reason, and if it gets out of control, I rein it back in."

"Spoken like a man who's never had a weight problem."

There's a sharp edge to my voice, and I wonder if he picked up on it. It's not his fault I'd been overweight my freshman year of high school and had worked hard to lose a total of thirty pounds. Joining the cheerleading squad had helped, but it'd not really changed the way people looked at me. It's not his fault I'd been passed over by every guy in high school I'd liked, and then still passed over once I lost the weight. It'd taken me a long time to come to terms with the fact that I had to have confidence in myself before anyone else would see it.

"Never have, and I don't believe for a second you have either," he admits. "To me, you're perfect. But if you listen to my buddy, Morgan, talk about me. He'll tell you I need to lose at least ten pounds."

"From where I'm looking, you look mighty fine." I give him a once over, and then let my eyes travel back up and down again, blushing when he notices me.

"Thanks for your vote of confidence." He pats his stomach again. "I will say this. We gotta get up and move, otherwise I'm gonna fall asleep before I even get home."

"You might have to roll me out of here," I groan as I lift myself up out of the chair and start putting my jacket on again, digging in my purse for some cash. When I hand him part of what the bill should be, he looks down at the money, almost like he's scared it's going to bite him.

"You remember that thing about my dad kicking my ass cause he's chivalrous? This is another one of those things. We eat, I pay."

Not used to this, I still want to do my part. "Then I pay the tip." I throw down part of my cash. "No arguing."

He holds his hands up. "Mom taught me never to argue with a lady. If you want to leave the tip, you go on and leave the tip."

We slowly walk toward the entrance of the restaurant, dodging people as we do. Even though it's after breakfast rush on a Saturday, there are still people milling about and there's a wait for a table. When we finally get past all the people, I turn to him. "It's still raining, but I'm up for a little window shopping if you are."

"Whatever you wanna do, I'm good with." He zips up his jacket and puts his hat back on. "As long as I get back home in time to take a nap, I don't care what we do. I just want to spend some more time with you."

The heat I feel on my cheeks says a blush is working its way up my neck, but surprisingly I'm okay with it. Caleb Harrison can embarrass me any day. "You ready?" he asks, reaching out for my hand.

"Sure am," I clasp our fingers together as we take off into the soggy mid-morning weather.

"Ya know I like rain like this. A soft drizzle, coating the streets, washing everything new again." He holds onto me tighter as I step down from the curb and we cross the street.

Downtown Calvert City looks like it could have been plucked from any postcard in the nineteen fifties. Mom and Pop shops have their doors open, even though the weather is wet and cool. Many of them have cider available or hot cocoa as we browse through their wares.

"I like this too," I admit, entwining my fingers in his. "A nice, steady, drizzle, it's my favorite. I have a tin roof on my duplex and I was listening to it come down this morning before you came to get me. It's the most relaxing sound." I turn him toward a small store I've been to a few times. "Over here, they have the best shampoo for curly hair. She handmakes it and it's got essential oils in it that curly hair needs. If I hadn't run out, my hair wouldn't look so insane today." I touch my braid with my free hand.

"Not insane, kinda cute." He tugs on the end of the braid. "I like this look on you."

When he smiles, the hint of a dimple shows on his left cheek, and I can't help but smile back. "Whatever you say," I laugh.

When we walk inside, he separates, looking at some of the stuff this shop has for men. He picks up some moisturizing oil I bought my dad not long ago. "I got that for my dad to use instead of aftershave." I glance at the bottle to make sure it's the right one. "Yeah, this one, and he loves it. Says it doesn't dry his face out, and it smells like the beach." I pick up another one. "I liked this one too; it smells a little spicier, sexier than the one I gave my dad."

I reach over, grab the bottle and lift it up to Caleb's nose. The hint of teakwood is enough to make me inhale deeply as I bring it under mine next.

It's one of my favorite scents, and I'd love to smell it on him.

"You like the way this smells, huh?"

"Yeah." I nod, blushing again. "Huge turn-on." I smack my hand over my mouth as I realize what I've just said. It's a little too early in whatever this is to be talking about turn-off's and turn-on's, but there's something about this guy and his deep brown eyes that makes me just want to keep talking.

A slow grin spreads across his face. "Is that right?"

"Ruby, I got your shampoo and conditioner." The cashier and part-owner of the store yells from across the room.

Saved by the bell, I turn around, thankfully hiding myself from his direct gaze to go and purchase what I need. When I feel him stand behind me, I turn around and get the bottle of oil. "Add this to it too." Deciding to go for broke, I am as direct as I can. "I'm the one who wants to smell it on your neck, I might as well be the one to pay for it."

His eyes darken when I lick my suddenly dry lips and I wonder just what the hell I'm doing. This direct person isn't me. Typically I play coy, make a guy chase me, and in the end, I push them away because they come on too strong and suffocate me.

But this guy? Maybe I want to chase him a little bit, maybe I'm feeling like it could be mutual, and when he catches me, I want him to take me. I want him to show me what I've been missing with these college guys, because there is no doubt in my mind, as I watch his big hand grab his bag, he's a man.

We walk back out into the weather, this time quieter with one another, but there's a tension that wasn't there before. It's not unwelcome. It's a string of sexual awareness we didn't have when we'd walked in. I can't even bring myself to regret I created the tension there, because I've never gone after what I want before. This will be the first time and hopefully it won't be a bust.

"You wanna head back?" I tilt my head toward his Jeep.

He pulls his phone out of his pocket and glances at the time. "We should, even though I'm having a really good time with you. I do need to get that nap in. If not, I won't be worth shit tonight."

The whole way back to my apartment, I grapple with what I want to ask. I want to see him again, but I've never been the type of woman to be forward. To ask the guy out on the date, more for fear that I'll get shot down, but I'm worried I'll let this moment pass me by.

Caleb takes the decision out of my hands, when he pulls up to my duplex and cuts the ignition. "I'd like to see you again, the next couple of days might be a little crazy for me after the weather we've had, so can we plan something for Friday night? Would that be okay with you?"

Inside my heart is pounding, I want to jump up and down and give the finger to the part of my personality that always expects the worst. But I don't, I keep it together. "Sounds good, what do you want to do?"

"We can check out the new bar, if that's okay?"

Recently a brewery opened up a few streets over from The Café, boasting its own bar. I've wanted to check it out, but I never wanted to go by myself. "Text me the time, when you get your schedule?"

We're staring at one another, so badly I want to lean over the seat and kiss him. Press my lips to his and know exactly what it feels like.

"What the hell," he mumbles as he takes the decision out of my hands once again, grasping my neck in his palm and pulling me close. His lips are soft as they coax mine open. His tongue tastes like the syrup he had on his pancakes and there's a hint of the coffee he drank. I moan softly in the back of my throat, wishing the console didn't separate us. When he pulls away, we're both breathing slightly faster than we were before.

"I gotta go." His voice is husky.

Mine is partially breathless. "That nap, huh?"

"Yeah." He sounds as if he regrets his job at this moment. "I'll text you though?"

"I'd like that a lot."

"Let me walk you." He makes to get out, but I stop him.

"Nah, I like to run." I give him a grin.

Getting out of the Jeep, I run to the front porch, dodging puddles as I go. He waits until I open the door and wave at him. As I make it safely inside, I can't help but feel like today was a life changer.

CHAPTER FIVE

Ruby

S UNDAY MORNING SERVICE is a tradition in my family, has been since I was a little kid. I'm not particularly religious, but even if you aren't, you're still expected to make an appearance.

"I promise, Mom, I'm fine!" I assure my mom for probably the nineteenth time since I showed up this morning. "The cop who helped me was nice, and there's nothing to worry about. He took me home, took care of everything, and made sure I didn't have to be scared. You don't have to worry."

"I'm just not used to you living on your own," she worries, pushing my hair back, out of my face. "It's an adjustment period for us, I'm not trying to crowd you, but please remember, you're still our little girl."

I want to tell her I've been on my own a while. When I was in college no one was there to make sure I came home at a decent hour, to make sure I went to class, or that I ate at a certain time. Funny how that worked out. I even had to make sure I did my own laundry. There was no one there to do that either. Moving back here has partially suffocated me, because now I have a whole family who's worried about me constantly. I know I should appreciate it, but at the same time, it's starting to get annoying.

"You were introduced to him from someone you work with?" my dad asks as he comes to stand next to us, resting his hands in his slacks pockets. "You didn't meet him off of one of those dating sites, did you, Ruby? That's so dangerous. I hope you have a better head on your shoulders than that."

Jesus Christ. All I want to do is get out of here, and away from the inquisition. If they think all of these things about me, how do they think I managed to make it through college? It's almost as if they still see me as a teenager.

"I promise I met him through a co-worker. I don't even have a profile on those sites, Dad, and believe it or not, I managed to take care of myself for almost five years and get a degree. I'm good!" I try to hold the irritation out of my voice, but I don't quite manage it.

My mom looks like she wants to say more, but wisely keeps it to herself. "I know we're a little overbearing, but you're our only daughter."

I've heard this my entire life. My older brother, Lance, could legit go impregnate the entire town and they would throw a celebration party, but me? I should have sensibilities. It makes me wonder what they would say if they knew I've thought about Caleb since he left, wondered what would have happened if I'd been bold enough to invite him in yesterday.

"You coming over to the house for lunch?" Dad asks as he and Mom start walking to their car.

"Not today, I have a lot of papers to grade, laundry to do and all that adult stuff."

I want to roll my eyes, but I keep from it. One day. One day they'll see me as the capable person I am. Education isn't the easiest program to go through, and I did it, graduating with honors. But nobody ever said anything about that, nope. Seems like they never will either.

As I wave goodbye to them, I get in my car, taking my hair down from where it's pinned up. Driving through town, I stop at one of the three fast food places we have, and as I pull out, I see a Laurel Springs cop car blowing past, lights blazing. I wonder if that's Caleb, or his dad. According to the text he sent this morning, he's working a double today, and as I see the car navigate traffic, see people not get out of the way when they should, my heart is in my throat. I've never had anyone I care about have a job where they could get hurt. This is going to take some getting used to.

SUNDAY NIGHT GRADING papers has never been my idea of a fun time, so when my cell buzzes, I hope it's Caleb. I know that he's what they call on-shift, and because of the crazy amounts of rain we've had, they're dealing with flooding. I don't think I ever realized the hours other professions put in. He had to do a double today after working the late shift on Saturday. No wonder he naps when he can. I'd be a walking zombie if someone had me mixing up my days and nights like that. What I don't expect to see is Karina sending me a message.

> *K: I heard through the grapevine you had a problem with the date that Trinity set you up on. My son was there to save the day?*
>
> *R: Yeah, it was a hot mess in front of everyone at The Café. I'll explain to Principal Taggert tomorrow morning, just in case. It was really embarrassing, but your son did save me. You should have heard how that conversation went he told me you're his mom.*
>
> *K: Ha! I bet there was a lot of explaining going on. I'm glad he was there though, I just wanted to check on you. See you tomorrow!*

As I say my goodbyes to Karina, I throw my phone on my coffee table. I haven't seen Caleb since we parted ways yesterday. I'm not even sure how late he's working today.

What I am sure of is that I want to see him again. Tucking my lip between my teeth and going to sit on my couch, I send a text with my heart in my throat.

R: *How was your day?*

My hands shake as I wait for him to answer, and I wonder if this is the newness of our relationship, or if this is *the guy* I'll have this with for the rest of my life. I don't have the experience to know which is which, but what I do know is I like it. I like the fluttery feeling in my stomach, and I like the fact that he's the one to give it to me.

Cruise

I'M COLD, WET, fucking hungry, and really done with this goddamn day when I get the text from Ruby asking how my day is going. For a few brief minutes I don't answer it. I contemplate lying to her, telling her it's been a good one, and then forgetting she even made the attempt to text. Then I look at my team, realize that every single one of them has had a shitty day too, and they have women at home they care about. They lay those problems down at the feet of the women they share their lives with. They don't sugar coat shit, they're partners in the ways that matter, and I know that if I want this to go anywhere with Ruby, we've got to be partners.

C: *Really fuckin' shitty. I can't talk about it right now, and I might not be able to text the rest of the night, but I want to see you. Soon.*

"Where the fuck did this shit wash up from?" Havoc stands to his full height from his crouched position. He's got his hands on his hips, looking down at a crate full of moonshine.

Over the past few years, we've almost eradicated the illegal sale and distribution of the shit that kills people. We've made huge strides and we've worked diligently with the state and county to get this shit off the street. This? This is a kick in the gut.

We responded to a call that said water had run over Pond Creek Road, and when we got here, that wasn't a lie. What we didn't expect to find were about five cases of moonshine floating for anyone to take. "You think it was hidden somewhere?" I crouch down to get a better look at it.

The bottles look old, reminiscent of the night when a friend of mine died after drinking a bad batch. To this day I can't look at glass bottles like this and not relive portions of that night. Most everything we see these days is in some fancy bottle, not many people embrace the old ways anymore. Just looking at it makes me shiver, gets me emotional, and makes me wonder what he'd be doing now. Would he be working with us? Would he have a family? That's the shit that sometimes keeps me up at night.

"It's got mud caked on it." Dad comes over to us. "But if it was in that creek bed, I mean it could have happened during the flood." He runs a hand through his hair. "What makes you think it's old?" He looks at Havoc, questioning the same thing I am.

"Don't know." He shakes his head. "A hunch maybe? This isn't the product we've seen around here the past few years."

"If you wanna get technical, we ain't seen this product since Jefferson went to jail. We can send it off for testing, see where it came from," Dad throws the suggestion out there. "For the most part we've eradicated production like this. If it comes into this town, it comes from out of state. We all know that."

"Jefferson's in jail," I protest. "He's still got a few more years left on his sentence, and Brooks is straight and narrow now. I mean he's not gonna fuck up what he's got with Trinity." Everyone who's seen them together and knows how happy they are knows he's not going to mess it up. He's worked hard to have a stable life; I don't see him doing anything to ever fuck it up again.

Havoc gazes out over the raging creek that's rushed it's banks and now sits over the road. "Doesn't mean he hasn't taught someone else on the inside and then instructed them on what to do once they got out. I don't know, I don't like the feel of this. Maybe he had all that stashed, and somebody was waiting for it to be found."

"I think you're paranoid." Dad claps him on the shoulder, leveling with his friend. "I think you're looking for something that isn't there. I mean we can investigate it, don't get me wrong, but don't let it consume your life. Things are going well for you and Leigh right now."

"That's why I'm worried about it. I don't want anything to mess up what we've got." He runs a hand over his mouth, almost like he can't believe he let the words come out. He and Leighton have been through hell and back with her family, and I completely understand why he's worried, but I'm with Dad; I don't think it's a source for concern at this point.

"Don't let shit like this in your head and it won't."

I'm watching the two of them, constantly amazed at how their friendship works. Forever impressed with the way they speak to one another and how they take each other's feelings into account, even when they don't agree with one another. That's the way mine and Morgan's friendship works, only we don't have a job together. Sometimes I'm thankful for that, because we do get a little shitty with one another now and again.

"So what do you want us to do with it?" I turn to Havoc for instruction. Ace and I found it when we responded, so it's up to us to take care of it.

"Take it to evidence, send off some to the state lab, and see what they come back with. Once the water recedes, we'll come out here and see if there are any clues or anything left. Right now you've worked nineteen hours straight, kid. Go home and get some sleep."

He's right, and I'm dead on my feet, but as I walk to my squad car, I realize I don't want to go home to my empty apartment. I want to go to Ruby's, have someone to talk to about this day. I wonder what she'd say if I laid my worries and my tiredness down at her feet. Would she make me dinner and put me to bed? Would she lay with me until I fall sleep? After long shifts like this, I sometimes have a really hard time turning my brain off. As evidenced by how it's running a mile a minute right now.

I wonder what the answers are to all these questions. Would she be the person who holds me when I can't sleep through the night? I want the answer, want it badly.

But tonight the answer won't come. School is in session tomorrow, and all I need to do is crash.

CHAPTER SIX

Ruby

"I'M SO SORRY!"

As soon as I walk into the library on Monday morning after going to see Principal Taggert, the apology is already coming from Trinity's mouth.

"I had no idea Seth was like that. We've known each other a while, he was my next door neighbor." She runs to me, enveloping me in a hug. "Brooks always says I'm too trusting, but I just never imagined he would be like that. And to think I could have gotten you hurt. I'm really, really sorry, Ruby."

"It's okay," I assure her. "All's well that ends well. I ended up having a great time anyway."

"It's all over town, that you left with Caleb."

My cheeks heat, I can feel it flush up my neck. There's no telling what people in this town are saying. "I did leave with him, he was kind of my knight in shining armor. If it hadn't been for him and his friend, things would have probably turned out a lot differently."

"Thank God he was there." She squeezes my hand. "Again, I'm so sorry. I never meant for it to happen, and I promise I'll never set you up on a date again."

I'm almost relieved, not to mention, I have a good feeling about Caleb. "Maybe I won't need you to set me up anymore." I shrug. Glancing up at the clock, I realize the bell will ring in a few minutes. "Gotta go. We'll talk later."

Hurrying along the same hallways I walked as a student, I wave and call out random hello's to the students I now teach. Turning down my side of the building, I run right into Karina.

"I was coming to find you." She steadies me as I hold my coffee in front of me, praying that it won't slosh.

When it doesn't, I breathe a sigh of relief. "I made it." I give her a smile.

"Honestly, I wanted to check on you. I know you told me you were okay and Caleb told me you were okay when I asked, but what happened to you had to be scary."

Karina is the mother hen to everyone in our module, but she's never overbearing about it. "It was." I'm never going to lie to her. She's been my mentor since I was a student here. "But Caleb saved me. Like I told you in the text, had he not listened to what was going on, it would have been a whole other story. I probably would have made the news, and not in a good way." A shiver runs through my body as I think about it.

"Have you talked to Principal Taggert yet?"

I take a drink of my coffee before answering. "I stopped by on my way in and explained what happened. He said as long as I wasn't arrested, we're all good."

A smirk tilts Karina's mouth as she leans in, her eyes twinkling. "Trust me, honey. You can get arrested in your bedroom anytime, and it's fun as hell."

It's hard for me to swallow the coffee, but I do. For a full minute I struggle with what to say to her. "I don't even know how to respond to that considering all Caleb and I have done is kiss, but I'll keep it in mind."

She winks. "He didn't even tell me you kissed."

When the bell rings I quickly make my escape.

Cruise

"THINK YOU CAN spot me?" I ask Morgan as the two of us workout in the gym at our apartment complex. I don't lift heavy anymore, but I do like to have a little bulk in case I have to throw some weight around with someone I'm trying to arrest.

"Yeah." He comes over to where I'm waiting on the bench and helps me lift the bar before I start, counting my reps. "So what happened with you and the girl from The Café?" he asks as we get started.

"I took her out the next day," I admit, a smile on my face as I think about our breakfast. "For breakfast, since I had to work the night shift."

"Wow dude, really? You ever had a date that fast?" Morgan asks as he holds his hands close to the bar, there to catch it in case I lose my grip.

"No, but there was something about her. How unsure she looked when I sat down at that table, how cute she looked in her porch light. I don't know, I thought she was hot, and I hadn't had a date in a while, so I thought I'd take it." I try to play it off. Truth of the matter was, she kept me going when all I'd wanted to do was go to sleep during my long-ass shift.

"Look at you, sounding like your pops." Morgan switches places with me, adding weight to his bar, before he starts his reps.

"My pops is a happy man," I remind him, thinking of how just about every day he's got a smile on his face.

"He is, and a damn lucky one," Morgan grunts as he pushes the bar up. "I don't know how you lucked out with a stepmom who looks like yours, Harrison, but fuck."

I roll my eyes, used to this. "She was my teacher before; I already had respect for her. Plus I mean, ewwww. This isn't porno, it's real life, man."

He chuckles as he sits up, panting. "I don't know about you, but I gotta get going. I'm working the night shift tonight."

"I'm in serious overtime because of the weather the last few days. They switched my shift with someone else tonight. I think I'm gonna go have dinner at my parents, if they're having something good," I tell Morgan as I watch him packing up his bag.

"Tell your mom I said hey." He says the "hey" in a really deep voice, coupling it with a wink.

"Dude, come on. My dad would kick your ass, let's not even joke around. You *know* he would kick your ass from here to next week."

Morgan laughs as he puts his hoodie on, shouldering his duffel and grabbing his bottle of water. We leave the fitness center and then walk up the stairs. Being next door neighbors also helps keep our friendship grounded, and it's nice to have someone who understands your job. "Your pops would throw down, and probably almost kill me."

Of that I have no doubt. "See you around." I give him a wave as we go to our separate spaces.

I'm about to climb into the shower when my phone rings, and because of who's calling, I answer it.

"Hey Caleb, it's your mom."

I roll my eyes. "Yeah, your picture shows up when you call, along with your name in my phone."

She laughs, because she knows it annoys me when she starts a conversation like that. "I made pot roast and corn bread," she says it in a sing-song voice. That had been one of the first meals Kari made us when she started staying with Dad, and to this day it's one of my favorites.

"You did, huh?"

"I did." I can hear her smile through the phone. "I thought you might like to join us tonight."

"I could eat." I rub my stomach that's already clenching at the thought of the meal I love so much.

"You're so full of shit." I hear my Dad's voice in the background. "Just get over here, we'll eat in an hour."

"Gotta take a shower, I just worked out with Morgan, but I'll be there very soon," I promise into the phone, reaching out to test the water. "In fact, my water's hot, I'll see you in a few."

"Great! Can't wait to see you and hear all about what's going on with Ruby!"

She hangs up before I can say anything, and I realize with great clarity that she played me like a drum. I soothe myself with the knowledge that while I'm facing the great inquisition, at least I'll be eating one of my favorite meals, and sometimes, that's the price you have to pay to get something you really want.

"WHO'S RUBY?" KELSEA asks as soon as I enter the house through the side door. She runs, jumps up, and locks her arms around my neck.

"Who've you been talkin' to Cupcake?" I tug on her braid as I sit her down. Damn I hope she has a growth spurt soon. She's way too short, and I don't want other kids picking on her.

"Nobody." She walks over to the breakfast bar, hitches herself up in the chair, and starts working on what appears to be homework. "I just heard Mom talking to someone else."

"Kels, you're not supposed to listen to my private conversations." Kari comes into the kitchen, wearing a MTF shirt and a pair of sweatpants. "That's why they're private."

"But you said it loud enough for me to hear it." She gives a look, as if that should solve everything.

"She's got a point." Dad says as he comes in the same side door that I just came through.

"Stop ganging up on me, or no one's getting dinner."

Wisely, we all shut up. Dad comes through, clapping his hand on my shoulder, giving Kelsea a kiss on the forehead, and then walking up to Mom. She puts her hands on her hips. "You think you deserve food after you sided against me?"

"You're not gonna tell me no, Rina, and I think we both know that. Doesn't matter what it is, you never tell me no." He cups the side of her neck and leans in for a kiss.

The two of them, at one time, embarrassed me with their displays of how they feel for one another. Growing up without a mother figure in my life, I hadn't known how to react to the public displays of affection they enjoyed with one another. Now though, as a grown man, I know I want a life like this, a wife who will let me cop a feel when she bends over to get something out of the fridge, one who won't stop me when I come up behind her while she's at the sink and press my body into hers. I want all of it, and I send up a little prayer, thanking God for letting Kari come into our lives, because without her I wouldn't be the man I am today.

"C'mon, Kels, if they're going to suck face and be all lovey dovey, we can do your homework in the living room."

She grabs her stuff quickly and hops down, following me as we get her stuff spread out on the coffee table. "What are we working on tonight?" I ask as we get comfortable.

"Just some history, I have to answer these three questions, and I'm almost done." She points to the questions. "I just have one more sentence to write, then I expect you to tell me who Ruby is." She grins.

I groan as I think about how I'm being annoyed by every single member of my family right now. "I guess I could talk to you about it."

She pulls her bottom lip between her teeth, hurriedly writing the last sentence, throws her pen down, and then looks at me, excitement in her eyes. "Now, who's Ruby?"

I chuckle, shaking my head. "Cupcake, she and I have only been out on one date." I try to manage her expectations. The only other woman I've introduced her to didn't work out so well.

"But you like her right?"

"How do you know that?"

"Because you get a smile on your face when you talk about her."

I try to think back. What are my facial expressions when I talk about Ruby? Do I really smile when I talk about her? "You think?"

"I saw it when Mom was asking you about her. Tell me about her." Kels turns around on her knees, looking at me. "Is she pretty?"

"She's super pretty, she's got blue eyes and blonde hair. She's short, but she fits right here." I put my hand at my collarbone, and that's when I realize it. I'm smiling as I talk about her.

"I'm smiling, aren't I?" I shake my head at Kels.

She giggles. "You are."

And that's when I realize that after one date, one moment in a lifetime of moments with this woman, I'm completely and totally fucked. It's finally happened to me. I've met the person who brings a smile to my face, and while on one hand, I'm scared to death – I'm also so fucking ready.

Hitching my head back against the couch cushions, I say a little "bring it on" to the big man upstairs.

CHAPTER SEVEN

Ruby

I'VE NEVER BEEN so excited for a Friday night in my life. This week has passed slowly, with numerous text messages between Caleb and me. Even if we can't see each other much, at least we have this as a means to get to know each other. We haven't been able to get together, and maybe that's why I'm so excited. He's busy, I'm busy, and we don't have just a ton of free time to devote to one another.

It's a commitment; I know I'm serious when I make one, and he seems to be serious too. This must be the difference in dealing with a man, rather than a boy who's unsure of what he wants.

So far, I have to admit I'm liking it. Grabbing my phone, I scroll back through our messages, grinning as I see some of them, thinking back to our conversations.

C: What's your favorite TV show?

R: Whatever I can watch on Netflix and don't have to wait for. I like shows that are already over.

C: Into that instant gratification, huh?

I grin as I think about what he's saying. To most people I'm not the least bit naughty. No one's ever seen me as a bad girl, but Caleb didn't know me in high school, he didn't know the girl who didn't believe in herself.

With him I can be anything I want to be, and that is a heady feeling.

R: Guilty as charged. I'm not a patient person at all.

C: I'll file that away for a later date. I'd love to try your patience out.

Is he flirting with me? Not many people have flirted with me, and I haven't returned the favor, which is why I can't spot it out in the wild.

C: Delaying gratification can make the ending that much sweeter, hotter, and offer so much more satisfaction.

He's definitely flirting with me, and I squirm in my seat.

R: Maybe with you, I'll give it a shot.

C: It would be my pleasure, Ruby. To try your patience out, see how you handle it.

My face is burning with the heat of what he's suggesting.

R: I'd like that.

C: I'll definitely keep that in mind. But right now I gotta go Ruby, I got a call.

R: Be careful!

As soon as I send the text, I say a little prayer that he's safe tonight.

I grin as I look at one of our other text conversations. In college, I never did the whole text conversation thing with any of the guys I dated. I saw them often enough between the dorms, what parties I went to, and study groups. But Caleb? He's a man with an important job, one he's got to work more than most people, and he's dedicated. His time isn't exactly his own. So when he's able to give me a little bit of it, I take all I can get.

R: Please tell me why I'm such a dork.

C: I don't know you super well yet, but I can categorically say *someone who looks like you isn't a dork, sweetheart.*

Little does he know, but he will totally learn. It's weird, the feeling that we've known each other for years, and I'm perfectly okay sharing things with him.

R: So today in front of my class, I was using the projector to demonstrate something I was doing, and I was typing. I was supposed to type dart, and I typed fart.

I give him a moment to let that sink in. Let him see how sometimes I stick my foot in my mouth, even when I don't mean to. How I even do it in a classroom full of kids.

R: You don't realize how immature your class is until they crack up at the word fart.

C: If you only knew how immature I am, because I'm cracking the fuck up.

A giggle escapes from my throat as I remember the entire situation. It had been hard for me to keep it together, but I'd managed to until I turned my back.

R: Confession: I laughed too!

C: Perfect answer, gorgeous. Perfect answer.

I'm dying, waiting for him to get here to pick me up. As we've talked this week, and I've gotten to know him better, I like him even more than I did when he saved me. When I hear his Jeep pull up outside, I grab my bag, fluff my hair, and do a quick breath check. The knock literally makes my heart beat triple time. I've never had a reaction to a man like this before, but honestly, the few relationships I've been in haven't been with a man. Not a real one like Caleb Harrison.

I force myself to slow down and walk to the door, not run.

When I open it, I feel that same spark I felt the other night at The Café. He's wearing a pair of black jeans, with a pair of black Timberlands, the laces lazily done up on his feet, a wallet chain hangs out of his back pocket, and a white thermal long-sleeve shirt covers his torso. Hand to God, this guy could be a cover model if he wanted to be. His dark hair is mussed, face covered with a day's growth of beard, those brown eyes of his dark and roaming my body just like I'm roaming his, and those pink lips? Kissable and full. Finally I speak. "Hey."

His lips hitch in a grin. "Hey yourself." His arm curls around my waist before he dips down, stealing a kiss. The feel of his lips against mine is something I've craved since I last saw him. He's warm, comforting, and everything I remember him being. Inhaling deeply I smell the oil I got him. It gives me a little thrill that he's decided to use it.

The kiss isn't long, or even very involved, but it's enough to interest me, and want to try it again. "How was work?" I know he worked an early shift today. I'm new at this, I'm not sure if he wants to talk about what happened, or not, but I figure he'll let me know if the subject is off limits.

"Blissfully slow." He escorts me out of the door and down toward his Jeep.

"Good, then hopefully you won't be too tired to hang out with me tonight." I bite my lip as he helps me in.

"I don't work until tomorrow night, so you've got me a while if you want me." His smile he gives me is pure bad boy, like he knows how hot he is, and makes no excuses about it.

I do want him, and I feel like there's always this undercurrent of need between us. Even though this is only the third time we've been together, only the second date we've been on. "Sounds good to me." I decide maybe that's a better way of putting it, rather than the creepy way.

He shuts the door, and as he walks around the front end of the vehicle, I admire the way he walks, his swagger, and the way his hair lays to the side probably from where he's run his fingers through it. When he climbs in behind the wheel, I almost hold my breath, hoping I enjoy watching him drive as much as I did last time.

Cruise

GODDAMN SHE'S HOT, with that curly blond hair, clear blue eyes, and ruby red lips. Ruby. Just like her. The sweater she wears shows off her curves, but not too much. It hugs everything in a way that makes me want to see more, but doesn't show everything she's got. If I'm honest, though, it's the jeans she wears that are driving me insane. There's a rip in the thigh. It's giving me a glimpse of smooth skin, and fuck if I don't want to see that skin with nothing hiding it.

Getting onto the main road, I keep with the flow of traffic, but I can't wait any longer. Her skin is calling me. I reach over, hooking my finger in the spot where the rip is. "I like this." My voice is gruffer than I mean for it to be.

She grabs at my fingers, holding them tightly in hers. Looking down I see her nails are painted either a dark gray or black. I like that, too. "My jeans?"

"No." I shake my head. "The skin it shows. It's a fucking cock tease, but I like to be teased. Now all I'm gonna be able to think about all night is what you look like with nothing covering that smooth skin."

She's quiet and I wonder for a minute if I've come on too strong. I've been accused of that before, but I'm an intense guy and I'm honest to a fault.

"Hopefully we can work that out for you soon." She lifts her eyes up to mine. Blue meets brown, and I see something flare in hers. Her tongue sneaks out to lick her lips. "I'd like to know what it feels like to have your hands touching my bare skin."

Her cheeks turn bright red, and as we come to a stop at a light, I reach over, dragging my finger down her cheek. It's hot to the touch. "What's wrong, Ruby? Embarrassed to admit that to me?"

"A little." She ducks her head, breaking our gaze.

"Don't ever worry about being embarrassed with me, Ruby Red," I say the words, and I know this woman is always going to be my Red. She'll be my passion, the desire to be around her, the color of her lips.

"Ruby Red?" She grins over at me.

"That okay with you?"

My dad's always called Mom *Rina*, and I've wanted a woman who deserved a nickname since she came into our lives. I learned the specialness of it from their relationship, and I've wanted that for so long. The nickname for her rolls off my tongue, and I know it's perfect. Waiting for her to answer is like waiting for paint to dry.

"I love it." Her smile is white behind those red lips, and in this moment, everything is right.

"WHY DO THEY call you Cruise?" She grins at me, over the mouth of her beer bottle. We've had a good time people watching, eaten some bar food, and now we're discussing our lives.

"How do you know my call sign?"

She shrugs, an impish look on her face. "Maybe, just maybe, I asked Karina."

I run a hand through hair that's a little shaggy. I'm at least three months behind on a haircut. Something my dad likes to bitch at me for every time he sees me. It's a thing we have. "When I played football at the University of Alabama, I was a running back. At one point, when I ran, I kicked it into a gear that everybody called cruise control. Once I was there, nobody could stop me." I shrug. "The nickname stuck, even if I haven't played ball in six years."

"You didn't go pro? Everyone in this town knows how good you were." She questions, her eyes bright from the liquor she's consumed.

Swallowing my drink, I shake my head. I've been asked this before, but never by someone like her. "Nah, I was actually drafted, but I turned the contract down. It wasn't something I ever wanted to do. I got the degree for my dad, but I never wanted to do anything other than be a cop. I was a good football player, but I think I can be a great cop. It's taken me longer than it would take others, because I entered after I'd already been on the force for a year. Everyone else had been in the military before they got on the force, so they automatically went onto the Moonshine Task Force. It's understandable, ya know? I don't have that military experience and I had to do some specialized tests to show I can handle myself, but I think in the last five years, I've more than proven I can."

"Hmmm." She slides closer to me, putting her hand on my thigh, caressing it slowly. I take notice, and love that she seems to like to touch me. "Football player, cop, and now a member of a highly specialized task force? You must have speed, and an extremely motivated personality to go with the stamina we've already determined you have."

Flashing her the smile that's gotten me into a ton of panties, I play the bashful guy, ducking my head. Straight up though, this girl does make me blush. "Little bit."

"Maybe one day I'll find out all about it. After all, you've been my knight in shining armor since you rescued me at the restaurant."

"Kinda my duty, ma'am." I give her my full southern drawl. "Ya know, protect and serve."

She leans in, whispering close to my ear. "How about you protect and I'll serve?"

CHAPTER EIGHT

Ruby

H E HASN'T GONE home, and I haven't wanted him to. We've been sitting on my back porch, watching the sun come up, talking about everything and nothing at all. Truth be told, I keep trying to come up with questions to keep him here. I don't want this night to end, don't want to let him go.

"You want kids?" I ask him, pulling a blanket around my shoulders that I went to get an hour and a half ago once it got too cold. My legs are in his lap and he's still playing with the rip in my thigh. He hasn't stopped doing it since we sat down, and I'd be lying if I said I wasn't feeling it in every part of my body. Each time he makes a trip forward and back, my nipples peak and my core throbs.

"At least two, probably three or four, if I'm given a chance. I want a family, something I didn't have until I was eighteen, when Karina came into our lives." His voice is deep with what sounds like the need to sleep. We've talked for hours, and even I have to lick my dry lips.

"I'm there for the two. I have a brother who's two years older than me," I reveal. "Our relationship isn't like you and your sister's, though. We're tough on each other, and he's a fuck up. I find myself cleaning up his messes, and my parents constantly make excuses for him. It drives me up the damn wall, but he's my older brother and I like to give him chances."

"Men mature slower than women." He plays with the skin of my thigh again, causing my breath to catch and my thighs to press together.

I laugh loudly because that's what my mom has told me almost every time I've complained about them coddling Preston. "Trust me, I know all about that. I hear it every time I complain about him."

Caleb chuckles deep in his throat. "Look at that sunrise." He extends his finger toward the sun coming up. I follow his finger, as it traces the horizon.

We sit there for a few more minutes, both yawning as we put our heads together. At this point I've been up for twenty-four hours and I'm pretty sure he has been too.

"I need to get out of here—" his words are broken up by a stretch, dislodging my head and legs from his grasp-"if I'm going to make it home before I fall asleep."

There's an idea floating around in my head, and I'm wondering if I want to ask it. Rejection is a thing, and I'm scared of it, but we're running out of time because I'm tired, and I know he is too. I don't want him to get hurt on his way home, so I go ahead and decide that it's time to grow a pair. We turn quiet, each lost in our own thoughts. With a deep breath, I work up the courage to throw it out there.

"You can stay here with me, if you want to. We can sleep, and then when you're rested enough, you can go home," I invite him, almost cringing at the way I sound. Not confident at all.

His eyes are wide, like it's the last thing he expected me to ask, and the silence stretches for too long. It embarrasses me and all my insecurities seep into my thoughts. If he'd really wanted to stay, he would have jumped on the chance. And now I feel stupid.

"Forget it." I reach down, grabbing a bottle of water one of us has gone in and gotten during our long night of conversation. I'm getting it so that I have a reason to get up and leave. So he can leave me without having to save face and make a quick exit. "Bad idea."

"No." He reaches out, stopping me. "Great idea. I haven't slept with a woman in a long time. I'd be honored to break that drought with you."

Little does he know, the pleasure is all mine.

Cruise

"IF AT ANY time you don't feel comfortable, just tell me." I follow Ruby into the back of the duplex, and immediately I feel as if I've been placed in a time warp. Earlier when I came in, I didn't pay much attention, but now I do, remembering us all moving Violet in when she'd been able to leave her husband. "Not much has changed since Violet lived here."

"Is it weird she lived here and now you're here with me?" She takes off her shoes, motioning for me to do the same and stick them next to the doorway.

"No, I wasn't here very often. I helped her a few times, move in, move across to Ace's side, and then when they bought a house all of us moved them out. It's been years since I've been in here, but I remember how proud she was of it."

She turns toward me, holding her hand out for my jacket. "That's kinda how I feel." She shrugs. "I went from my parents' house to the dorms, and now I'm here. I'm lucky though, so many of my classmates weren't able to find jobs, and they've had to move back home. Even if Laurel Springs doesn't pay a lot, I didn't have to move back home. I'll always be thankful that it worked out this way."

"Oh my God, isn't that the truth? I live in an apartment across town, it's a really small two-bedroom, but I would rather live there than live with my parents again," I commiserate with her. "I sleep naked now, and there's no way I could do that under my parents' roof."

She laughs loudly, putting her hands over her face, as she runs her eyes up and down my body. "You sleep naked?"

"Well, once we get to know each other well enough, you'll find out for sure." I give her a wink. I'd like both of us to sleep naked right now, wrapped up in one another. After talking to her about anything and everything, I feel closer to her than I have anyone else I've been with in a long time. It's just I don't know how she'd handle the request. Soon though, we'll know each other that well. Until then, I tell my wayward dick to calm down.

"I don't know what I'm going to do with you." She walks farther into the living room, and I follow her like a puppy.

"Just let me stick around. I'm gonna end up being one of those things you can't live without," I say, making her a promise.

"You think so?" Ruby asks, stepping close to me this time, hooking her arms around my waist.

"Count on it." I loop my arms around her waist, holding her close.

★　★　★

"SURE YOU DON'T want to take your jeans off?" she asks as we get situated in her bed. She's changed into a pair of the shortest damn shorts I've seen, and a shirt that slips off her shoulder. When she moves a certain way, it shows the lace of a black bra underneath. I run my hand down my stomach, barely able to stop myself from reaching down and adjusting my package.

"I think they should stay on, I don't want to pressure you into moving too fast, because of how I react to you." I let my eyes do the talking as she flits around the room, closing the curtains.

"I kinda like how you react to me."

When she gets done, she comes back over to where I'm lying and slides in next to me. "You set your alarm, right?"

"Yep." I pick up my phone and make sure one more time I set it correctly. "We can sleep almost eight hours, then I have to get out of here and go change for work."

Slowly, she scoots over to where her head lays on my chest. Circling my arm around her neck, I hold her close.

"You're the first guy I've ever had in this bed," she whispers softly a few minutes after we cuddle up with one another.

"What about in this apartment?" My voice is deeper than it should be, the answer she's about to give me means more than it should.

I've always been the guy who's taken my responsibilities seriously, and I've been accused of having a hero complex more than once. But the night when I saw her scared to death, it did something to me. The first glance I had at her, I saw a future. One I've never let myself think about, one I wasn't really sure was ever for me. Everyone always told me when I met my match I'd know it, and damn if I don't know it right now.

"No men besides family have ever been in the living room, much less the bedroom." She scoots in closer to me. Maybe she's like me, feeling more comfortable because of the darkness of the room, the quietness encompassing us.

"That makes me happy." I run my finger up and down her arm.

"You should go to sleep," she says quietly before tucking her face into my neck, hooking her leg over my abdomen.

Chancing her pulling away, I put my hand on her thigh, squeezing, where it lays against a cock that's starting to pay attention to what's happening between us. "I should," I agree with her. My eyes are heavy, words a little slurred, because I'm starting to drift off. I have presence of mind to lightly push my fingers through her hair, and level her gaze to mine. "But what I really want to do–" I stop, letting her pull away if she wants. When she doesn't I go forward with what I've been wanting to say all day. "–is kiss you. Is that okay with you?"

Her smile is lazy, and she doesn't open her eyes, but she tilts her mouth to mine, letting me take control. Control is something I like, it's something I crave, and her giving it to me so easily? Maybe Ruby's made for me in more ways than one. Leaning slightly into her, I brush my lips against hers, slightly pressing for entry. When she allows it, I take. My tongue dances with hers as I slightly tighten my grasp in her hair. Slowly she melts into me, hugging me tighter with her hip across my waist. My hand there tightens on her thigh, and it takes everything I have not to pull her across me, sit her up, strip her of her shirt and bra, and end up with her tits in my mouth. She strains against me, digging her fingers into my skin, moaning softly in the back of her throat. When I pull away, she chases me, but I hold her back.

"As much as I would love to explore this mouth, and making out with you, I seriously gotta get some sleep."

My voice is wrecked, deep and regretful.

"I know."

"If I didn't have to work tonight…" I release her hair from my grip and let my hand fall to the front of her shirt. Through the material, I cup her breast, running my thumb over a nipple that's peaked against my touch. "I would explore all the ways we could both make each other feel good, but I do have to be decently rested to work a shift."

She moans, easing back from me, grabbing my thumb. "Then don't tease me, Caleb. Get some sleep so I don't have to worry about you so much."

"You gonna worry about me?" The thought spreads a warmth across my chest and into the pit of my stomach.

"Yeah, hot stuff," she sighs as she situates herself against me again. "I'm gonna worry a lot about you."

"I didn't see you coming," I whisper in the stillness.

"Didn't see you coming either."

And as I listen to the sound of her even breathing, I drift off into the best nap I've ever had before a shift.

CHAPTER NINE

Cruise

I'M DREAMING, WRAPPED in the fogginess of whatever my subconscious wants me to know. My mouth is slanted, claiming the mouth of another, my fingers are thrust into hair I know, blonde and a mass of curls, as I tilt her face to the side so I can get in deeper.

"Caleb," she moans, and as I feel her hands at my biceps, I know this isn't a dream.

"Ruby," I hiss as I feel her legs part, allowing me to slide in between them.

Sometime in the afternoon we've spent sleeping, we've rolled toward one another and started kissing. The kissing must have been going on for a while, because my cock is hard, pressing against the zipper of my jeans, and as I pry my eyes open I see love bites on her chest and neck. The belt at my waist is undone, and the button on my jeans has been popped. I'm thick against my boxers, searching for her core.

"Don't stop," she whispers as I lever myself away from her body. With the admission, she's bold, reaching back for me. "I've wanted this all night while we talked. I initiated while you were asleep," she admits as she wraps her legs around me.

She may have initiated, but I'm sure as fuck gonna finish it. I don't have as much control as I like to have as I reach in between us and work on pushing both sets of clothing we're wearing down. I may have teased her earlier, but now she's teasing the fuck out of me. Somehow I strip us both of the barriers between us and manage to reach into my jeans to grab the condom I keep there for those "just in case" times.

"Take off your shirt." My voice is strangled as I push the latex down over my length. When she's left in just her bra, I realize I want that gone, too. "Bra too, let me see you Ruby."

Her gaze is on my thick hardness as she takes the bra off, licking her lips as she sees me give myself a few strokes. "God, I can't wait." Her eyes are hooded.

"I can't either." I push up on my knees, allowing her to fall back against the pillows. "How long has it been for you?" I ask her before I position myself at her entrance, my fingers in front of my cock.

"Few months." She bites her lip as I slowly work a finger inside her. She accepts it, moaning as I push all the way in. "Keep going," she begs.

With two fingers, and then three fingers down, I know she's ready. And I definitely know I'm ready. Removing my hand, I slowly press into her, and we both moan, straining against each other. "Feels so good, so tight around me," I pant against her neck.

Her nails score up and down my back as she pulls me closer to her, and as she opens wider, I know I'm completely lost to this woman.

Ruby

THERE'S A PART of me that really should be ashamed. I knew he was asleep, knew I was playing with fire when I started kissing his neck and rubbing against his stomach. I've never been the type of person to literally take what I want, but I want Caleb, and I know he wants me too. So when he responded, I gave myself a small pat on the back.

Now though? I know I'm in over my head. No one else has ever played my body the way this man is. Ever made me feel like I could break apart with just a few thrusts, and here I am, opening wider, giving him more access to my body.

"Don't stop," I beg him. Most of the guys I've been with always stop before it feels really good. But with Caleb, it's been feeling magnificent for a while. "Please don't stop."

"I'm not going to, Red, not until you come all over me," he whispers darkly in my ear.

Reaching up, he grasps my hand and pulls it down in between us where we're connected. "Make yourself feel good, Ruby, show me what you like."

Getting over the embarrassment I would normally feel when asked to do things like this, because I want it so fucking much, I reach down and work my clit as he presses into and then pulls out of my body.

"Yeah, loosen up for me, let yourself go there," he encourages me.

When I lift my eyes up to his, I see him looking down to where I'm working myself. He's propped up on his arms, watching everything that's going on between us, his eyes glued to where we're connected. The flush of his face says he likes what he sees.

"You like it?" I ask, surprised at the question coming from in between my lips.

"Fucking turns me on, can't you tell?" His length grows, presses deeper into me.

I wonder what would happen if I took my other free hand and cupped my breast with it. With that idea in my head, I do exactly what I'm thinking, but before I do, I reach forward to his mouth, holding a finger up to his lips. He obliges sucking it deep, twirling his tongue around it, before letting me go. Knowing I have his attention, I make a production out of bringing that finger to my nipple, flicking it, circling around it, and moaning deeply as I arch my back. The show I'm putting on for him is turning me on too as I see his eyes darken, as I feel his pace quicken.

I realize that we're both in the driver's seat for each other. Hooking my legs tighter around his waist, I bounce against him, thrust up, closing my eyes and throw my head back. I'm feeling him touch, rub, and slide along every part of my body, letting him and my fingers play me like an orchestra.

"Ruby, you're so fucking hot." His hand goes to my other breast, palming it as he buries himself deeply inside of me.

No one has ever called me hot before, and hearing it come off his lips is enough to turn me on even more. "You're hot too," I whisper. "Everything about you."

When the pace quickens again, his angle changes, hitting a spot inside my body that no one else has ever managed to reach. "Oh fuck, Caleb, right there!"

With a few more thrusts, I feel his body stiffen, and as he pulses into the condom, I'm right there with him. We're both moaning, groaning, scratching, and completely decimated by what we've experienced as we lay beside each other, trying to slow our breathing.

Eventually there's a sound that breaks into my conscious. "Caleb, is that your alarm?"

"Oh fuck." He scrambles, trying to find where the noise is coming from.

The sheets and covers, along with our clothes are every-where, and eventually we find his phone under his jeans, which are under the bed. The alarm has been going off for over an hour, and he's officially late. There's two missed calls, and he's trying like hell to get rid of the condom and put his pants on.

"I hate to run, Ruby, I really do, but fuck I'm late."

I laugh as I watch him try to put his clothes back on and kiss me at the same time. "I wish I had the whole afternoon here with you." He cups my face.

"I understand. You've gotta go. I'll see you soon?"

He nods, before his face gets serious and he stops rushing. He palms my neck and forces my eyes to meet his. "I don't take what we did here lightly, and just because I have to rush off doesn't mean shit in the grand scheme of things. Thank you for giving me a piece of you."

I lean in kissing him on those lips of his. "Thanks for giving me a piece of you too."

He blushes, the first time I've ever seen him do that, before he goes back to putting his clothes on and then rushes off to work. When the door closes, I lean back against my bed and smile the biggest smile ever. I'm a supremely happy woman.

CHAPTER TEN

Ruby

TODAY HAS BEEN one of the longest days ever. It feels like every teenager I've spoken to has been a smartass to me, and I'm beyond ready to go home. Unfortunately, I have to submit my grades for the quarter, and it has to be done before I leave.

My kids are doing well, and that makes me smile. History has always been one of my loves, and to know my kids are doing well with it, makes me incredibly happy. Maybe I'm doing something right. On days when I totally question it, I can look at these grades and know I've helped them accomplish this success.

As a first-year teacher, this is everything I can hope for. Maybe I'm not changing lives, but more than anything, they're listening to me. It's enough to bring a smile to my face. Glancing at the clock on my computer, I give myself a goal of getting these all entered within the next hour. If I do, then I still have time to take a spin class at the gym. Putting in my earbuds, I crank the music on my phone and get to work.

I'm into it, moving my head to beat as Justin Timberlake talks about summer love (hey, I like the oldies), when I feel lips on the side of my neck, the scrape of stubble against my smooth skin. I jump, but don't scream as I smell the beard oil I gave Caleb. His arm snakes around my neck, my eyes fluttering down to check for the ink on his arm to confirm it's him. Closing my eyes, I lean my head back against him, exposing my neck to his lips. Reaching up, I take out my earbuds.

"Hey." My voice is hoarse, as I feel his tongue play against the pulse beating just beneath.

His moan is a deep sound in my ear that causes goose bumps to pop out on my arms, all the way down my body. I feel it in every part he's touched of me. My nipples harden against the cups of my bra, my core hums with the knowledge of how only he can possess me. I've only had him once, but I want him again, again, and again.

"Hey yourself."

God that deep growl of his is enough to make any mere mortal fall to his feet and offer to worship the ground he walks on. When he loosens his hold on me, I physically feel the loss, but turn in my chair, to look up at him as he extends to his full height. Sitting here, I'm eye level with his flat stomach, just below is his belt buckle and I can see he's just as affected by me as I am by him. My lips are dry, and my tongue sneaks out to moisten the bottom one. He groans, reaching forward with his hand to curve it around my jaw, his thumb swipes against the wettened flesh. "So, is this how it's going to be?" Caleb asks, that voice of his is deep, hoarse, dark.

"What do you mean?" I'm genuinely confused, fighting to make sense of what he's asked. Pushing back the brain fog only this man can give me, I glance up, my eyes meeting his.

He leans down so that we're even with one another. Immediately my gaze goes to the pink fullness of his lips. I'm hit with a memory of them being wrapped around my nipple as he thrust into my body. As his eyes flash, it's like he knows what I'm thinking.

"I mean–" He tilts my chin forward "–now that we've had a

piece of each other, is this how it's going to be all the time? Sparks flying, heart pounding, goose bump-inducing awareness between the two of us? It'll calm down, right? Because if I get hard every time I see you, this is gonna be a problem."

"I don't know," I admit as I shake my head in his grip. "I've never experienced it before, you're the first, hot stuff." I give him a grin.

The side of his mouth tilts in a smirk, before a brilliant smile spreads across his face. "Yeah?"

"Yeah."

He nods. "I like that shit."

A giggle rips from deep in my throat. "I like that shit, too."

He laughs along with me, before he straightens up and we physically take a step apart from one another.

"What are you doing here?" It's not very often I see him at school.

"Picked up Kels after her play practice at the elementary school and brought her over for Mom. Dad's working, and Mom said something about having to get quarter grades in. I'm assuming that's why you're here."

He drags an empty chair over and has a seat. "It's been a long day," he sighs. "It's nice to sit down, I've been on my feet forever."

"It has been a long day," I agree with him, and suddenly I'm happy that I have the option of basically sitting down whenever I want.

"What's your plans?" He leans forward, putting his hand on my thigh.

I love that he always seems to have to touch me, to want to be connected whenever we're together. "I have about ten more minutes to go here, and then I was going to hit up a spin class, but it looks like I'm not going to make it." I frown as I check the clock. Caleb interrupting has put me behind, but I can't be sorry to see him today.

"Well that's easy, come work out with me and Morgan," he says as if it's no big deal.

"Have you lost your damn mind?" My voice is as high-pitched as I've ever heard it. "Why would I want to go embarrass myself like that?"

He tilts his head to the side, before he huffs out a breath. "Yeah, you do spin class, we don't. To do spin, you have to be in decent shape. Trust me, you'll do fine with us, and you'll get to spend time with me," he says with a cocky grin.

"Okay," I agree. "Don't make me regret this, but give me a few minutes and then we can go."

Cruise

"IT'S NOT MUCH," I warn Ruby as we stand at the front door of my apartment. "But I don't really need much, since I'm not here half the time."

"It's fine," she laughs. "What you have can't be much different than what I have."

What she says is true, but for some reason, I'm a little embarrassed to show her where I live. Opening the door, I enter and hold it open for her. I left a light on before I went to work, in case I had to stay late. I hate coming in to a dark house.

"It's very you." Her eyes are taking in the sparse furnishings. "There's not a lot of clutter, very no-nonsense," she teases me.

"You're so funny. I'll have you know I spend most of my time in the bedroom."

"Oh, I bet you do." She winks.

"Look at you, getting that personality." I crowd her into the door I just closed. I allow myself a moment to capture her lips, to let my tongue tangle with hers, to feel the grip of her nails in my shoulders as she hangs on. When I pull back, we both seemed dazed, and that's honestly the way I like it.

"We should probably change and get that work out in." She licks her lips, and I imagine she's tasting me.

"Yeah, c'mon. Maybe we should change separately."

"Sounds like a good idea."

"You take Kelsea's room. It's hers when she's here."

Showing her to Kelsea's room, I leave, to give her privacy before I go to my room. When I shut the door, I take a deep breath, leaning my head against it. No woman has ever affected me the way she does, and it's throwing me off. Groaning, I let my forehead hit the door, before I go grab some clothes, and hope to God I'm not tortured for the next hour.

"I THOUGHT YOU said you weren't in good shape," I huff as I run on the treadmill next to Ruby's.

She's keeping pace with me, possibly going a little faster. Morgan has abandoned us to work on his abs; he's not much of a runner.

"I didn't think I was." She gives me a look.

"You just don't give yourself enough credit. Obviously you're in good shape." I let my eyes linger on her ass in the pair of leggings she wears. I'm not a huge fan of workout clothes as regular clothes on women, but if she wore those all the time, I wouldn't complain. When we finally break the five-mile mark, I slow the pace down, holding my sides as we cool our bodies and stealing glances at her as she does the same.

"So what else do you normally do?" she asks as she holds her arms above her head, stretching them behind her back.

"Today is pull-up day. You can hang out with us for a few

more minutes and then we can go grab some dinner, or you can head back to my apartment and get changed. Your call."

Her eyes show interest. "I think I'd like to watch you do some pull-ups."

I'd be lying if I didn't admit the fact she wants to watch this is a turn-on for me. I like that she likes my body; I enjoy hers, I want her to enjoy mine. I try to keep my head in the game as I walk over to where Morgan is, and he helps me strap the weight around my waist. He and I have been working out together a long time, we move like a well-oiled machine. I jump up, grabbing the bar and start counting my reps, feeling the burn in my arms and abs.

"Is that as hard as it looks?" Ruby questions from where she sits in front of me. "I mean the way all your muscles are rippling, the way your veins are showing. It looks like you're working pretty damn hard."

"It's not easy," I huff out. "But this is the best way for me to stay lean and take down those guys who like to run away."

"Plus he likes showing off for you," Morgan inserts his voice in the conversation.

"He's not wrong, but he should totally shut the fuck up," I groan as I finish up my reps.

The three of us are taking a rest, drinking water, and trying to let our bodies recover slightly when Morgan looks over at the two of us. "So dinner, or did you two have something planned?"

"When he says dinner, he means The Café," I clue her in on what we do most nights. "You want to come with us?"

"Sure, I was going to eat a frozen organic pizza, but I'll take The Café any day."

When the two of us get back into my apartment, I grip her hand in mine. "Thanks for coming with us. It's weird to say, but neither Morgan nor I have had a woman in our lives for a while and it's been the two of us as best friends for the last six years."

"Since you joined the MTF?"

"No, I had to do a year on the police force before I could move to the MTF. I don't have military training like everyone else, so there were special qualifications I had to fulfill to be a part of it. Not that it really matters, I would have done whatever, but..." I shrug. "Morgan and I have always had each other's backs when no one else was around, ya know?"

"I get it. He's important to you." She wraps her arms around my neck, leaning in for a peck on the lips.

"You're important to me too." I hug her around the waist.

"We can co-exist, I promise."

And right then it hits me how lucky I am to have her in my life. Someone who gets it. Some women would be pissed, but not Ruby, and I'm beyond thankful she chose me.

CHAPTER ELEVEN

Cruise

October

"YOU SURE YOU'RE okay spending the evening with my family?" I ask Ruby as she climbs into my Jeep and gets situated. "I know this is kind of moving a little quickly for us, but Halloween is a family affair in my house."

"No, I'm excited!" She reaches back to put her bag down in the back seat. "Plus I'm super excited to see that you're wearing your old football uniform. And I'm excited to wear my old cheerleading one for you."

Truth be told, I'm kind of excited to wear it for her. I can only imagine what life would have been like when we were in high school if she had been my girlfriend. Maybe we would have fucked under the bleachers, maybe I would have had the guts to actually go all the way with someone in my house. I like to think I wouldn't have paid attention to the rules my dad laid down, and I would've done whatever it took to be with her. "So is that what you're really wearing tonight?" I question as I turn from her duplex toward my parents' house.

"Isn't that obvious?"

"With you, not a damn thing is obvious." I give her a grin.

"I'm really gonna be the head cheerleader to your captain of the football team. When you told me, I dug out my old cheerleading uniform, and I'll be damned if it actually fit."

Immediately I'm hard thinking of the role-playing that could go in this scenario. Maybe tonight I *will* get a chance to fuck her under the bleachers. Not able to help it, I put my hand on her thigh. "Oh really? Where'd you come up with that idea?"

"Like I said, as soon as you told me you were pulling out your old football jersey and stuff, it was the only thing I could think of." She puts her hand on top of mine. "I went back and forth on whether I should be a cheerleader or not, because let's face it, I don't really have the body I used to have for it, but I think I found one of my old uniforms that was flattering."

"Get the fuck outta here with you saying you don't have the body for it. Your body is fucking bangin', Ruby. Don't let anyone tell you different. You're perfect for me, I don't want you to change a damn thing." I pull her hand in between my legs, letting her feel my length. "I'm already hard thinking about you wearing it, and I haven't even seen you in it yet."

I wonder if anyone's ever told her that before, because she doesn't quite meet my eyes. I know she had issues with how she looked before, but I want her to know without a doubt she turns me on.

"I can't wait to see you in it tonight." I lean over, giving her a kiss as we stop at a red light. "Actually, I can't wait to get you out of it, and get in you tonight." I move my nose along her jawline, nipping at her skin.

"Anyone ever tell you you're a bad boy with a one-track mind?"

"Only for you, Red, only for you." I pull her hand up to my lips and drop a kiss on the back.

"I kinda like how you do it only for me."

He pulls his sunglasses down so I can see those brown eyes of his. "I kinda like it how you lose all your inhibitions with me, and even when you try to keep it from happening, it happens. You trust me with your pleasure, and there's nothing I value more."

I AM IN hell.

That's the first thought that comes to my mind as Ruby walks out of what once was my room. The skirt is shorter than I imagined it would be, and the top hugs her body like a mother-fucking glove.

Kelsea grabbed her hand and begged her to help with her outfit as soon as she saw Ruby's. They've been in Kelsea's room for the last thirty minutes, and all I can think about is how she looked in that costume. It's giving me thoughts I shouldn't have around my little sister, much less my mother.

"You sure you're okay to take her while I sit here and hand out candy?" Kari snaps me out of my thoughts as she empties bags of chocolate into bowls. Snagging a Snickers to give me something to do, I pop it into my mouth, chewing as I talk around it. I'm chomping harder than I should, just to take my mind off those smooth legs. "Yeah, we don't mind. Honestly this is probably the last year for Kels anyway."

"Bubba, I'm ready." She comes running out of her room dressed as a University of Alabama cheerleader. Ruby following behind her.

"Hang on," she cautions. "Let me put your sticker on your face."

The sticker is my old number, and I can't help but grin when I see Ruby's got one on her face too. I watch as Ruby quickly puts it on, before she hands Kels her pom poms.

"You two lovely ladies ready?" I ask as I take a good look at them.

"We are when you are, hot stuff." Ruby leans in, giving me a chaste kiss.

It's the first time we've kissed in front of my family, and Kari gives me a knowing smile when she and I pull away from one another. "Okay Mom, we're leaving. We'll be back in a bit."

"Have fun, y'all. Mason should be home by the time you get home, so we'll grill some burgers and hot dogs, if that's okay?"

My stomach growls as I think about eating. It's been a super busy day and I barely got lunch. "Okay with you?" I look back at Ruby.

"You're drivin', I'm ridin'." She winks.

Immediately I have a vision of her riding my dick in my head. It's the fucking skirt, everything about the skirt and seeing so much leg exposed is driving me nuts. Hopefully I'll be able to get through this night without embarrassing myself.

"Grab your bucket Kels and let's get out of here."

She does as she's told and the three of us walk out of the house, down the porch steps, and to my Jeep.

"Are we going downtown?" Kels asks as she straps herself into the back.

All the businesses downtown set up a row of sorts that any kid can use as a one-stop shop to completely fill their buckets up. Because it's so crowded, many parents still choose the old way of trick-or-treating, which is why Mom is at home with a bucket and bags of candy, but this, this is more my speed. "Yup, I'm gonna do my best to park as close as we can, and then we'll hoof it over. I heard Leigh say she's giving out goodie bags. Not gonna lie, I'm down for that too, so we're definitely hitting up The Café."

Kelsea giggles. "I can't wait until I look like the type of cheerleader Ruby does," she mentions out of the blue. "Right now my chest doesn't fill out this top," she pouts, her voice letting us both know how upset she is.

"What the fuck, Kels? You're ten. Your chest isn't supposed to fill out the top." I glance at her in the rearview mirror, my heart racing like I've run five miles. These type of words shouldn't be coming from my little sister. I don't want her to grow up on me, because then I'll have to fight the boys off.

"Don't worry, Kelsea." Ruby turns around to face her. "My chest didn't fill out this top until my freshman year of college."

"How old were you?" she asks, awe in her voice.

"Almost eighteen, so you've got a way to go, chick. You're perfect just the way you are, Kels. Don't compare yourself to others. There's a quote that says comparison is the thief of joy. If you spend your whole life wondering why you don't look like someone else, you're going to miss out on a lot of good times. Trust me, I did."

It looks like Kelsea is taking her words to heart, and I'm so happy Ruby is here with me to help me through this process. I wouldn't have known what to say if it had just been the two of us, and right now I'm thanking my lucky stars she's with us. Reaching over, I grip her hand in mine.

"Thank you," I whisper.

She grins over at me. "Believe it or not, I've been through this more than once in my life, and I'd hate to see her almost kill herself trying to be perfect the way I did."

Ruby

I'VE NEVER MET Mason officially and to say I'm nervous is an understatement. A part of me had hoped to change before I got to meet him; I'm still in this damn cheerleading uniform, and it makes me self-conscious as hell. Although this is only the first time I've hung out with Kelsea, I have a feeling she's easier to win over than her dad.

"Why are you so quiet over there?" Caleb asks as we drive slowly through the remaining kids trick or treating.

"I'm nervous about meeting your dad." I've met more people than I care to remember since the school year has started, but somehow, not Mason. We've seen each other in passing, but never had an introduction. I'm more nervous than I thought I would be, and I'm having a hard time explaining why.

"Oh babe," he laughs as he reaches over and grabs my hand, bringing it up to his lips. "Don't be nervous to meet my dad. He's like the quintessential dad. You'll be fine. There's nothing super special about Mason Harrison, other than the fact he's a regular guy who loves his family."

"So not true. He's your dad, Caleb, and that right there makes him super special."

Our eyes meet, and I can tell what I've said touches him, the way his eyes dilate, the way he can't force words out of his mouth.

"Ohhhh she's good," we hear from the backseat.

I laugh as I turn around and look at Kelsea. "It's true though. I like your brother and I want all of you to like me too." I've never thought about it so much, but these people mean a lot to Caleb, I want them to know they mean as much to me. It's obvious he's a family man and he likes to spend a lot of time with them. It makes sense that I want to make a good impression too.

"I like you," she assures me. "He's only ever introduced me to one other girl. Cassie was nice," she mentions what I'm assuming is the name of the ex-girlfriend. "But she couldn't handle the stress of being with a cop. It made her too nervous."

I didn't exactly expect those words to come out of her mouth, but she's surprising the hell out of me. Obviously her brother has taught her well, and not to hold her tongue.

"What the fuck, Kels?" He sounds as if he can't believe what his sister has said.

"It's true! Ruby though, she can handle it, I can already tell."

My grin almost breaks my face. This kid is one of the best kids I've ever met in my life.

"What do you know about any of that? You were five," Caleb meets her eyes in the rearview mirror.

"Doesn't mean people don't say things around me, and I'm not stupid," she reminds him.

From the mouths of babes. They recognize so many things that none of us give them credit for.

"Well I'll promise you something here and now." I turn around so that I can look at Kelsea. "If you're ever worried I can't handle your brother's lifestyle, call me on it. Because I want to be what he needs, and I'd really like to hang around and be your friend."

She holds out her small hand and we shake on it.

CHAPTER TWELVE

Ruby

W E PULL INTO Karina and Mason's home, and immediately I see a Jeep that reminds me of Caleb's. Glancing over at him, I give him a grin. "Exactly how much are you and your dad alike?"

"So much!" Kelsea says as she jumps out of the backseat. "Sometimes I think Bubba and Dad share a brain."

"She's not wrong." He hitches his chin toward the house. "C'mon."

I'm slow getting out of the passenger's side, and I'm not sure why. I've seen Mason around school before, and I know we've said "Hi" a few times, but I'm nervous. After Caleb and I spent the night talking, I know how much his dad means to him. I know the relationship they've had with one another and just how much he seeks approval from Mason. It makes me want that approval too, and also gives me a fear that I won't live up to what Mason sees as the woman for his son.

Caleb comes around to meet me, taking my hand in his. He turns me so that we're facing one another. His free hand comes up under my chin, tucking a finger there, tilting me up to meet his gaze. "It's gonna be fine, babe. Trust me."

I take a deep breath wondering just how fine it'll be. We follow Kelsea in through the side door, and she yells for her dad as soon as she sees him.

"Daddy! You're here."

He turns from where he'd been talking to Karina, and once his eyes land on Kelsea, he scoops her up in his arms, holding her tightly. I don't know this man, but the way he closes his eyes and hangs on to her, it worries me slightly. He's still wearing his uniform, and it's obvious he just got off-shift.

Karina locks eyes with me, and I can see she's been crying. Discreetly she wipes her fingers under her eyes, and as Mason sits Kelsea back on the ground, she pushes Kelsea's hair back. "Why don't you go get changed and we'll cook some dinner. Then you can show us all the candy you got."

"Dad?" Caleb asks, standing behind me, sticking his arm around my neck and pulling my back to his front.

I can tell by the energy in the room that something has happened, I'm just not sure what it is. I'm nervous as I wait for either one of them to speak, and when they finally do, I'm not prepared for what I hear.

"Be thankful you didn't have your radio on you tonight. A teenager got hit over on Calhoun by a drunk driver. He Was life-flighted to Birmingham. The scene was a fucking mess. In all the years I've done this, I've never seen so much damn blood, never heard someone scream so loud."

"You responded?" Caleb moves from behind me, walking up to his dad.

Seeing the two of them there, facing one another, I'm struck with how much alike they look. Mason's only a few inches taller than his son, but Caleb's more muscular, wider, and just seems to take up a little more room than his dad.

"Yeah." He holds a hand behind his neck, his voice hoarse as he answers. "I was first on scene. It wasn't anything I'd wish on my worst enemy."

"Shit." He leans in, wrapping his arms around his dad, comforting him because they both know what this feels like.

"It was Tanner." Karina pushes between her lips, her throat sounding like it won't let the words come out.

"No…" I feel tears come to my eyes. Tanner Sumner is loved by everyone in our school. He's the heart of Laurel Springs High, a sixteen-year-old with special needs, he's doted on and everyone has taken him under their wing. He helps the football team, the cheerleaders, he runs the concession stand – where no one gets annoyed with him when it takes him a few seconds longer to count change; he's everything good about everyone. The tears are slipping down my face. "Is he gonna make it?"

Mason clears his throat, as he looks at me for the first time. "They aren't sure. Blaze was on scene, and I know she'd do whatever it takes to stabilize him until they could get him to the heli-pad. The asshole had Moonshine in his trunk, was drinking it in a water bottle." He puts his palms to his eyes and rubs hard.

All of us adults are trying to get our emotions under control when we hear Kelsea running back through the hallway. It's obvious by the way she's quiet and unsure of whether to approach her dad that she knows something has happened.

"I'm gonna go take a shower, Kels, and I'll fire up the grill when I'm done," he tells her as he quickly walks back to what I assume is their bedroom.

Karina glances at the two of us, her eyes pleading. Caleb looks as wrecked as the rest of us, and he seems to be having trouble figuring out what needs to be done. Glancing around, I notice Kelsea's bare nails, and on impulse I reach into my purse. I have an assortment of nail polish in there, it's what I do when I'm bored, but I have a favorite. Rose gold glitter – I always feel like a million bucks when I'm wearing it. "How about we go outside, wait for your dad, and I paint your nails? This color would look so great on you." I shake it up and hand it to her.

"Mom?" she glances at Karina, who has such relief in her eyes.

"That would be so much fun! You go out there with Ruby, and I'm gonna go check on your dad."

Caleb snaps out of it when she mentions Mason. "I'll go ahead and get the stuff ready to grill, Mom. Tell him to take his time."

She comes over, kissing him on the cheek, before she all but runs to the bedroom. Karina's a strong woman, and I can't even begin to imagine how many times she's had to comfort her husband after he's come home from a rough shift. It makes me wonder if I have what it takes. Immediately, I know I do. I'll never give up on what Caleb and I could build together.

"Is he okay?" Kelsea asks, glancing at the two of us, shuffling on her feet, putting her hands in her pockets.

"He had a rough day, Kels. You know sometimes, we just do." Caleb squats in front of her, pulling her into his arms. "But he'll be fine because he's got us, and he'll definitely want to see how awesome your nails look when Ruby gets done with them."

She pulls back from him, and then motions for me to follow her out onto the back porch. As I'm about to leave the kitchen I hear Caleb's voice.

"Ruby?"

"Yeah?" I glance back at him, waiting to hear what he wants to say.

"Thanks, you don't know how much you taking her mind off of how he acted when he came home helps. She gets really upset when she can't figure out what's going on with him."

He's right, I'm new to this. I don't know what it's like to deal with the hard, emotional stuff that comes with being someone who dates a cop, but I do know the toll has to be enormous. If I can't handle this, how can I handle things that may or may not happen to Caleb? That's the thought that runs through my head; this was a test and I've passed. I don't know how I'll handle it when it's him, but I hope I do as well as I have today.

"No need to thank me, hot stuff. When you're ready, we'll be out here waiting on you."

"Now?" Kelsea asks as she looks at me.

"Few more minutes." I giggle when she squirms in her seat. "Beauty takes time, girlfriend, but if you like this and it's okay with your mom and dad, I'll take you to get your nails done sometime. They have little dryers that fix you up in no time at all."

"We'll have to ask." She nods to me, her tone very serious. "I'm not sure I can handle this every freakin' time."

"Be right back." I get up and go to where Caleb is manning the grill for his dad. "You okay?" I ask as I stand beside him, running my hand up and down his back.

He wraps his arm around my shoulders, pulling me in close. "Should probably be asking if you're okay, I didn't know Tanner."

"Yeah, we'll definitely have to do some counseling at school. He's a big part of Laurel Springs High. Right now, though, I'm more worried about you and your dad. While you don't know him, I don't know what it's like to see someone who's been hit by a car, so I think in the grand scheme of things, we're even. Plus it can't be easy to see your dad affected by things."

"It never is." He flips the burgers, sighing heavily. "He's always been such a strong person, and it never occurs to me that this shit bothers him, until I see it bother him. None of what we do is easy, but that is the hardest. Especially when moonshine's involved. We take that personally, and it just hurts me to see him hurt. He's always been this larger-than-life guy who never lets anything get to him, it just hurts," he explains.

"I can see that." I curl into his chest, wrapping my arms around his waist. I lay my head on his chest, listening to the strong beat of his heart. "I can handle this," I assure him, at the same time assuring myself. None of what's happened here tonight has scared me away from being with him.

"I know you can, you did amazing today."

I preen under the praise he's given me. To know he understands that I'm willing to do whatever it takes to prove to him I'm serious about our relationship means everything to me.

He drops a kiss to my forehead as his parents come out the back door. Karina sends Kelsea inside to wash up, and Mason walks toward the two of us.

"Sorry you walked into a shit storm." His lips tilt to the side, and the move is so much like Caleb's, I feel like I'm seeing my boyfriend in sixteen years."

"It's okay." I return his grin. "Life isn't always rainbows and unicorns."

"No, it's not. I'm Mason." He holds out his hand.

I untangle myself from Caleb, holding my hand out too. "Ruby, nice to meet you."

We talk for a few minutes about how we've seen each other around school, and then Mason smacks his son in the stomach. "Move over and let your old man work."

Caleb hands him the spatula. "I'll have you know I had this shit locked down. Don't need you coming out here and telling me what to do."

They share a grin, and I know this is their way of making sure the other is okay. It's endearing and totally makes me want to melt that Caleb can be this way with the man he looks up to so much.

"Ruby, can you help me bring the sides out?" Karina yells from the door as Kelsea comes back out, her hair out of her face and it looks like her hands washed.

As we assemble the meal and I have a seat next to Caleb, I look around thinking I definitely could belong here if given the chance.

CHAPTER THIRTEEN

Cruise

"Y OU SEEM TENSE," Ruby comments as we pull out of my parent's driveway.

She's right, I am. There are some days I hate what I do because of the emotional toll it takes on me and the men on my team. Then there are days I love what I do because of all the shit we take off the streets. We make life safer for the citizens of the town we live in. No day is perfect, but this one was super shitty for my dad. I hate that he had to see what he had to see, and now he's gotta live with it. He'll need to process it and figure out how to not take it with him the next time he goes out on the streets.

"Just the stress of the job sometimes. Even though it didn't happen to me, I know what my dad's going through, and I worry about him." I shrug as I drive us along the deserted streets of Laurel Springs.

At this hour everyone's closed up shop, the candy's all gone, and what's left are the reminders of a Halloween that's over. There are jack-o-lanterns sitting on steps, candy wrappers here and there on the ground, and a couple of teenage stragglers walking the streets.

"How do you deal with the stress when it's you?" she asks softly as she reaches over, running her nails along my neck.

Do I want to be completely honest with her? Do I want to tell her exactly how I deal with it? There's a part of me that realizes this is more than she bargained for. But if I want this woman to know me, the real me, I have to be honest, don't I? If not, we'll never make it, and I desperately want to make it.

I stop at a red light, grip the steering wheel, and decide to fucking go for it.

My voice is soft, rough, wrecked when I answer her. "Sex, but not just any sex. I like it a little rough and a little adventurous."

Her blue eyes widen, her mouth is slightly open, those teeth of hers taking her lip between them. "How have all your other girlfriends dealt with it?" she asks softly.

"They haven't." I shrug. "I've never told anyone else. Like I told you, I haven't really had a girlfriend for a long time. You're the first one I've trusted enough to tell."

Her eyes lift up to the light, still glowing red. She leans forward, turning her body to me. "Thank you for trusting me, Caleb."

"You trusted me from the first moment we met," I remind her.

"Which is why I want to be everything you need."

She takes my hand in hers, pulling it between her skirt-covered legs. "Is this adventurous enough for you?" she asks as her fingers move her panties aside and place mine against her bare skin.

I lick my lips as I feel her arousal. Behind us a car horn honks, but I don't remove my fingers as the costumes we're wearing gives me an idea. "Ruby Red, we're gonna see exactly how adventurous you can be."

"HERE?" HER VOICE is almost a shriek as I pull around the back of the high school.

"I use the football field sometimes to work out on; I run the edges, trust me no one *ever* comes back here." I remove my hand from between her legs. "C'mon, you don't even know what I want."

She moans as I put the Jeep in park and get out, coming around to her side. Reaching into the back, I grab a blanket I keep behind the passenger's seat for emergencies.

"Where are we going?" She unbuckles, turns, and spreads her legs to let me in between them.

I allow myself to capture her lips, before I put the blanket over my shoulder and grasp her around the thighs. "You'll see, head cheerleader."

A blush works its way up her neck. As I carry us under the bleachers. "Caleb." She wraps her arms around my neck, burying her face there.

When I get us deep enough under the bleachers so that we can't be seen, but we can see, I tell her to put the blanket down behind her, on a small concrete seat.

"Back when I was in high school, I'd come out here and smoke," I admit to her, as I set her down.

"You smoked? God, you're just every girl's dream guy. Dark, brooding, smoker – the ultimate bad boy." She runs her hand down my chest, until she encounters my belt buckle.

"You're about to see how bad I can be." I close my eyes, enjoying the feel of her fingers on my body. My cock punches against my zipper. Opening my eyes, I look down at her. "You okay with this? I don't want to do anything you aren't okay with."

I'm unbuckling my belt as I gaze down at her, waiting for her to tell me yes or no.

"I'm okay. I told you, I want to be whatever you need me to be," she answers as she spreads her thighs wide. "I want whatever it is you want to give me."

It's all I need to hear as I push my pants down far enough to extract my cock. She breathes deeply as she sees how hard I am, licks her lips when she notices the drop on the tip. "This won't be pretty, Red," I warn her as I take myself in hand, stroking up and down. "Not everything in the world is pretty."

Understanding sparks in her eyes. She gets this is how I get rid of those desperate feelings. I fuck them out, let them go as I cum, and bury myself in something that's good and decent. "I don't want pretty," she whispers.

Her blue eyes are now closed as she leans her head back, and I watch as she moves her hand down her body, pulling aside those panties for me. Her skirt is hitched to her waist, and underneath the tight top she wears, I can see her nipples peaked. This is turning her on as much as it's turning me on. Maybe she has to fuck a little of the bad in the world out too.

My hands are shaking, and I'm fumbling with the condom I've taken out of my back pocket. Shaking because I can't wait to get inside her, fumbling because I'm about to lose my cool. I move the hand that's holding her panties to the side to her core, extend her finger and encourage her to play with her clit. "Make sure you're ready, baby."

There's a noise in the back of her throat, and I'm surprised as fuck when she goes for it. She's not shy in the least, maybe it's because of where we are, what this situation is, and what we're doing, or maybe it's because she wants me as much as I want her. Pushing the condom down my length is literally almost enough to undo me, but I grit my teeth and move on. Holding the base, I push my legs apart to put me level with her, and then press my cock inside her.

We both moan loudly as I press home. "Shhhhh."

"You moaned too," she points out as she grabs hold of my biceps when I start to pound.

"I know, I know." I lean my head against her shoulder, letting her take my weight since she's sitting down. "But we have to try and be–" I grunt when she widens her legs. "*Fuck me.*" My eyes roll back in my head slightly. "Quiet."

She buries her face in my shoulder, just like I've done to her. Both of us moaning, grunting, groaning, fucking like something you see on Tumblr. My hands grip her hips, my fingers tilt her ass as I use her and she uses me. It's the most primitive fuck I've ever had. Her breath is hot against the shirt I wear, and I know mine's hot against her skin.

"Caleb." She runs her hands up and down my arms. "Feels so good, I didn't know this would feel so good," she breathes out.

I can't speak in full sentences, not with the way her pussy is gripping my dick, but I do my best. "Forbidden. Could get caught. No finesse. Just fucking. Sometimes it's better."

"Yes." she tilts her head back, exposing her neck, and I go to town. Nipping and biting, flicking my tongue against the wild pulse there. Open-mouthed, I suck at the flesh, knowing I'll mark her. Knowing that tomorrow when she wakes up, she'll bear proof this night happened.

"Ahhh," she groans out. I hit a particularly sensitive spot.

Taking one of my hands off her body, I move it to her mouth, gently covering it, so that it muffles the noise of what we're doing. Not that it helps a whole lot, the sound of my balls slapping against her is loud in the still of the night, but if I absolutely have to, I can slow down. She can't seem to stop voicing her approval of what I'm doing to her, and truth be told, I don't want her to.

"I'm gonna come," I whisper in her ear, pushing my thumb against her clit as I work the both of us. In that instant, I can feel her tighten against me, can feel her let go, and it makes me want to beat my chest and scream to the world I did this to her.

But instead, I thrust. Once, twice, and on the third withdrawal, I come. Hard. Fast. More. With a ragged grunt, I feel the release everywhere. My stomach muscles and ass jerk as I empty into the condom. We both look down, watching me fill it as I can't seem to stop myself. My nipples are tight and I have to throw my head back as I continue to thrust into the air, my cock searching out her warmth again as my fingers grip her thighs tight. My mouth is open, heaving in deep pulls of air, trying to come down from whatever this orgasm is. My body is trembling, my skin is sensitive, and my dick is still fucking hard when my gaze falls on Ruby.

Her makeup is smeared, those panties are now ripped, and her hair is a mess. She's trembling too. I step closer, because I don't want to leave her so exposed, using my body to block hers, in case anyone were to happen upon us.

What I don't expect, is for her to reach around me, stick her hand in my jeans pocket and pull out another condom. I watch in a blur as she takes the first one off, using those wrecked panties to clean me up, and then puts another one on.

"I need you again, Caleb. Having you that wild one time wasn't enough. It'll never be enough." She scoots closer to the edge, angles my cock down, and pulls me into her using her hands.

Fuck me, this woman. She's everything, literally everything.

And minutes later, when we both come again, I know without a doubt, I'm never letting her go.

CHAPTER FOURTEEN

Ruby

November

WHEN I WAKE up the next morning, I feel like I'm a different person. Not only am I a different person, but I'm closer to Caleb than I've ever been to anyone else. Rolling over, I grab my cell phone, seeing I have a text from him. For a moment, I inhale the scent of the pillow he slept on, loving that now my bed smells like him.

Glancing up at the clock, I see it's past ten; he's already been at work for a few hours.

C: Morning, Red. You okay? You looked peaceful, and I didn't want to wake you up before I left.

R: I'm good! I promise I would let you know if you hurt me. You so could have woken me up, it would have been fine.

The way he commanded my body last night did frighten me, but not in the way he thinks. I've never had someone make me so aware of how another person can pleasure you so much.

C: Did you like it?

I contemplate lying to him. I really do. Not because I'm embarrassed at what we did, but I'm a little self-conscious at how I reacted to him. One thing I'm learning though, is I have a need to be honest.

R: *I did, but only with you. I don't think I would have trusted anyone else as much as I trusted you last night.*

C: *That's good, and I'm glad I didn't scare you off.*

R: *No! Not at all, I wouldn't mind doing it again.*

C: *All good to hear, Red. I gotta go, I'll talk to you later.*

Sighing, I fall back against my bed and let the smile spread across my face. I'm lazy as I contemplate getting up and moving. My plan before what happened last night was to do some shopping today, but I'm having a hard time motivating myself. When my phone beeps beside me again, I make a grab for it, hoping it's Caleb. Instead, I see Karina.

K: *Hey! Mason's working today, so Kelsea and I are doing some shopping. I was wondering if you want to go with us? We're going to Birmingham.*

Karina and I have been friendly since I started student-teaching. I was lucky enough to do my rotation at Laurel Springs and then slipped into a full-time job there, so the two of us have known each other for almost two years. We, however, haven't been what I would call the type of friends who get together outside of work. We're acquaintances who help each other out when we need it. I know she's making an effort to get to know me outside of work because of Caleb, and I find I want to get to know her as well. Which is why I text back an *I'd love to* when before I may have made an excuse and not moved from my bed.

K: *Great! We'll pick you up in about an hour if that's okay with you?*

R: *I'll be ready! I've been told it's the old duplex where Ace and Violet lived, if that means anything to you.*

K: *Perfect! I know exactly where that is.*

And with that motivation, I hop out of bed, and get ready to go about my day.

★   ★   ★

"THANKS FOR COMING with us," Karina says as she backs out of the driveway of my duplex. "When I mentioned we were going, Kels threw out the idea to invite you and I got excited about it too. Typically it's just the two of us, and she falls asleep on the way home." She shoots a glare through the rearview to her daughter.

"It's just because you make me shop 'til I drop."

"Pretty sure it's the other way around, kiddo."

In the back seat, I watch as Kelsea puts on a pair of ear buds and starts watching her iPad.

"Another reason I needed another adult to come," Karina laughs. "I get bored on the drive with no one to talk to. She'll be engrossed in that thing until we get to the mall."

"No problem." I situate myself in my seat, and put the drink I brought with me into the cupholder. "I tend to go by myself, so it'll be fun to go with someone else."

"By yourself?" I can tell she wants to ask why.

"Most of the friends I had in high school have either taken longer to finish college than I did, or they've moved on from Laurel Springs, and me being the youngest teacher doesn't help. There aren't a lot of women around my age, if you think about it."

I can see her doing the math in her head, going over who's around my age. "You're right, I never thought of that. Well, never fear, we're here now. We're actually meeting a couple of the MTF wives in Birmingham. I hope that doesn't scare you off."

Scares the fuck out of me. "No, I'm good," I answer, reaching over to take a drink from my to-go cup. At least she didn't tell me before I agreed to come, then I may have backed out.

"How did last night go, after what happened with Mason? Sometimes that kind of stuff affects Caleb too, I'm glad he had you to help him."

I can literally feel the warmth in my neck, working up to my face. "He was upset, but he's okay now, we worked it out."

She gives me a knowing glance. "Yeah, I can tell you did. You missed a little spot on your neck where you tried to cover up that beard rash."

My hand immediately flies to where Caleb had been biting and nuzzling my skin. Immediately I want the attention off me, so I turn to her.

"How did you and Mason meet?" It's something I've wondered since I found out who she was married to. I want to know how she came to be Caleb's mom.

"Smooth," she giggles.

Her gaze shifts back to where Kelsea is still watching her iPad. Karina says her name once, and when she doesn't even flinch, she starts talking. "We met off a dating app. We talked for maybe two weeks before we met in person, at a restaurant in Birmingham, actually." She gets a nostalgic smile on her face.

"What happened then?"

She turns to face me, whispering. "We had an amazing date, then we fucked in the parking lot in the back seat of his Jeep, and I ran because I was scared of how he made me feel."

"Holy shit, Karina!"

"Yeah." She grins. "He's still got that Jeep. It's not the one he drives now, but he refuses to trade it in. Every once in a while, he and I take it out for a spin." She winks.

"How did you get to know Caleb?" I intentionally put a

curve in the conversation, just because I'm not sure how much I want to hear about her and Mason's sex life.

"That's a funny story, I thought Caleb was a little kid. Mase had mentioned being a single dad, and I just assumed it was to a little kid. Caleb was my student, and when I had a career day, in walked Mase wearing his uniform."

"Oh hell." I can just imagine, because I know what Caleb looks like in his.

"Yeah." She nods, obviously remembering the situation well. "He confronted me about running and told me I wouldn't be running any longer. Then when I realized Caleb was basically an adult, Mason and I had some serious conversations about what he was doing as a teenager."

I laugh loudly at that. "Obviously not what I was doing," I mumble.

"Me neither, not at least until I was eighteen." She checks her blind spot as we merge into the lane that will take us to Birmingham. "But I mean, come on, you see what my husband looks like. You see what Caleb looks like. Even as a teenager, Caleb had girls who wanted to be with him."

"I bet he did." Now this I'm curious about.

"I don't know what his college life was like," Karina continues speaking. "Because he never really talked to me much about the girls he was dating or screwing around with while he was there. But he did have a high school girlfriend. That ended when she went to Ole Miss and he went to Alabama. She didn't love Laurel Springs though and said she'd never live there. I always knew he'd be back to Laurel Springs."

"Yeah, we had a conversation not long ago about how he was drafted, but all he ever wanted to do was follow in his dad's footsteps."

She sighs. "He's always had a huge case of hero worship for

his dad. Mason doesn't understand it. Like any parent, he wants better for his son than what he was able to give him. I don't know the full story, but they had some really lean years when Caleb was little, Mason was away serving, and things just went to shit. But I'd say Caleb is a very well-adjusted grown up today."

Unless you count the fact he likes rough sex to take the edge off. But that's our secret to keep, and I'll guard it with my life.

"He is, he's a good man," I agree with her. "Mason did a great job with him."

"I can't wait for you to hang out with him more. Last night was awful and he wasn't himself. Usually those three have me in stitches, and the way Caleb talks to his dad? They're best friends, and you can tell. Back when I first started dating Mason, I was kind of amazed at the conversations the two of them had together. Eventually I realized it was because they'd actually grown up with one another, and while Mase did lay down the law when he needed to, more than anything they were friends. It's how I try to raise Kels, but it's harder because of the age difference and she's a girl."

"Girls are so different than boys."

"Oh my God, I know. There are things that are completely different for her and Caleb. Even though Caleb was older, there are still some parallels for the two of them, and the way she handles it is like night and day. He's really good with her, though."

"I noticed that last night. There's nothing hotter than a guy who's good with his little sister and even has a bedroom for her at his apartment."

She flashes me a grin. "If he gets wind you said that he'll totally use it to his advantage."

"Trust me when I say, he doesn't have to do much."

She giggles as we take the exit to the mall and begin the

search for parking.

Cruise

I'M SITTING IN the MTF headquarters doing some paperwork I'm behind on when my phone vibrates next to where it's sitting on the desk. When I see a picture of Kelsea, Ruby, and Karina, I can't help but smile.

> **R:** Wish me luck! I'm going shopping with them and with the MTF wife crew.
>
> **C:** You're gonna need it! Stay strong, don't let them pull you into discussing shit you don't wanna discuss. Those ladies and even the kids are sneaky. Before you know it, you've agreed to host a sleepover at your apartment for Stella and Kels, along with feeding them, and letting them watch scary movies they have zero business watching.
>
> **R:** You're a good brother.
>
> **C:** I'm a sucker....don't make my mistakes, Red. Learn to say no!
>
> **R:** LOL!

I glance up, when the main door opens and in walk my dad and Renegade.

"What's up?" I yell at them from where I'm seated.

We've been so busy, I'm behind by at least a few weeks, so much that I'm not out patrolling today. After last night though, I can't say that I'm completely sad to not be on the streets.

"We got back the sample from the creek bed," Renegade says as the two of them have a seat in front of my desk.

"Oh yeah, and what was it?"

"Really old 'shine," Dad supplies the answer. "Like probably from back when Jefferson was hiding it. There are some markers in it that can date it, and it's not new product. Which is a relief."

We've basically eradicated most of the big operations that have come and gone since Jefferson and the Strathers were making big money selling their supply. A few suppliers have come and gone, but for the most part, we dismantle any of the operations before they can get too big. It's why they keep us together, and it's why we all still have jobs. Nine times out of ten anyone we catch with moonshine now is from out of state, moving it in, or they're working on their own. It doesn't mean we don't still have some sometimes, and it doesn't mean that it still isn't dangerous. People can still die, and dealers can still kill. We're proud of what we're doing here.

"Anyway, we don't want to interrupt you, just wanted to come by and let you know." Renegade gets up from where he's had a seat. "I'm gonna hit the head and then we can be back out." He lifts a chin to my dad.

I wait until he's gone before I turn my gaze onto the man who's raised me my entire life. "You good after last night?"

His answer is slow, and I can tell he thinks about it for a few minutes. "I'm good. I'm glad you and Ruby were there last night, it helped with Kelsea. Really sorry I didn't get more of a chance to talk to her."

"Nah, it's okay, she gets it."

"She's pretty," he needles at me. "I've see her around school before."

"Dad…"

"What? I'm just saying."

"It's new," I warn him. "It's new and I don't know where it's going."

"Yeah well, at one point Rina and I were new too, and you see how that ended up."

Before I can say anything else, Renegade comes out, and the two of them head out. Leaving me alone with thoughts of a blonde haired, blue-eyed vixen that, after last night, has me all tied in knots.

CHAPTER FIFTEEN

Ruby

"**G**ET IT!"

I'm not sure who's talking to me. I'm surrounded by a group of women, all telling me I need to get this dress I just impulsively grabbed and tried on.

"Whitney, don't pressure her if she doesn't want to," the red-head who we met at the mall, I think they called her Blaze, tells her friend.

"No, someone needs to pressure her, because if Caleb saw her in that? Oh my God, he'd be all over her. It'd be great for Valentine's Day. I mean he could take the skirt off and still keep the top on. Ya know, some men like that!"

"Hello! I'm his mother!"

There's too much noise around me, but I do like the way this dress I picked up looks. It's on clearance for much less than its original price tag, and the deep pink color shows off the little bit of a tan I keep year-round. What's throwing me is the fact that it's a two-piece and where they meet in the middle, you can see a good portion of my stomach.

As I listen to everyone voice their opinions behind me, I quickly take a picture and send it to Caleb, wanting his opinion to what he thinks I should do.

R: Toss or buy? What do you think? As you can see by the

peanut gallery's faces behind me, there's a heated debate going on.

I hope he's not busy, and it doesn't take him too long to get back to me. I'm pretty sure Whitney will throw down in a minute, just to prove a point. She's very, very loud in her belief I should buy this dress.

C: *Fuck, Ruby! Get it! I love everything about it. Especially the little strip of skin you see between the two pieces. Please, get it.*

R: *Will do! Thank you, hot stuff.*

C: *Wear it for me? Soon.*

I would probably wear it for him tonight, but I do like Whitney's idea of wearing it on Valentine's Day. So instead of just telling him that, I decide to play a little coy.

R: *Ehhh, we'll see. Thanks for telling me to get it!*

"Alright." I turn around, facing what has almost become a firing squad. "I'm getting it. You can all stop pleading your cases."

A cheer goes up, and people in the store look at us. I'm not used to being the center of attention, but I've had a good time with these ladies today.

"I love it," Kelsea tells me as I come out of the dressing room, after putting my own clothes back on.

"Thanks, Kels! I love it too."

As we're standing in line to pay for it, she puts her head on my thigh and wraps her arms around my waist. It's a show of trust I'm not exactly prepared for, but as my eyes meet the group of women who are waiting for me to check out, I can almost hear them welcoming me to the group.

★ ★ ★

"LET ME ASK her," Karina is saying into her cell phone as we're walking out of the mall. She got a phone call from Mason, and she's been talking to him the last few minutes.

"Mase wants to know if you want to have dinner with us. He and Caleb are prepared to make some spaghetti, if you do. Caleb's over at the house with him. After last night, I think we'd all like a little bit of a do-over."

"I'd love to," I answer immediately. One, because that means I get to see Caleb. Two, because I really would like to get to know Mason. He's a huge part of Caleb's life, and I'd never dream of holding what happened last night against him, but I'd like to see him on a normal day.

"We'll be there in the next hour or two, depending on traffic. I'll let you know when we get closer." She finishes up the phone call, and we all head out to the parking lot to make the trek home.

Cruise

C: *Thanks for agreeing to dinner tonight. I can't wait to see you.*

Does that make me whipped? I saw her last night, but now I'm dying to see her again. More than anything, I want to see her relaxed and in the home I shared with my dad for so long. It's important to me that they like each other. More important than I ever thought it would be.

R: *I'm excited to hang out with you all again tonight. Plus, I'm really excited to see you, and see what you can cook.*

C: *Hey, Dad and I are capable of cooking a few meals. We may* *not be gourmet chefs, but we're passable.*

R: *That remains to be seen, hot stuff.*

She sends a little winky emoticon, and again she's surprised me. There are certain things she does, almost two months into this relationship, that surprise me.

"Rina just texted that they should be here in about thirty minutes." Dad comes into the kitchen, fresh from the shower. I took one before I came over, and it's obvious he wants to get dinner started.

"What do you want me to do?" I go over to the sink and wash my hands.

"Start the salad and garlic bread while I get the other stuff going?"

"Can do."

For a few minutes the two of us work in silence, both concentrating on the tasks at hand, until Dad breaks the silence. "So you like this girl?"

Like is too weak of a word, but I don't think I've fully admitted it to myself yet. I've never been much a liar to my dad, and I don't want to start now. "You remember you telling me you were insanely hot for Mom? Well that's how I am with her."

"I remember those days." Dad gives me a grin. "Happy you're having them."

"Kinda never thought it would happen," I confide in him. "Just wasn't sure."

"Caleb, it hadn't happened because you weren't ready for it. Cassie," he mentions the last relationship I had, "would have probably given you whatever you wanted, but you weren't ready for it."

"I don't think she could have handled it," I admit. "Like what happened to you last night, she would have crumbled. There would have been no helping Kelsea get over it, none of that. But Ruby, she's got what it takes, she gets every party of me."

"Every part?" Dad asks, the eyes so much like mine looking at me.

After last night, I can definitely say an affirmative. "Yeah, every part. I'm a lucky man to have found her."

"Hold on tight to her, woman like her don't come along every day."

"I know. I got it, and I don't plan on letting her go."

"WHAT ARE YOU doin' here?" Kelsea asks as she walks in through the garage, looking at me with a smile on her face.

"We're makin' dinner. What are you doing here?"

"I live here…duh!"

"Well I lived here before you," I argue with her. "Sometimes I like to come back and have dinner, ya know?"

"Just didn't expect to see you tonight."

I crouch down to her. "Just couldn't wait to see you again." I grip her nose between my pointer finger and middle finger, pulling on it.

"Stop!" She giggles as she runs down the hallway with her bags in her hand.

When I stand up, I'm face-to-face with Ruby. "Hey." I reach out, pulling her into my arms, hugging her around the neck.

Her hey is muffled by the cotton of my t-shirt. When I release her, she sniffs. "Something smells really good in here."

Kari laughs from where she's standing next to Dad. "That's because Mase can cook like five things well, and one of them is spaghetti. He's passed that on to Caleb, and I daresay, it's some of the best spaghetti you'll ever eat."

"C'mon, Rina, give credit where credit is due. We even make

our own sauce from scratch," He slings an arm around her neck, pulling her close, almost the same way I did to Ruby. The similarities are sometimes fucking scary.

She rolls her eyes. "You make it using a can of tomato paste."

"We mix multiple ingredients together to make a sauce that's not readily available in a jar. Hence, we make our sauce from scratch. I challenge you to tell me that's not the definition, Mrs. Harrison."

I glance over at Ruby who's grinning at the two of them.

Dad makes a production of looking at his watch. "Still waiting, babe."

"Oh shut the fuck up, Mason, and just get the stuff on the table."

He chuckles as she turns her back to him and smacks her on the ass.

"Ouch!" She turns giving him a glare.

He tilts his head to the side. "Don't even, Rina."

I put my mouth next to Ruby's ear. "Welcome to a *real* dinner at my house."

"I think I'm gonna like it here."

LATER ON, KELSEA'S gone to bed, while the four of us adults sit on the back porch, each enjoying a beer. It's cold, but a few years ago, they put in a firepit, so it's warm enough.

"Do we have to tell Ruby about all the stupid shit I've done?" I groan as we sit snuggled together in one of the chairs. She's on my lap, curled into my chest, and I'm burying my face in her hair.

"You've done plenty," Dad busts my balls as he takes a drink of his beer.

"Getting my squad car stuck on the railroad tracks was probably the most embarrassing," I admit.

Dad laughs loudly. "They had to call the train company, because one was headed that way. It stopped a good twenty feet from Caleb's car. I mean we all stood there watching. Me, him, and Havoc. We were screaming and waving our arms, hoping like hell this guy wouldn't hit this car and it would blow up. When he put the brakes on, the train smoked. We thought we were all fucked."

"And they never let me live it down."

"Oh hell no." Dad shakes his head. "You will never, ever live that down, just like Havoc will never live down when Dale asked to speak to a supervisor, knowing damn good and well Havoc is the supervisor."

"I bet you get some really belligerent people," I make an observation.

"We do," we both say.

"There was a guy not long ago, who was threatening to kill Renegade's whole family."

"Oh my God," Mom inhales deeply. "Why?"

"Because–" Dad's gaze settles on the two women with us "–Renegade told him to drop his weapon. It turned out the weapon was a small flashlight, that in the dark, looked like a gun. The guy didn't take too kindly to being arrested for resisting and started spewing a shit ton of threats. Said he'd kill all our entire families and he'd do it with a smile on his face, anyone we cared about would be dead."

"What did they do with him?" Ruby asks softly.

"He's in the psych ward of the prison right now. Luckily the judge agreed with the doctor who gave the evaluation. That's not always the case." My voice is somber as I again remind her of what she's signed up for. "None of what we do is easy."

"It's just like being a teacher, hot stuff. It's not glamorous and you don't make a lot of money doing it, but without any of us, the future of this nation wouldn't have a future."

I tighten my grip around her, because she does get it. Out of anyone, she gets it, and it's nice to know the person I want to share my time with, doesn't begrudge the civic duty I owe to this community.

I just have to prove that when the time comes, I can love them both equally.

CHAPTER SIXTEEN

Ruby

Late November

"I'M WARNING YOU, my house isn't like yours." I fidget with my fingers as I hold my hands in my lap.

Caleb's driving us to my parents' house for Thanksgiving dinner. Because of my extended family, we're actually having it on the Saturday after Thanksgiving. Which is good, since he wasn't scheduled to work today.

"I know, in the years I've been hanging out with friends and stuff, I've come to realize my family situation is way different than most. I'll be able to handle it, Red, it's okay."

My parents are so much less laid back than Mason and Karina, they take things way too seriously when it comes to me, and let Lance run around like he has no responsibilities, or any kind of care in the world. It isn't fair, but it's what I live with. "I just hope you won't want to say fuck it with me after this."

He reaches over, grabbing my hand. "I'll always want to fuck you, Red; you're hot as hell."

My face flames. I'm still not used to the way he talks, even a few months into this relationship. I think Caleb will always heat me up, and even I know that's something most people never get. "Ditto." I grip his fingers in mine now.

I direct him down a tree-lined road on the opposite side of

town from where his parents' house is. My parent's own a farm, and even though there isn't much money in it anymore, they still work the land like it's the best gift they've ever been given. As the white house I grew up in comes into view, I try to look at it from Caleb's eyes. It's old, been in my family for generations, and while there have been a few upgrades, most of what's there has been there since the early 1900s. It used to embarrass me, but I learned it's a part of our heritage.

"Wow," he breathes deeply as he gets a good look at the wrap around porch.

"It's mostly the original design." I give him a brief history. "Of course they've had to replace the wood over the years, but mostly, this is the house my great-great-grandfather built for his family."

"Do you know what I would give to have that kind of history for my family?" he whispers.

And in this moment, I realize that maybe the two of us are fulfilling roles in our lives that both of us needed filled. He makes me not take myself so seriously, makes me push at the boundaries both myself and my parents have set for me my whole life, and I give him the history, the sense of belonging he's always needed.

"I never thought about how truly important that is, but you can bet I am now. C'mon, Caleb." I hitch my head toward the front door as we park. "Be your normal charming self and my mom will love you. Don't worry about my dad and brother; once they find out you played for Alabama, you're golden."

"HE'S REALLY CUTE," Mom whispers to me as we finish up the last of the side dishes.

Caleb had offered to help, but the men in the family had

commandeered him and not let go.

"He is." I look back at the living room, hearing his deep voice explain why the team on the television had run a play opposite of what the consensus had been they would run.

"He seems to be a good man too, good manners, I like the way he held the door open for you when you came in the house. Seems like he's very polite."

I fight the snicker that wants to come out. He's polite all right, until we get naked and then Caleb can be downright demanding, but I'd be lying if I said I didn't need that in my life.

"He's everything and more, Mom. I'm lucky he was there that night, at The Café."

"Yes you are," she agrees as she wipes her hands on her apron. "Maybe we should invite him to Sunday service. You think he'd come?"

I think he would probably do anything I asked him to do. "I can, if you want me to. It's not a promise he'll be there, but I'll put the invitation out, because I know that's important to you. He's busy and it would depend on his schedule."

She smiles at me and calls the men to the table, while we set the dishes out. As I'm lifting the big platter of turkey, Caleb swoops in, grabbing it from my hands. "I got it, Red. Where does it go?"

I literally fucking swoon at how hot he is when he's being a gentleman to impress my family. "Over there." I point to a bare spot on the table. "Thank you."

"Any time." He gives me a wink over his shoulder.

As we have a seat and my dad prays over the meal, I'm starting to relax.

"What's it like being a cop here?" my brother asks, being as polite as I've ever seen him be. "There was a time when I thought about trying out at the academy, but I'm needed to work around here."

I know he doesn't mean it as a slight to me, but I feel it as Lance reminds us all he's expected to work the land. He hadn't really been given an option, as the male child, and maybe that's why he is how he is. He wasn't really given a choice. I had no idea that had ever been something he wanted to do. While I've been judgmental of him, maybe I should listen instead when he speaks.

"We aren't a big town, so we don't have a lot of the problems other cities do. That's not to say there aren't situations that are dangerous. We have our fair share of domestics, drugs, and just people who are mean, but I'd never want to do this anywhere else. My home is here, my heart is here."

"Was the academy hard?" my mom asks, as she fills his plate with stuffing.

"Not any harder than playing football was." He shrugs. "I kind of had a physical advantage because I was already used to most of the fitness stuff. My dad taught me to shoot when I was young, so I had that advantage too. I had a hard time with the ten-codes and statutes. Other cadets gave me a hard time because of who my dad is and thought that I'd be treated differently. I wasn't; I had to pass all my classes and do everything else that the rest of them did. But, in the end I figured it out and graduated. It was one of the proudest moments I've ever had."

"Watching Ruby graduate from college was one of our proudest moments." Dad looks over at me. "As a family, it was one of our proudest days ever. Even though it wasn't that long ago, it'll be one of our better memories."

"Really?" I ask, genuinely surprised.

"Yeah." He smiles. "It wasn't easy to get you there. Just like most everything else, there were sacrifices that had to be made, but we knew we wanted to do it for you. It was a decision we made as a family. Me, your mom, your brother. We wanted you to have your dream."

I'm speechless as I think about what that probably meant for Lance. Now, I understand why they give him such leeway, why they let him do the things he wants to do. He sacrificed so much for me, and I never gave him credit for it.

"I'll make you proud," I promise them all.

Lance gives me a grin from across the table. "You already do."

As we all get back to our food, I realize that without Caleb being here, without him starting this conversation, we never would have had it. It's just one other way he's brought new perspective to my life, and I grow more thankful for it every single day.

Cruise

"THANKS FOR INVITING me," I tell Ruby's parents as she and I prepare to leave. "And thanks for having your dinner on another day, to help accommodate. Unfortunately in my line of work, sometimes I'm not available on holidays."

"You're talking to a family of farmer's son, I think we get it." Phillip puts my mind at ease.

One of the things I had been most worried about when it came to meeting her family was them thinking I couldn't give her everything. My job has been a deterrent for most of my adult life, but I'm willing to admit the deterrent has been because of me. Because of what I've wanted, not because of what they've wanted. Now I'm ready to give in and experience it all.

Ruby stands next to me as her mom reaches in and gives me a hug. "Hopefully we'll see you at church?"

I've never gone to church in my life, not regularly, but I'll do whatever's expected of me to get in the good graces of this family. Just so they know I'm serious about their daughter.

"As soon as I can make it," I promise as Ruby and I head out the door, down the porch steps and to the Jeep.

Once we get in and shut the door, we both breathe a sigh of relief.

She leans over, kissing me fully on the mouth. "We made it!"

We sure did.

CHAPTER SEVENTEEN

Cruise

Mid-December

"S ORRY I COULDN'T come and pick you up," I apologize as Ruby meets me outside the only Baptist Church in town.

I had been cutting it close, working overnight. As it is, I've made it with ten minutes to spare, after going home, taking a shower, and changing into a pair of khakis and a button-down. My hair is still wet, and I didn't have time to shave, but they'll have to take me how I am.

"It's okay, I had Mom and Dad pick me up so I could ride back with you." She smiles up at me, leaning in for a kiss. She's wearing a modest dress with a cardigan over it, her hair half up in braid across the crown of her head, her curls a little unruly, just the way I like it. I like this buttoned up version of her; it makes me want to mess her up.

It's been a few days since I've seen her, and if I let myself, I'd take what she's offering right now way too far for the church parking lot.

"You look tired." She runs the palm of her hand against the stubble on my face, her eyes concerned.

"Been up for about fifteen hours, will probably pull a full twenty-four by the time we hit the parade," I admit. "But I've got a couple of cans of Red Bull in the Jeep, and since school's out for the break, I'm hoping I can convince you to take a nap with me when we get done."

"In your bed?" she asks. "It smells like you."

God, this woman. "If that's what you want." I rub my thumb against her pink lips, before leaning down to take another kiss from her.

"It's definitely what I want." She tilts her head toward the two doors that are starting to close. "We better get inside before the service starts."

Her hand in mine, she leads me up the steps and through the doors, directly to the pew her family sits in. We exchange quiet greetings, before having a seat. I get comfortable, putting my arm around her shoulders, pulling her hand with my free one onto my thigh. She crosses her legs toward me and leans in, as we both look ahead and pay attention to whatever's being preached today.

I've done my best to keep my attention focused on the pulpit at the front of the church, but I'm having a hard time not wanting to close my eyes for just a few minutes.

"He's almost done," Ruby assures from beside me.

"Now we have an update on Tanner, a young teenager that was hit at Halloween. We've been praying for him, and I heard from his mama the other day he'll be heading home at the end of next week. We'd like to get together, provide them with meals for the their first couple of weeks back, along with some gift cards to help with day-to-day purchases. I'll post something about it in the church's Facebook group tonight," he finishes off.

"Oh thank God," Ruby whispers. "I was worried about him, and we hadn't had an update in a while."

Leaning in, I kiss her on the forehead. Knowing that she's relieved, makes me relieved too.

"ARE YOU ALL coming to the parade?" I ask her mom and dad as we stand outside the church, waiting for Ruby to change into something warmer. It's colder today than it has been in the past few weeks, and it rained last night, leaving a chill to the air. I've changed into some jeans, a long-sleeve shirt, grabbing an old hunting jacket and put a beanie on my head.

"Nah, too cold for us." Susan smiles as she takes Phillip's hand in hers. "But hopefully we'll get to see you again soon, young man?"

"I hope so too," I tell her as she leans in to give me a kiss on the cheek. Phillip gives my hand a shake, and they are off.

Going over to my Jeep, I lean against the passenger side door, waiting for Ruby to come down the steps. When she does, I can't help but smile at the picture she makes. She's wearing those jeans I like, with the rip in the thigh, and a North Face jacket, along with a beanie on her head too.

"I love those jeans." I pull her into my arms, looping them around her waist. My hands itch to reach down, and palm her ass cheeks, pull her so close to me that there's no space between us. My mind warns me that this isn't the place for that.

"Just like I love this chain you wear." She reaches down, grabbing the wallet chain I have.

"Yeah? You never told me that."

She shrugs. "Always kinda been my little secret. Here's the thing though, for most everyone else you're this officer of the law, you uphold all the rights, punish all the wrongs. All of that inherently makes you this really good guy, but for me? You're a bad boy, you make me do all the things I always told myself I would never have the courage to do. You make me drop all my inhibitions and encourage me to trust you. So the tattoo on your arm" – she runs her fingers along where she knows the ink is –

"and this chain you wear" – she tugs on it, and for some reason that tug goes to my groin too – "they're some of my favorite parts of you. I consider them mine." She leans up on her tiptoes, circling her other arm around my neck, pulling me down.

Before our lips meet, I let her know the truth. "They're completely and totally yours. No one else gets this side of me."

"Good." I can feel the smile against my lips. "No one else gets this side of me either."

There, in the parking lot of the church, I take the kiss I've wanted all morning. Tongue, nipping, even a little teeth involved, and for the life of me, I can't help but think since God knows what's in our hearts, he's probably, definitely okay with this little public display of affection.

"YOU WANT A hot chocolate?" I ask as we exit the Jeep and start walking to what will be the main thoroughfare of the parade. I've got my Red Bull in one hand, her hand in my other.

"Oh yes, that would be awesome." She snuggles next to my body, allowing me to block the wind that's coming between the buildings.

When we round the corner, there's a line, but Leighton is working the hot chocolate booth. She sees my head over the sea of people and gives me a smile. "Officer Harrison, how many you want?"

I hold up one finger, and she sends Ransom over with one for me. "Mom says it's on the house."

"Tell her I said thank you." I hand it over to Ruby.

"Come watch me play and we'll call it even?"

The kid drives a hard bargain. There's still a few games left in the football season, and I can't tell him no. "Have your mom or dad text me your schedule, and I'll be sure and make it to one."

Ransom gives a smile and a thumbs up.

"You're such a good guy, Caleb. You do your best to make time for everybody."

"They make time for me." I shrug. "So many times in my childhood nobody had the time to give to me, they didn't care whether I had it or not. I do my best to let people know they matter. Even if it's just showing up to some football game."

She leans up, kissing me on the cheek. "Whether you want to admit it or not, you're special. I'm so happy to be here with you today."

And those words? They make me happier than anything else has made me in a long time. "C'mon, let's go find Mom and Kels."

After a text conversation and a little walk around where we are, we eventually find them.

"Bubba!" Kels greets me, running up to us and throwing her arms around the both of us. You would think she hasn't seen us in months.

I give her a hug and then go over to where Mom sits in one of her camping chairs. "How's it going?"

"Cold, why is it so cold?"

I laugh. "You're from Philly, you should be used to this."

"Nope, in the years I've been here, I've lost what I used to be able to tolerate. Now the temp gets below forty and it's freezing."

"Where's Dad?"

"He's at the roadblock, keeping traffic from coming down here. I'm surprised you made it, didn't you work last night?"

"I went to church with Ruby and her parents." I hold up the Red Bull. "And I brought reinforcements."

Her gaze cuts to me, surprise across her face and in her

voice. "You? Went to church?"

Somehow, I feel like I'm never going to hear the end of this. "I did. Can we drop it?"

"She's more special than you want anyone to know, isn't she? Damn, Caleb. You went to church. You know what that means, don't you?"

That I'm completely and totally serious about her. Everyone saw us there today, together. It was the equivalent of giving her my letterman's jacket in high school.

"Yeah, I know, and I'm good with it."

Her mouth is hanging open as she reaches in and grabs my hand. "I'm happy for you. I'm so happy that you've finally decided to let someone else in. I know with the fear your mom put in you about people leaving."

"You're my mom," I remind her. "And you gave me zero fear."

She knows by the way I've spoken that I don't want to talk about the woman who gave birth to me any longer.

"Then I'll just say I'm happy for you, and we'll leave it at that?"

"That I'll gladly take."

The crowd shifts as the parade is about to start. Kelsea sits in her chair next to Mom's and I have a seat on the curb, motioning for Ruby to come sit in my lap. She does so without hesitation, sitting sideways so that my arms go around her thighs. As we watch the parade, I play with that patch of bare skin, grinning when she giggles, burying her head in my neck.

"That tickles." She kisses me softly on my Adam's apple.

"Where?" I whisper.

We're around hundreds of people, but it feels like we're totally and completely alone.

"Everywhere," she answers, those blue eyes of hers shining

bright.

With her newfound boldness, I know I won't lose the smile I have for the rest of the day.

"WHY DON'T YOU let me drive?" Ruby questions as we make our way back to my Jeep. I've already been through the two Red Bulls and I'm dead on my feet.

"You sure you can handle this big boy?"

"I can handle you, can't I?"

Catching her around the waist, I pull her to me. "This mouth you've got." I cup her jaw. "What am I going to do with it?"

"Kiss it, own it."

Looking around, I see we don't have an audience. My lips to her ear, I whisper. "Fuck it? Cause I think you'd kinda like that too."

"You'll never know until you try, hot stuff."

With those words, she takes off at a run for my Jeep, sliding into the driver's side.

"Be careful with him." I hand her the keys.

"I'll be as careful with him as I am with you," she promises as I let my seat lay back.

Before we're even out of the parking lot, I'm asleep. Content in the knowledge I trust this woman with everything.

CHAPTER EIGHTEEN

Cruise

New Year's Eve

"SHE NEEDS TO be in bed by eight," Karina tells me as Ruby and I wait for her and Dad to leave for their date.

I shoot Ruby a look, before I put my hand over Karina's mouth. "Mom, I've watched my sister before, in fact, I watch her probably more often than most brothers do. I think I got this."

"I know." She wraps her finger around her curl, before her eyes cut to Dad's. "It's just... I feel bad asking you to watch her on New Year's, especially when you have Ruby," she admits, looking apologetically at the both of us.

"I think we'll be fine." I roll my eyes. "You and Dad go out, have a blast, rent a room if you want. We got this."

"Listen to your son." Dad puts his arm around Mom, pulling her toward the door. "He's got this."

"I know he does," she worries again, biting on her nail. "I'm just really sorry you're spending your first New Year's together, watching your little sister."

"Karina," Ruby laughs. "It's fine, I promise. We're gonna have a good time here. You two go out and have fun, like he said, we got this."

"Okay, okay, I'll stop apologizing. If you need anything we

have our phones on."

"Rina." Dad's voice is soft, but commanding. "If you don't stop, we're gonna miss our reservation. Trust me when I say, we'll make it up to them. Let's go, babe."

"Okay, I got it!" She grabs her phone and purse. "You two have fun."

Dad looks at me, a twinkle in his eye. "You remember what I told you the last time you stayed here with a girl? Same rules apply."

"Fuck that," I laugh, giving him the finger. "I'm watching your offspring so you can go have a good time, you can forget it."

He laughs loudly as he looks at me. "Just keep it quiet." He winks.

"Whatever, Dad. Get outta here."

They finally leave, and I lean my back against the door. "I never thought they would leave. Cupcake, where are you?" I yell for my sister.

"Did they finally go, Bub?" she asks as she comes in the kitchen. "I never thought they would leave. What are we doing tonight? Is Ruby staying with us?"

"She is." I reach down, picking her up in my arms. At ten, she's still small for her age, and I'll hate the day that I can't hold her like the little girl she is. "What do you want to do tonight?"

"Since Ruby's here, do you think we can paint my nails?" She glances down at Ruby's, which are a bright pink, glittering in the light.

"You're in luck, I brought my nail stuff, because we had such a good time talking about it last time." Ruby lifts up the bag she brought with her.

"While you ladies are doing your nails, I'll order us a pizza and find something to watch on TV. Sound good?"

"Yeah." Kelsea grins, and by her look, I know she's excited to spend time with us.

I watch as Kelsea and Ruby go into the living room and start setting their stuff up on the coffee table. "Is pepperoni okay with you two?"

"Sounds good to me." Ruby gives me a thumbs up.

"Cupcake, you want the apple streusel dessert?" Kelsea is a sucker for all things sweet. She's a lot like me.

"You know me, you know I do," she answers as I log into my account on my phone. Within minutes, I've ordered pizza, cheese bread, and a dessert for us.

I think twice about it, but I still go ahead and make Ruby and I drinks. We're not planning on going anywhere for at least a few hours, so I feel like it's okay for us to have some Jack and Cokes. Walking back into the living room, I watch as Ruby and my sister play on Kelsea's phone.

"Stick your tongue out" Ruby grins as they take a picture. "I love these filters, I keep trying to get your brother to try them with me, but he won't." She shoots me a look.

"Forgive me if I don't want to look like a dog or a panda bear. I'm good the way I am."

"You sure are." She shoots me a wink.

Turning the TV on, I queue up *Pitch Perfect*, because I know it's a favorite in this household. Basically I check my man card at the door, when it comes to Kelsea. Ruby and my sister sit down on the floor with their nail stuff spread out across the coffee table, I lay on the couch, so that I'm close to them. As I situate myself, I put my arm around Ruby's neck, laying on my stomach so I can touch her as she helps Kelsea do her nails. I've never been the type of guy who's had to be touchy-feely with a woman, but Ruby's changed all of that for me.

"I *love* this movie," Kelsea looks back at me, giving me a grin.

"I know you do, Cupcake, it's why I picked it."

Situating myself on the couch, I sigh, but it's a content sigh. Never in my adult life have I felt so settled, felt like I was where I should be. That's what Ruby gives me; she gives me a peace I've never had. There's always been this anxiety bubbling under the surface. It's been there since I was a kid, constantly at the back of my mind, always making me wonder when things are going to go bad. Finally, I'm not waiting for the other shoe to drop, I'm comfortable in living my life and being happy in it. Curling my hand against her neck, I lean in, kissing her softly.

"What's that for?" She turns slightly so I can see her face.

"Just for being you, Red. Just for being you."

When the doorbell rings, I gladly go get the pizza for these ladies in my life, and I love that I'll get to spend my New Year's Eve with them.

"DOES THIS TAKE you back?" Ruby asks as we lay on the couch wrapped up in each other. My hands are on her ass, and she's turned into my body, touching each part of me she can. Kelsea went to bed, and it was like game on with my lady.

"Not really," I admit. "There's only one other girl I've ever had in this house. She and I didn't curl up on the couch. We spent the night in my room." I drop a kiss on her forehead.

"Ohh really?" She lifts herself up on her elbow. "This I gotta hear." My girl is inquisitive about almost everything, has been since we spent the night after Halloween together.

"Long story short, she was at a party and things got a little too serious for her. She called me and asked me to come and get her. Her parents weren't home and she didn't want to go home to an empty house. Dad offered to let her come here, but he warned me that we better not sleep together, or fuck around." I chuckle, remembering him warning me. "But we slept in my room with the door shut that night."

"And what did you do with her?" She puts her hand under her hair, looking down at me, her blue eyes shining bright. Seeming to dare me to tell her the entire truth. I have nothing to hide, so I have no problem with telling her all about my night of rebellion.

I think back to that night, remembering Jess with fondness, a smile on my face. She and I saw each other once or twice when we were in college and Alabama played Ole Miss, but we never managed to recapture what we had those few months in high school. "We fucked around," I admit. "She gave me the best blowjob I'd had up to that point in my life, and I had to keep quiet for fear my dad would hear. It was kinda hot."

The memory of us messing around while trying to keep quiet is fresh in my mind. As a teenager that had been the hottest thing I'd ever done, as an adult, it cracks me up that I'd had the guts to do it, knowing my dad would have beat my ass.

"Such a bad boy." Ruby grins before she leans down, placing an open mouth kiss on my neck. Her tongue and lips are a huge turn on as she nips, nibbles, and soothes.

"Maybe I was." I thread my fingers through her hair, holding her tightly to my flesh as she begins nibbling.

Pulling back, she licks her lips. "The question is, are you still?"

"Now? Now I'm adult who takes my pleasure seriously."

"Hmmmm, funny enough, I take my pleasure seriously too." She kisses me again, running her hand down my chest and stomach, stopping when she encounters the buckle of my belt. "And maybe I feel like this Jess girl, laid down a challenge for all the girls to come after her."

Immediately, I stiffen, grabbing her around the neck, tilting her chin up to meet mine. "I can promise you, I'm not the type of man to compare, but at the same time I can tell you no one has ever made me feel the way you do. You get me off harder than I've ever gotten off, and I wake up every morning wanting to bury myself so deeply inside you we don't know where each other begins and ends. Whatever happened in my past, there is legitimately no comparison to what I have with you."

It's important she know what she means to me. That when I fall, I don't fall easily, but at the same time I fall hard and completely.

Ruby

THIS MAN CONSTANTLY turns me on and makes me want to explore the edges I have within myself. I want to be the first, the last, and the only thing he thinks of. So I feel slightly that there is a challenge that's been thrown down when he tells me what happened in this house with his high school girlfriend. That's on me, not on him, but I still want to blow his mind. It's a point of personal pride.

"Trust me, Caleb, whatever I do, is something I want to do. To prove to myself I can, and to prove to myself that there aren't any boundaries between us."

He inhales deeply, the inhale sharp and encompassing his whole body. "You don't have to prove anything to me, baby, but if you want to prove something to yourself, far be it from me to stop you."

I fumble with the buckle of his belt, but I eventually get it unhooked, and his jeans unbuttoned and unzipped. A sly smile on my face, I lean in, claiming his lips for my own, before I pull away and work my way down his body. When I realize how tall he is will encumber what I have planned, I get up off the couch and kneel in front of it. He gets the idea, sitting up so that his legs are spread with me in the middle.

"Remember you don't have to do this." He cups my neck in his hand as he situates himself, pulling his jeans and boxers down.

His cock stands erect before me, hard and tall. Licking my lips, I lean forward, grasping the base and closing my lips around the head, testing the resistance against my tongue.

"Son of a bitch, Red," he groans out as his head falls against the back of the couch and he spreads his legs farther, putting his feet flat on the floor. "Baby." He tangles his fingers through my hair, as I come up and then go back down.

Using my tongue, I lick down and then up, circling the head, before I pull my mouth off and use my hand to jack the length while I glance up at him. Our eyes meet, and my body heats up as I see what I've done to him. "Feel good?"

"Fucking amazing." His eyes are already hooded, chest already heaving, and I can tell how excited he is. It's obvious he's a fan of head, and I can't believe he's never told me.

Taking him down my throat, he moans loudly, pushing his hips up at the same time.

"Shhhh," I giggle. "Don't wake up Kelsea."

"If you knew how warm, wet, and absolutely amazing your mouth felt around my dick, you'd know it's almost impossible to keep the sounds to myself. God you get it so wet." His head lolls against the couch as he digs his fingers in my hair.

Lifting my eyes up to his, I pull his cock out of my mouth, my hand around the base. If there's one thing I've learned, he likes to be in control. "Show me, Caleb. Show me what you want."

His eyes darken and those fingers in my hair grip harder as he pushes me down on his length. The excitement of proving to him what I can do helps me take him deep. Saliva helps to lubricate his way as he pushes his hips up and my head down.

"Yeah, Ruby, just like that." He pushes my hair back from my face, moving his hand down to my jaw, tilting me the way he wants me to go.

Turning my head to the side, I make a huge production of taking him, as my eyes flutter up to his. I feel like a fucking porn star as I put on a show for him.

"Oh God, yeah, look at me as you take my cock down your throat. Get it wet, Red," he encourages as our pace picks up. My jaw hurts because he's so large, so thick in my mouth.

Pulling him loose, I pant heavily. "You're so thick, my jaw." I point, my chest heaving, my heart pounding.

He chuckles as he grips the end of his cock, lazily stroking it as he glances down at me. "I never wanna hurt you," he assures.

And I never wanna leave him wanting. Reaching to the hem of my shirt, I grasp it, pulling it over my head, before I pull the cups of my bra down.

"Oh fuck, Red, seriously?"

Leaning with my hand against the back of the couch, I dangle my nipples in front him. He grabs one in his mouth, twirling his tongue around the peak. Taking my knees again, I lean over his cock, grasping the sides of my tits.

"Oh fucking shit," he moans deep in his throat as I enclose his hard length in between my flesh and start to move up and down around his cock.

Another thing I've learned about Caleb is he's very visual and he's a very dirty boy. He likes sex, he doesn't mind getting messy, and he loves telling me what to do. "Like this?" I gaze up at him, taking in the passion on his face, the sweat dripping off, and the way he's pulled his bottom lip in between his teeth.

"Fuck yeah, Red, don't stop." He's given up the façade of

trying to hold his shit together as his hands come down over where mine are, pressing my tits around his cock. The way he's pressing up into them, he's got no rhythm, no finesse. It's as if he's lost all semblance of the guy who normally fucks me until I can't see straight. I've finally done it, finally made him lose his control.

"Give it to me, Caleb," I hiss out in between my teeth, rubbing my tits up and down his length, enjoying the slippery feel of him there.

His head punches back against the couch as he runs a hand up his t-shirt covered chest. He's grabbing his nipple in between his fingers, tugging roughly on it. I wish I could reach up and take it into my mouth, the way he takes mine. Right now I wish I could swirl my tongue around the hard nub, bite his flesh the way he bites mine. Doubling up my efforts, I go after his orgasm hard, stopping once to push his length back into my mouth, to replace the moisture lost by him jacking it between my tits.

"You want it?" His neck is strained, his words breathless as he pushes up in between the tight space.

"Yes!" And I realize I don't know what he's asking, but I want whatever he's willing to give me. His pleasure is my pleasure.

Caleb pulls back, taking himself in his free hand, jacking up and down furiously. "Push those tits together, Ruby," he hisses between clenched teeth.

Immediately I know what he wants, and I want it too. To feel his pleasure across my skin? It's what I've been aiming for since we started this rendezvous with one another. "You want it?" he asks me again, his eyes open wide as he looks down at me.

"Yeah." I give him a grin as my eyes drift down to where he's holding himself, his big hand running up and down his length. It always amazes me when I watch him jack off, he's much rougher on his flesh than I dare be. Probably because he knows what he can handle. Offering my flesh up to him, I lean in close as his hand goes up and down in a blur. "C'mon, Cruise," I use his call-sign. The only time I use it is when we're getting intimate like this, and as such it affects him like no other. His hand goes faster, his hips push harder. The veins in his neck are standing out, and his whole body is tightening as he works for relief.

"Ahhh yeah." The words come out in a rush as I feel the heat of his release on my skin. His lip is clenched between his teeth, and I'm panting as he paints my tits with the evidence of his pleasure.

CHAPTER NINETEEN

Cruise

I'M WRECKED AS I lay panting, my head resting against the back of the couch, trying to figure out exactly where I am. If I've ever come that fucking hard, it's been a long time. When I hear a giggle, I pry my eyes open, seeing Ruby still kneeling in front of me. Her breasts are wet with me, and I wish we were alone, back in my apartment or her duplex. I would think nothing of jerking my shirt off and pressing our skin together. We aren't alone though, and we're lucky Kels hasn't woken up yet. I struggle out of my shirt, using it to clean her off, since we don't have anything around to do so. As good as I can, I stuff myself back into my jeans, before zipping, buttoning won't be happening for a while. I sigh, running my hands through my hair.

"You okay?" she asks, raking her nails along my stomach muscles. They contract roughly against her touch and my body instinctively wants to seek more from her.

Leaning down, I capture the edge of her jaw with my fingers, holding her still for me. "Fucking perfect."

"Did you come harder?" she asks, those blue eyes dark in the flicker of the TV playing behind us. "Ya know, than you did with her?"

I see this is a point of pride for her, and instead of getting annoyed she brought up Jess again, I drag my hand down her neck, over the swell of her breast and press her nipple in between the pads of my fingers. "I always come harder for you than I ever have anyone else. That's what happens when you care about the person who's blowing your mind, or your dick." I give her a grin. "There's no comparison, please don't think there is. You get me more than any other woman ever has, and because of that, you get a part of me that no other woman ever has. Fuck, you're so special to me…" I trail off as I capture her lips with mine.

She moans deep in her throat as I coax her tongue out to tangle with mine. When I pull away, her lips chase mine, and I can feel her warm breath on my skin. "C'mon, let's take this someplace a little more private?"

She nods, grabbing my hand when I stand up, reaching for her. Together, we make a path through the house, turning off lights, checking on locks, and then quietly we look in on Kels. When I see she's slept through our living room blow job, I close the door and drag Ruby to my teenage bedroom. When we get inside, I flip the lock, and push her up against the door, shoving my thigh in between her legs.

"You're in luck, Red, there's a small bathroom attached to this bedroom. The shower is tiny, but it'll work for what we need to do. Which is clean you off." I run my finger along the swell of her tits, feeling a bit of the stickiness of me left behind. She moans, closing her eyes and licking her lips as I let my palm caress the weight. Not able to stop myself, I give into the urge to lean forward and take one of those nipples into my mouth. My tongue circles the hard nub and I suck hard, hollowing out my cheeks as she grabs my hair and holds me tightly to her.

The cry she gives when I nip slightly is guttural and that's when I make a decision. My hands on her ass, I pick her up, carrying us to the bathroom, not removing my mouth from her flesh until I have to sit her down.

She's breathing heavily as she watches me turn the water on, and then a slight film of steam fills the room.

Without words, we disrobe and step into the shower. Once we're there, it's comical how small it is. We manage to get shampoo and body wash on us, but it's a tight fit. I have to hold my arms up and she has to stand in the shadow of my body, almost putting her arms around my waist. I love being this close to her, love sharing this moment, and I know it's one I'll never forget.

"How did you even jack-off in here?" she asks as she grins up at me.

My face scrunches together in a laugh. "That's a seriously personal question."

"I got seriously up close and personal with you a few minutes ago, so I think you can answer it." We switch places as she gets under the flow of water and quickly washes off.

"I didn't." I wink. "That's what laying in my bed was for. Then I'd come take a shower. You have to make do with what you've got."

"Oh is that how it is?" she laughs as she tilts her head back to get the shampoo out of her locks.

When she does, she offers her tits up to me, and I'm an enterprising man. I take what's offered. Swirling my tongue around the tip, I reach down to her ass, grab her up, putting her legs around my waist. As I reach to turn the shower off, she squeals when I turn with her in my arms, taking us to my bed. "That's exactly how it is." I toss her on the mattress I spent most of my teenage years on, and then look my fill. Her legs are slightly parted as she looks up at me, her elbows holding her weight. "And just so we're clear, Ruby Red." I get down on my knees, ignoring the hardwood under my wet skin, spreading those thighs to make room for my shoulders. "I'm about to get seriously up close and personal with you."

For a few moments, I stare at the feast before me. Letting my gaze travel from the top of her head to where I'm situated between her thighs. Her blue eyes meet my brown ones, her eyebrow raised. "Do you need a roadmap?"

My grin tilts into a smirk. I love the sassiness of her, the way she tells me what she wants in her own way. "Nope, just takin' my time."

Her legs widen farther, a smirk covers her face. "Then maybe I can entice you." Her hand scoots down her body, her pink nail extending, almost touching her clit before I reach up, grabbing it in my grasp.

"Oh no, babe, this is all mine." I run the flat of my hand along her pussy, covering it completely, before running my index finger along the little piece of skin that's begging for my touch.

"Then take it." She thrusts toward my mouth. "Please, take it."

At that loss of control, I angle my head to the side, use my free hand to expose her clit, and dive in for a taste of what I know will become an obsession. "Caleb," she whispers as she reaches down and threads her fingers through my hair, holding my mouth as close to her as it can be. I give her what she wants, circling her nub with my tongue and then suctioning hard and deep.

Pulling back with a loud pop, I let go of the fingers I'd captured, placing them on her breast. "Make yourself feel good." I bring my other hand back down to where my mouth is. Extending two fingers and pulling the rest back into my palm, I test the tightness of her channel, moaning deep in my throat when I feel how fucking wet she is. Blowing me turned her on, and mother fuck if that doesn't turn *me* on. Even though I just came not long ago, I can feel my dick hardening again, the head bumping the edge of the bed. It feels good, so I keep thrusting as I continue to work her.

Using the tip of my tongue, I circle her nub, flicking the flesh as I push my fingers in and out of her body. Her moans are loud in the room, and I worry that Kelsea is going to hear, but I also can't stop the way I feel, the way she's feeling. When I push even deeper, she lets out a guttural cry, forcing me to remove my mouth. "Red? Kels, remember?"

"Fuck Caleb, you do that so good." She extends her leg and hooks me around the neck, bringing me back down to her. When I give her a pointed stare, she grabs a pillow, shoving it over her face. There's a chuckle in my throat, but when I get back to the business at hand, I find I have to tell myself to stop moaning.

She's so sweet, everything I've ever wanted in a woman, and her taste was made for me. Her pussy too, almost completely bare, just a little patch of hair at the top, neatly trimmed. Makes me glad I take my time to do my own trimming. With everything I have, ignoring the pain in my knees, the cramp in my forearm, I go after her, because I can feel her tightening, can feel her getting close. I want to give her what she gave to me. And that's when I hear her, even through the pillow. I can't wipe the smile from my face, even when I wipe my mouth. She puts the pillow to the side, chest heaving, stomach going concave as she looks down at me, running her hands up and down her body.

"Where did you learn that little tongue and then suction, and then thrust gimmick? Because, oh my God!" She's gripping her skin, almost like she has to touch herself, and it's hot as fuck.

"I've got a few tricks you haven't seen yet," I assure her, as I walk over to where I left my jeans, going into the back pocket and fumbling with my wallet. This is one of those times where I wish we'd had the birth control discussion, where I wish I could sink into her bare, and not worry about any consequences. Feel myself shoot inside her body, feel her take every bit of myself I have to give her. It's something we'll need to discuss in the future, but right now, the cock against my stomach is demanding fucking relief.

"God, Caleb Harrison." She looks over at me, eyes hooded, lips pink, face flushed with the orgasm I just gave her. I'm going to give her more, and she's going to look like my very own porn star before I'm done. "If I knew your middle name, I'd call you by that too." She shakes her head. "You're amazing at what you do."

"It's Matthew. My middle name is Matthew."

The smile she gives me is dazzling. "Mine is Josephine."

I stop what I'm doing and give her a smile back. "That's you, an old soul."

The tender moment is completely unexpected, but it's everything I've come to understand makes up Ruby.

I snag the condom I'm looking for and suit up as I walk back over to where she lays, spread out for me like an all you can eat buffet. Pushing her thighs apart, I dive into the space that's been left for me, curling my arms around her head, putting my palms flat and pushing up. She accepts me easily, a small grunt leaving her throat as she adjusts to my size.

"Okay?" I strangle out, feeling her squeeze against my fullness. It's almost enough to set me off, but I hold back, clenching my ass, trying to focus on anything other than the way she feels.

"Yeah." She nods, lifting her head off the bed, pressing our lips together.

Pushing deeper, I pull back, and bury my head in her neck. "Hang on, Red, I can't wait any longer."

And as we both groan into each other's skin, I realize with everything I have, I don't want to let this woman go.

CHAPTER TWENTY

Ruby

February

I'M NERVOUS AS I smooth the dress down my torso, examining the way it shows the bare patch of skin at my stomach. Caleb is supposed to be here to pick me up in an hour. Excitement bubbles up in my throat as I think about how he's going to play my body after our dinner reservation. I bought special lingerie for tonight, and I can't wait to show it to him.

I'm finishing up my hair when my phone rings. Seeing his smiling face, my stomach immediately sinks. Foreboding hits me hard, and I know he's about to cancel.

"Hey," I answer, trying to sound much more positive than I feel.

"Red." The regret is deep in his voice, like he wants to tell me anything other than what he's about to.

"You have to cancel don't you?"

He sighs heavily. "I do. There's been a bad wreck on sixty-five, and they've called everybody in. There's some fatalities, Ruby. Dad and I are both responding."

Carefully I control my emotions, because I don't want him to know I'm upset. There's nothing he can do about this, and honestly, it's the reality of our relationship. If I let this get to me, I'll never be able to handle anything, and there's no point in us even being with one another anymore. "It's okay," I soothe him. "We can plan for something else; it's not a huge deal."

"It *is* a huge deal," he argues. "And I feel like shit that I'm doing this to you."

"I know what getting involved with you entails, and there are sacrifices that sometimes have to be made. It'll be okay."

He's quiet for longer than I like before he speaks again. "I bet you look gorgeous. Can you at least send me a picture?"

He's killing me. "I'll do it as soon as we hang up. I'm not mad, or disappointed. This is life, babe."

"Okay." He sounds resigned.

"Just let me know when you're safe, and done. Maybe we can hang out later."

"I'll keep you informed," he promises, and I can hear people in the background telling him they're leaving.

"Go, Caleb. I'll see you soon."

"Bye, Red. I'm sorry," he apologizes again.

"No need, be safe."

"Always," and then he's gone.

When I make sure the phone's been hung up, I let out a little cry, because I am disappointed and upset. Not at him, but at the situation. Then I feel awful, people have died, and I'm feeling sorry for myself for not going out on a date. "Suck it up, Ruby."

My phone vibrates with a text. After the news I just got, I wonder if I want to see whose messaging me now. When I look over, I see Karina's name.

K: *Wanna come hang out with me and Kels? We lost our V-Day date too.*

R: *Be right there!*

And in this moment, I'm so thankful to be a part of this family.

Cruise

THE SCENE WE'VE encountered is awful. A couple obviously on their way to a date for the night. She's wearing a dress, he's dressed up in a suit, and as we search the scene, trying to find ID so that we can notify next of kin, we find an engagement ring in his pocket.

This is the shit I hate. People who get stopped in the tracks of their lives. I'm sure they started this night, especially the guy, thinking that it would be the best night of his life. It's a reminder of how quickly life can turn in the complete opposite direction of what you assume it will.

"Caleb, I need you to go over there and start directing traffic around some of that debris." Dad throws me a vest and points to where there's a bottle neck.

I put the yellow vest on and move quickly to get to work.

"LOOKS LIKE RUBY is at the house." Dad comes over as we're finishing clearing up the scene.

"Is she?"

"Yeah, Rina invited her over. The three of them decided to spend V-Day together, since we ended up having to work."

At least she didn't have to sit at home by herself, and I'm thankful she had my family to be with. "Good, then I'll head to the house with you. I'll follow behind."

I'm beyond tired and beyond ready to see my family as we pull up into the driveway of the only house I've ever been able to call a home. Dad gets out of his Jeep slowly, just like I do. He puts his arm around my neck, pulling me into his side.

"You don't gotta turn it off just because you've had a rough night and you have a woman in there waiting for you. It's okay to feel whatever it is you feel. You start lying to yourself and her, then you're fucked. Whatever we walk in to, is what we walk in to. She may be upset, she may be angry, but then again she may be okay. This sets the tone for the rest of what you two have, but don't let it ruin anything. Got it?"

I nod, thankful for the advice he's given me. "Love you, Dad."

He gives me a grin. "Love you too. You're a good man, Caleb. The two of you will figure this relationship shit out."

We enter the kitchen through the side door where the three women in our lives look to be having the best time ever. Kari and Ruby are drinking margaritas, and Kelsea's got what looks like a slushy in her glass.

"You're home!" Kelsea yells as she hops down from her chair at the bar, running to me and Dad. We both hug her before we each go to the respective woman in our life.

As I greet Ruby, my gaze lands on some flowers and cup-cakes on the bar. "Good job, Dad. Those flowers and cupcakes look amazing."

"I will take credit all day for the flowers." He wraps his arms around mom's neck from behind. "But the cupcakes, I didn't do."

"Ruby did them," Kelsea lets us know as she bites into one. "And they are totally amazeballs. Chocolate covered strawberry."

I let go of Ruby, moving in to inspect the cupcakes sitting on the counter. They look like they were bought at a bakery. The chocolate frosting layered on, with little pearls on top, sitting in Valentine's day cupcake sleeves. "You did these?"

"Yeah." She looks at me like I'm crazy. "We never bought desserts at my house, you've met my parents. I can bake, if I do say so myself."

My eyes flutter to Mom and Dad, both standing there, looking at me with looks on their faces. Dad gives me a grin before he speaks. "No ugly-ass cupcakes for birthday parties, am I right?"

The pounding of my heart inside my chest seizes, as I wrap my arms tightly around this woman who's changed so many things in my life.

"What in the world are you two talking about?" she laughs as I bury my face in her hair.

"Just a little inside joke," Dad saves me from having to put voice to my feelings.

Kissing her on the temple, I pull myself together. "Let's give one a try."

Reaching forward, I devour the sweet treat, moaning as the flavors hit my tongue. My eyes almost roll into the back of my head, it tastes so good. "That's it. Cupcakes every night, forever."

"Not happening," she laughs, smacking the stomach I'm so proud of. "You'd have to be way more dedicated to working out than you are right now."

She's not wrong, and I concede defeat easily.

★   ★   ★

WE'VE DECIDED TO spend the night here because I'm tired and she's a little tipsy. I hand her a shirt to wear, watching as she takes off her jeans and gets comfortable.

"Oh, I almost forgot." She reaches into her purse, pulling out a card. "Happy Valentine's Day." She pushes back her hair nervously. "I've never had a Valentine, so I wasn't sure what to get you."

Going over to my bag, I pull out a card for her too. "My big present was the dinner we had to cancel, so I'm sorry you're getting just the card now." And I feel like complete shit over it, but as Dad said earlier, there's nothing that can be done.

"Just promise me we'll go back sometime?"

"That I can promise." I lean in, kissing her softly.

I slip between the covers and pull her into my side, curling my arm around her shoulders, holding her close. Her fingers play with my bare skin, trailing her nails back and forth. "Can I ask a question?"

"Anything." I kiss her forehead, grasping her fingers in mine, just wanting to feel close to this absolutely amazing person who's come into my life.

"What was the deal with the cupcakes?"

My throat works hard as it swallows roughly, but I know I have to be honest with her. Even if I don't tell her the whole story, I have to give her what this means to me. "You know some of the situation with my birth mom. One thing that always bothered me, that seriously sucked was Dad couldn't make cupcakes for the class on my birthday. I mean he did," I amend my statement, "but they sucked. They were so shitty," I laugh. "Somehow over time, that became something that stuck out to me. You were a very lucky person if you had someone to make you cupcakes that didn't suck."

She pushes herself up on her elbow. "Caleb, if you want me to, I'll make you cupcakes every day."

I laugh loudly. "How about on my birthday and maybe on a few holidays? It's really not that big of a deal."

"It is a big deal." She sees right through me trying to joke this out. "And what's a big deal to you, is a big deal to me. You'll have those cupcakes whenever you want them."

She comes off her elbow, pressing herself to me, holding me tightly around the waist. And for the first time, in a very long time, I feel like I can breathe. I inhale deeply, the scent of her shampoo, and drift off into one of the best sleeps I've had in years.

CHAPTER TWENTY-ONE

Cruise

March

IT'S BEEN A somewhat quiet night on shift, and I have less than an hour to go. I'm really looking forward to going home and crashing, this is my third twelve-hour night his week.

"We have a report of shots fired from a silver colored Impala, in the vicinity of Callahan and Miller."

The info from dispatch makes my ears perk up, I'm two streets over from Callahan. "Dispatch, do we have plates?"

"The only thing anyone got was a possible W as in water, and a H as in Harry."

Up ahead of me, a silver Impala turns into my line of vision. I accelerate, until I can see their license plate. There in the glow cast by my headlights is a W and an H. "Dispatch, can you run this plate? I believe I have the vehicle in sight."

Giving them the plate number, I know this is the shooter in question. I can feel it in the way my body tenses, the way my hands grip the wheel, the acceleration of my heartbeat. It's an intuition everyone told me I would get once I'd been on the force long enough – and they were right.

"They're driving on suspension, Caleb."

"10-4, I'm initiating the stop." I flip on my lights and hope they pull over. When they take off like a bat out of hell, I groan.

The police package in the Camaro I drive responds as I punch the gas. "They took off, traveling north," I calmly relay to the hub of the station, hoping other officers can respond.

"I'm coming south." I hear my dad's voice respond. Typically we aren't on shift together, but his is starting right as mine is ending.

We take a left, and I keep the information coming. My heart is pounding, but my voice is calm. It was probably the hardest thing for me to learn, to not let what other people are doing affect me. I have to keep a level head about me, have to be the voice of reason, even when speeds are topping ninety miles an hour. This time we take a right, and I have to slow down to keep from hitting the car in front of me.

"He's gonna lose it," I warn everyone listening.

And as he pushes the limits of the car he's driving, making a sharp left, he loses control and rolls over. "Roll over," I quickly shout into my radio.

Hopping out of my car, blue lights and sirens blaring, I see that the driver has gotten out and is turning to run. I lunge forward, pushing us both against a chain-link fence.

"Don't resist me," I groan as he does just that, stiffening his arm so I can't get it behind his back. He flings my hand off and sprints to the left, but I manage to tackle him and we hit the asphalt hard.

"I can't go back," he's screaming. "I can't go back, just let go."

"Stop resisting!"

I've got him down on the ground, but he's strong, trying to flip me over, and I can't get his arms behind his back. We're still for a moment, each of us trying to get the upper hand on the other. I use my feet to brace against the asphalt, put the legs that managed to almost let me be a pro football player as leverage.

Risking it for a moment, I manage to key my radio. "I need assistance, I can't get him cuffed."

It's the longest seconds of my life as I hear other officers calling out where they are, and I almost cry with joy when I hear the stomping of boots in my direction. "I'm here, I'm here!" It's my dad, and I've never been more thankful in my life.

He and Tank were riding together, both take over as I roll off the guy, completely wasted of strength, and trying to regain my surroundings. Adrenaline is flowing through my body, and I'm shaking with the exertion it took to hold him still. As Tank and my dad get him cuffed, other officers arrive.

"You okay?" Dad asks me quietly as he bends down so that we're eye-level. He reaches out his hand, helping me up.

"Yeah," I pant. "He was strong, I just couldn't get him cuffed."

He pulls me into a hug while Tank waits his turn. "Lost fuckin' years off my life when you said you couldn't get him cuffed and we didn't hear anything else on the radio. Thought he'd hurt you."

"I'm a big guy, but he was strong." I lean over, pressing my hands against my knees.

"Not wanting to go back to jail makes you do things. You're bleeding, and your pants are torn. You sure you're okay?"

"I think so."

"Let Blaze check you out." Tank grabs me in for a hug around the neck. "Fuck that was scary, man."

"Yeah, try being there," I laugh, because now that's all I can do.

"C'mon over here, let me check you out, stud muffin," Blaze yells from her ambulance.

I'm not even sure when they got here, but as I have a seat, I'm feeling very lucky that I wasn't hurt. This could have gone a very different way.

Ruby

"ARE YOU OKAY?" I ask Caleb, as he walks through my front door.

We were supposed to meet after work, and while I was at the grocery store, I ran into Morgan who asked me how Caleb was doing. It was a shock to find out what had happened, and I've been losing my mind ever since.

"I'm fine," he answers, enveloping me into his arms. "I've never had a scare like that before though. I couldn't get him cuffed, and I was scared I wasn't going to get him cuffed."

"When Morgan told me what happened, I was worried he was going to tell me you'd been injured."

I'm shaking as I hold him in my arms, running my hands all along his body, making sure he's okay.

"It's just part of the job, Ruby. There are days like this when things happen, and then there are days when nothing happens. I'm glad to get to come home to you, though. It made filling out all the reports and waiting to get checked out worth it."

"What do you need from me?" I ask, my eyes searching his, looking to see if he needs me to be what I was after the hard night his dad had.

"I need you," he answers, his voice hoarse. "I need you to be exactly who you are, and us to be exactly who we are."

He's got the stench of sweat on him, probably from the adrenaline that pumped through his body and the exertion of trying to save his own life. "C'mon." I grab his hand, leading him to my bathroom.

I sit him down on the toilet, as I start to fill my bathtub up. He's despondent as he gazes off to the side, not focusing on much of anything. I can understand he's got a lot going on in his head, and I want to help him work through all of it. But I know him, he's not ready to talk about any of it. What he's ready to do is not have to think.

Once the tub is full, I go to work on taking his shoes off, then his pants, and finally his vest and shirt. When he's naked in front of me, he seems to come back to the present. "Sorry, I'm a little out of it."

I kiss the space over his heart. Before I move to the road rash spots on his arms and knees. I'm so thankful he wasn't hurt worse. The reality of the situation is scary, but I also realize how lucky we are. "You're fine, let me help you."

When we're both naked and I've put him the bathtub, I kneel next to it, taking the time to wash him off. I massage the tight muscles and do my best to ignore the one between his thighs that's now resting on his flat stomach. Every once in a while, I watch as he reaches down and gives himself a few strokes, but I want him relaxed before I do anything. Finally, his head leans back against the tub, and his eyes close.

His hand is still on his cock, jerking slowly, to a rhythm only he hears in his head. It's hot, watching him do this, knowing that he's doing it for me. Knowing that he's completely lost all inhibitions around me. Quickly I jump into the tub, hoping to not disturb him. I know I've accomplished that when I learn forward, take his length down my throat, and he levers up out of the water.

"Son of a bitch, Ruby, I wasn't expecting that."

It doesn't take him long to get with the program though. His thick fingers dig into my hair, pushing me up and lifting me down. "Stop, stop," he pants, pulling me up by the thighs to straddle him.

"We've never…" he swallows roughly. "We've never had the

conversation, but I would really like to go bareback in you tonight. Can I do that? Are you protected?"

God, just the words he uses is enough to turn me on.

"Yeah, I am. I'd love to do that with you."

There's no hesitation, in one push he's inside my body, mouth at my breast, and the world as I know it has completely turned on its axis. Because unprotected sex with Caleb? Feeling him with absolutely nothing between us? Better than I ever imagined it could be.

CHAPTER TWENTY-TWO

Ruby

May

"OKAY LADIES AND gents, you have five minutes before the bell rings, and that's all I have for the class. Talk amongst yourselves, but please keep it down," I tell the juniors that make up my history class.

History isn't my first love. If given the choice, I would have taught English, but I can do both and there was a need for a History teacher, so here I am. Using my five minutes wisely, I go ahead and start in on next week's lesson plans, because I plan to spend as much of this weekend as I can with Caleb. A smile toys against my lips as I think about the guy who has so unexpectedly come into my life. We've been going strong for months now, definitely longer than any other relationship I've ever had. With other guys, I didn't stay at their places, they didn't stay at mine. I know part of that is growing up, not being in the dorms anymore, and not having to worry about roommates, but I feel adult in this with him. Like he and I could make a go of this, if we continue to travel down the path we are. I've never felt that with another man.

The bell rings and my class dismisses. As is my custom, I watch them as they leave, and then stand out in the hall until most of the crowd disperses. I broke up a fight once, and since then I've continued to do this. It's important that none of the students get hurt on my watch. I take it very seriously.

"Ruby!" I hear a loud voice coming down the hallway, and it's a voice I'd know anywhere, one that's started to make me smile.

"Hey Kels." I wave as I see her and Caleb coming down the hallway.

Lord I love to watch Caleb approach, it's nice to watch him leave too, but watching him approach legitimately makes my heart beat faster. The asshole, he knows it too, I can see his smirk from where I stand.

He's working today, wearing his MTF uniform of tactical pants and a t-shirt with a bullet-proof vest reading MTF on the chest in bright yellow letters. His badge hangs around his neck, and goddamn if he isn't sex on a stick. I watch as he slows his walk down, the loose-legged gait becoming lazy as he eats up the distance between us. Kelsea beats him to me, and I reach down to give her a hug.

"See ya, Ruby, I gotta go find Mom."

"See ya." But my eyes aren't on her, they're on her older brother.

He hasn't shaved today, and it makes his brown eyes pop against his tan face. When he's finally within a few inches of me, he reaches out with his left hand, the exposed ink on his arm catching in my peripheral, and cups my jaw, before shoving his fingers into my hair, tilting my head to the side and claiming my lips with his. The kiss, compared to many of the others we share isn't even steamy, but this is Caleb. Everything he does is a turn on. When he breaks away, his voice is deep, rough. "Missed you today."

Not able to take it, I step forward, wrapping my arms around his waist. "Missed you too," I answer, before leaning in for another kiss.

When we break apart again, he pulls his bottom lip in between his teeth after he licks the fullness. "Sucked not waking up next to you this morning. We're gonna have to do something about that, Ruby Red."

"At some point we will," I agree, because I hate waking up alone too.

"Soon?" he moves his hand forward, using his thumb to wipe at my bottom lip.

"Soon, hot stuff, really soon."

He sighs. "I'm gonna go say hi to my mom, wanna come with me?"

"Yeah, just let me lock up my classroom."

He's a gentleman, standing in the door until I've done everything I need to do and then shutting off the light and closing the door for me. I fumble with the key because he's standing so close. There's something about his presence that rattles me, but in a good way. As we walk down the hallway, he puts his arm around my neck, pulling me close.

For a moment, I flash back in time, wondering what it would be like to walk these halls with him when I was in high school, if I had been just a little older. He and I would have at least been in this school at the same time. Chances are he wouldn't have even noticed me, but I can still imagine what it would have been like walking these halls with him.

"Did you walk down this hall with your high school girlfriend?" I tease him.

He throws back his head, groaning. "Yeah, we walked down this hall, but I wasn't nearly as excited to see her as I am to see you."

I'll take what he's giving me, even if sometimes I don't fully believe it. Unfortunately I'm a cynic, but it's gotten me this far in life, so I'll take what I can get.

Cruise

"I'VE NEVER TOLD a woman about my past, never managed to get close enough one to trust her enough with the information. Opening up about how I grew up isn't easy, at all." I hold her close, kissing her forehead to give me comfort as I consider opening up and baring myself to Ruby. I'm not even sure why I'm doing it tonight, but the things we've been through recently have made me want to share every part of my life with her. Knowing she doesn't judge me and she doesn't blame me are huge parts of why I trust her.

"You and your dad seem like you had a decent life before Karina came along." She leans up, kissing me on the neck.

I'm torn between her believing these things about me and being completely honest about the path I took to adulthood. "My parents had me at sixteen and my mom left before my second birthday. I've only ever seen her once, and never officially met her." I lay my dirty secret down at her feet, wondering if this will change her perception of me.

She pushes herself up on her elbow, her blue eyes moving up and down my body. I wish I knew her thoughts, could see inside her mind and see if it surprises her. "She left?"

"Yeah." I reach over, running my fingers through her hair. "She left. Which is why Dad and I are so close now. It was just us for a long time, except when I was little and he was deployed."

"Who took care of you then?" she questions softly, running her fingers along my bare skin.

"My grandmother. We don't have a relationship now because of some things that went down between my dad and his dad, but at least I had someone to take care of me when he was gone."

"Did you like staying with her?"

I swallow roughly, tightening my arms around her. "No, I hated it. The only thing I wanted back then was my dad. I didn't understand why he was gone, what he was doing, and why I had to share him with the world. I remember him and other people trying to explain it to me, but I could never get it to compute in my head. I always thought he was *my* dad, and there was absolutely no reason I should have to share him. I felt the sacrifice early, and I reacted badly to it. The second time he was deployed, I was a complete shit. I acted out, got into fights, and was literally a holy terror. After that, Dad didn't take another deployment and got out."

"From there, where did you go?"

It's hard to explain this vagabond life to someone who's only known me as a person who's had a stable existence, but I want her to know me. The real me. "We lived in a few different towns in Texas before we ended up settling in Laurel Springs. It wasn't until we came here that I realized what a home was and felt like I belonged."

"I'm glad you did." She finally relaxes, putting her head on my shoulder. "If you hadn't, I never would have met you. I'm a firm believer, given the way I grew up, that everything happens for a reason. Your mom leaving directly brought you and your dad here. To the Moonshine Task Force. To Laurel Springs, and in the end, to me. I can't hate her for that, Caleb. I just can't. I can tell you she missed out on knowing an amazing man, but I can't hate a life that directly affected bringing you into mine."

Wrapping my arms around her, I realize how blessed I truly am.

CHAPTER TWENTY-THREE

Cruise

June

"WOW!" HER GAZE falters on me as she hops into the Jeep and gets a good look at the shirt I'm wearing. "That shirt is bright."

"Yeah, I know." I look down at the hot pink shirt covering my body. "The Hurricanes got to pick out their colors, and they decided on hot pink and black. I'm very well aware that I look like a goddamn highlighter. The perks of coaching *and* having to attend softball games."

She laughs, covering her mouth with her hand. "Mason wears it too?"

"What can I say? Kels makes us do shit we never thought we'd do. Like wear hot pink and spend our weekends during the summer and fall with ten-year-old girls. But I'd rather them be with us than some tyrannical coach who doesn't give two shits. I did that enough in football. These girls are learning valuable lessons. Even if I do catch a few of their moms checking out my ass."

Her blonde hair whips around. "I'm sorry? What? They're checking out your ass?"

"Well I mean, it's a nice ass." I give her a wink. "But just in case, I got you a little something to wear today." We come to a stop at a red light, and I reach into the backseat of the Jeep, holding another hot pink shirt.

She opens it up, smiling big as she sees that it has the team name on it, and then turns it around where it sports Kelsea's number and it says *Coach's Girl* on it. "Great, so now people will think I'm with your dad."

"We're both coaches," I correct her.

"Aren't you assistant?" She giggles, busting my balls.

"Fuck that, I'm out there on the field, in the hot sun every day. Besides, Mom has one that says *Coach's Wife*; he wouldn't have a wife and a girlfriend. Everyone knows that. Mom would cut his dick off. Everybody will know you're mine. Especially when we walk in together and you give all those women the evil eye for staring at my ass."

She reaches down, managing to grab a little bit of skin to pinch. "Damn right, Harrison. That ass is mine, and they may as well just get used to it."

Damn, I love this woman. Love the way she makes me feel, the way she's fully integrated into my family, and the fact she's not ashamed to be with me. If I'm honest that's something that's hindered me for a lot of years. Because my mom left, I always got the feeling people were ashamed to be seen with me. That they didn't love me as much as I loved them. Ruby is showing me that I'm capable of being loved. I'm capable of accepting love, and maybe just maybe, I can take it at face value and not question it. After all, I was able to get it with Karina, I give it to Kels, and my dad with no question. To a point I give it to Ruby too, but opening myself up is hard. I'm learning though, with this woman, and it's worth it.

Ruby

"I SEE YOU graduated to the official shirt," Karina greets me as I make my up in the stands to sit next to her.

"I did." I take a drink of my water bottle and pull my sunglasses down further on my face. "When he gave it to me, I had to give him shit and tell him that people will think Mason has both a wife and a girlfriend."

Karina laughs, throwing her head back. "Oh my God, I told him that too. I told him he should have put assistant on there."

"He got made fun of by both of us." I smile softly as I gaze out onto the field.

"It's cool, he's used to being made fun of." She smirks. "That's basically our relationship."

"At least he's a good sport."

"Caleb's always been a good sport about everything. When I tell him and other people that Kelsea's lucky she got the brother she did, I'm not kidding at all."

The two of us people watch as other parents, friends and family members arrive for the game that's about to start. I want to talk to Karina about Caleb, but I'm not sure how to approach the subject.

"So I went by Caleb's the other day, but I saw your car parked beside his Jeep and was scared I'd interrupt something if I went in." She gives me a grin.

I try to think back to what day she's talking about, wondering if she would have really interrupted anything. Chances are, with us, she would have, but I don't want to tell her that.

"It was Saturday, and I knew he had to work that night. It was late enough in the afternoon that he was probably taking a nap."

Immediately my face burns, because I do remember that day.

He'd tied me up and shown me what nipple clamps can do, something I'd never experienced before, and probably never will with anyone but him. Instead of taking the nap he'd wanted, he'd ended up being fifteen minutes late to work.

"Feel good, Ruby?" he whispers into my ear as he circles my nipple with his finger. The clamps have been on long enough that I can't feel anything anymore, but I'm straining against the Velcro he's wrapped around my wrists. If I can just get my finger underneath, I can get lose and take the clamp off, feel the explosion of pleasure that borders on pain he's told me I'll feel when he does.

"Yes, God yes, please," I fight against the restraints again. "I want this."

"You sure?" His brown eyes are almost black, his cheeks red underneath the stubble. He's as excited as I am. I nod, wrapping my legs around his waist.

When he fingers the metal release on the clamp, and then presses it, I about come up off the bed. The rush of feeling is overwhelming and I'm not sure I can deal with it, until he clasps his mouth over the tight bud, soothing it with his tongue. His other hand goes down to my pussy, where I'm as wet as I've ever been. And when he bites roughly on the sensitized skin, I come, in a shivering quivering mess against him. It takes me by surprise, and I scream loudly.

"Yes," he encourages me. "Let the whole fuckin' complex know."

And when he takes off the other clamp, I'm pretty damn sure I do just that.

"You would have interrupted something," I whisper under my breath.

"Things are going good with the two of you? He doesn't really talk much to me about it, which makes sense. I'm the mother figure in his life, but I'd like to know he's happy."

"I'm happy, and I hope he is. I haven't ever been with someone like him before. He's something else." I shake my head.

"He's a lot like his dad. I'd never met anyone like him before either, and he blew my carefully laid plans and world totally up.

"That's Caleb if I ever had to describe him. He's definitely blowing up my plans and rocking my world."

"Girl, I know all about the world rocking when it comes to a Harrison boy."

And that's when Caleb and the girls take the field. He's coaching the third base line which is where we're sitting, and as he bends over, hands on his knees, I get the best look at his ass. Today is definitely a damn good day.

CHAPTER TWENTY-FOUR

Cruise

Fourth of July

"DO YOU NEED my help?" I ask Tank as I sit around a patio table at his parent's house. The entire MTF and their families have descended upon their pool, and have taken over their bar-b-cue. Somehow all of us got the afternoon and night off. Many of us worked the early morning and previous overnight hours, so there's some tired faces but we're all extremely happy to be spending this holiday together.

"Nah, I got it." He closes the lid to the grill and heads back into the kitchen.

I'm glancing around, half paying attention, with my arm around Ruby, when a conversation starts that gets my interest. Renegade and Whitney are talking about a teenage boy Renegade found stealing at a local department store.

"I don't doubt that," Ruby is saying at my side, in response to whatever is being discussed. My girl is fired up about whatever this is, because she's leaned forward in her seat, away from my arm around her shoulder. The tank top she wears pulls at the back, and shows the skin between the edge of it, and the beginning of her bikini bottoms. I rub the exposed flesh, trying to calm her down. "I taught Nickolas." She sits her glass down on the table. "He was in my class and I tried to get his piece of shit parents in there, I reported them to Principal Taggart and made a CPS complaint."

"I'm sorry." I lean forward with her. "I totally missed what happened, can somebody fill me in real quick. Why's Red so pissed?"

Renegade takes a drink of his beer. "It's that kid I picked up the other night. The one who was stealing? He was stealing food, socks, and underwear, man. It wasn't like he picked up a video game system. When I got there–" Renegade takes a moment to shake his head "–he reminded me of me, at his age. I asked him, ya know, why are you taking this stuff?"

Ruby interrupts him. "He's takin' it because school is out, he has no food to eat, and I can guarantee you the kid hasn't had new clothes since my freshman year of college. He's Caleb's size." She hooks her thumb at me. "Remember when I asked you if you had anything you weren't gonna keep? The stuff you gave to me, I gave to him."

My heart breaks for this kid as I listen to everyone talk about him. "Did you charge him?"

"Nah, I talked to the owner, told him what the kid told me, and paid for what he'd stolen."

"You paid for it?" That's big. It happens every once in a while with us, but we really have to believe the situation.

"Yeah, and I took him home, where I witnessed some not so great things happening."

Whitney picks up the story as she grabs hold of her husband's hand. "We've spoken with some people we know, and we've contacted a lawyer. He's going to be emergency placed in our home as a foster child next week. That's how bad it was."

"No shit?" I'm amazed that this has gone so fast, but it couldn't have happened to anyone better than these two.

"Yeah." Renegade smiles at his wife, as he runs his hand

along her arm, and then they clasp them together. "We wanted more kids and it never happened for whatever reason. Maybe this was it. When I presented what I had to the supervisor over at CPS, she made things happen. Nickolas was taken out of their care yesterday. He'll get looked at today, have all the paperwork filled out tomorrow, and we'll take custody of him after the hearing on Monday."

"I wish we could have just taken him today. So he could have met all of you and everything." Whitney worries her bottom lip between her teeth.

"I know, Princess, but we gotta do stuff by the book."

Beside me, Ruby speaks again. "If he needs some help to get to where he should be for the upcoming school year, my summer class is almost over. I'll do anything I can to help him. I'm positive he wasn't getting the help he needed at home."

"Thank you, I'll text you and set something up." Whitney grins over at my girlfriend.

Having her willingly put herself in our group is one of the best feelings I've ever felt. As we all go back to talking to one another, I lean in. "You wanna go get in the pool?"

"Sure!"

We get up and go over to the lounge chairs, me taking off my shirt, kicking off my flip flops. I watch as she puts her hair in a ponytail and kicks off her own flip flops, but never moves to take the tank top off. "You gonna get in with that."

She nods. "I've never been fully comfortable with my stomach."

That pisses me off. Walking over to her, I tilt her chin up to look at me. "If you're uncomfortable, then you're uncomfortable, but know I think you're fucking gorgeous, perfect, and everything I've ever wanted."

"Thank you." She leans her forehead against my chin. "I'll

think about it."

"You do that."

A few hours later, when I come out of the house from using the bathroom, I see my brave girl has finally taken that tank top off, and damned if she doesn't look amazing playing volleyball with all the other ladies.

Ruby

"SOMETIMES, I SIT back, look at you, and wonder how in the hell I got so lucky." I lean my head against Caleb's shoulder, wrapping myself around his body. His big hand rubs against my back, and I can't help but feel the goose bumps appear.

We're sitting in the bed of Ryan's truck, waiting on the Fourth of July fireworks to start. He laughs deep in his throat as he takes a drink from his beer bottle. "You wonder that? Babe, that's my life. Like why in the hell did you decide to even go out with me after what happened to you that night. I'm a lucky motherfucker."

"I think we're both pretty lucky." I reach over, taking a drink from his bottle of beer. It tastes better when it's his; I can't explain it, but there's a taste that's just Caleb's.

His eyes follow the motion of my throat, and I can tell by the way his eyes dilate, he approves of me sharing it with him. Wrapping his arm around my neck, he pulls me into him. "That's sexy as fuck," he whispers in my ear.

"What is?" I'm not sure what he's talking about.

"Sharing my beer with me, not being afraid to do what feels good. I've never been with a woman like you before." He pulls me closer into his body.

Glancing around at the group with us, I notice no one's really paying any attention. He picks me up, sitting me crossways over his lap. I circle my arms around his neck, leaning in to take his lips with mine. It's a hot night, but I don't mind being close to him, don't mind being in his lap sitting so close. "You think I'm sexy?" I question, when he tugs on the end of my hair.

"Always, you're always sexy. Doesn't matter what you're doing, you just being you is the sexiest thing I've ever seen."

My cheeks heat at the mention of him thinking I'm sexy. This relationship that the two of us have, is so different than anything else I've ever experienced.

"Bubba." I hear Kelsea's small voice beside us and pull back, respecting the fact she wants her brother's attention.

"Yeah, Cupcake?"

"Will you go ride the Ferris Wheel with me?"

"You want Red to go with us?" He gives me a wink.

I pinch him on the side. "You know I hate heights."

"I'll be there with you and..." he trails off. "Cupcake's going, so I mean you'd be hanging out with a ten-year-old."

"Oh, so that's how it's going to be?" I give him a saucy smile. "You're trying to shame me into riding the Ferris wheel with your little sister by acting like she's braver than me."

"Actions speak way louder than words, Red."

"Alright then." I stand up, holding my hand out for Caleb. "Let's get this show on the road."

"C'mon, Kelsea." He jumps down from the tailgate of the truck, holding his hands up to help me down too.

It's the annual Fourth of July celebration for Laurel Springs, and while I have no intentions of riding the Ferris Wheel, I'm really happy to be here with Caleb and Kelsea. He holds my hand as we walk through the crowd of people.

"I can't believe we walked these same paths, did all this same shit, but a few years apart, and we never knew each other." He lets go of my hand and pulls me by the neck into his side.

"You were older, and away at college," I remind him. "What would you be interested in a high school kid like me for?"

"Young Caleb was fuckin' dumb Caleb," he growls as he nips at my ear.

"And I wouldn't have had the confidence back then to let you make a play for me. I would have just faded into the background," I try to explain to him. "Even though I was a cheerleader, I totally hid in the back row."

"You're my cheerleader, babe. You would have been front and center, right here for me." His eyes heat as he looks at me.

Where we are on the main thoroughfare isn't far from the football field, and I can tell by the heated look we exchange, we're both thinking of Halloween. But tonight we have someone else with us.

"Can we get some cotton candy?" Kelsea asks as we see a line waiting to get the sugary treat.

"Yes!" I let go of Caleb and run up to walk next to her. "We can get all the cotton candy there is."

As we walk away, I turn around, throwing a smirk and a wink back at Caleb.

Cruise

I LOVE THE way she's taken to my sister and my sister has taken to her. They're two peas in a pod, and I've always known if I wanted to keep someone in my life, Kelsea would have to love them. Right now, I'm pretty sure she loves Ruby more than she loves me. After all, what do I know about nail polish, braids, and clothes? It makes me think things though, as I watch the two of them walking ahead of me.

They look almost related, because Kelsea has a major case of hero worship right now. She wants to do everything Ruby does, and that includes wearing whatever clothes she can find that match any of my girlfriend's. They're both wearing cut-off shorts and tank tops. The thing it makes me think about? What if in ten years that's Ruby with our kid?

Never, in the almost twenty-nine years I've been on this planet, have I thought long-term about anything other than the Moonshine Task Force. Never have I thought past what I wanted to do once I made it. After I said goodbye to a pro football career, all my time and energy was spent making my dad proud. Making him see I understood the sacrifice he made for me, for us as family.

Now? I'm thinking about my future, what I want out of life. And I'm more sure than I've ever been that it's a curvaceous blonde spitfire, small enough for me to rest my chin on her head, bold enough to make me hard with just a look. She's sweetness mixed with sassy, and her blue eyes can see right through my soul. And she's completely perfect for me. She fits me, she fits my family, and without me even realizing it, she's become one of the most important people in my life.

"Hey ladies," I yell as they've gotten ahead of me, standing in line for what looks like the largest cotton candy I've ever seen. "Wait for me!"

"Hurry up then, slow poke," Ruby yells back as she and Kelsea giggle, sharing what appears to be a private joke between the two of them.

When I get there, they're next in line. I pay for what they order, and then wait with them while it's being made. I watch in awe as the person makes cotton candy fucking art. He gives a small heart to Kelsea, which makes her immediately fall in love, and then I watch as the fucker makes a flower for Ruby, handing it to her with a flourish.

"For the beautiful lady."

She smiles at him, gratefully accepting it, before she takes a bite. I scowl at him over her head, mouth a *WTF dude*, and turn them toward the rides.

"How did that guy know my favorite flowers are pansies?" she wonders as she continues picking at the different colors, before putting them in her mouth.

I watch as she licks her lips to rid them of the sugar, and then I wonder, why the fuck didn't *I* know pansies were her favorite flower? Why the fuck haven't I gotten her flowers before, and why am I so jealous of some guy who works at a carnival?

God, love is a crazy fuckin' thing.

"C'mon let's go to the Ferris Wheel." Kels directs us through the crowd, to where we stand in line.

"Are you really going to go?" I ask Ruby, knowing from a few conversations we've had, she truly hates heights.

"No." She grins as she shakes her head. "The two of you have totally got this taken care of. There's no way." She puts her arms around my waist. "Even with you, I'd probably pee my pants and get so scared I wouldn't be able to physically get off the ride."

I can't imagine this woman that's come to mean so much to me would ever be that scared of something, but we all have our quirks. "I'd keep you safe," I remind her.

"You're not God, Caleb, and there's no safety net under this thing. Sorry, but you're not getting me up there. I'll gladly watch the two of you with my feet safely on the ground down here."

She's still eating her cotton candy, and it's turned her lips a different color. Unable to help myself, I lean forward, licking the sweetness off of them. Glancing around, I see that Kelsea is talking to one of her friends from school. "I wonder what that would taste like around your other lips." My voice is pitched low, and I can tell the moment she understands what I'm saying. Her gaze becomes heated and she stops with a piece of the candy half-way to her mouth.

"Caleb Matthew." Her voice is scandalized. "I can't believe you just said that to me."

"Believe it." I lean in, getting a taste of the sweetness myself. The line is moving and it's our turn. "And you best believe I'm picking up another bag before we leave. Tonight, Ruby Red? We're gonna have some fun."

TWO ORGASMS AND a bag of cotton candy later, we're both laying in her bed, trying to get our breath back.

"You're gonna kill me one day," she accuses as she rolls over to rest her head on my shoulder.

"Nope." I hold my hand to my chest. "Pretty sure my heart is going to beat out of my chest. That, was one of the best ideas I've ever had."

She makes a noise in her throat. "True, but it's sticky."

I snort, tilting my head down so that I can see her. "Newsflash babe, most everything that's fun without clothes on is sticky. If that's your only complaint, I'm not accepting it."

"Then don't." She shrugs. "Just come join me in the shower."

She gets up, slipping out from under the covers. My gaze is immediately drawn to her naked ass and the two dimples above it. When she turns around, looking at me over her shoulder, I'm a goner. I'm out of bed so quickly I almost trip over the covers, and all I know is one thing: I'm gonna clean her up, just so I can dirty her up again. It's become one of my favorite things about being in a relationship.

CHAPTER TWENTY-FIVE

Ruby

I T'S A HOT summer day, as I walk onto the practice field. Since school let out in early June, I've been catching up on sleep, taking a summer class, and spending as much time with the man in my life as I can. Neither Mason nor Caleb are here today. Both are on duty, so another parent has offered to help the girls practice. Karina is sick with a summer cold and me? I'm here, not sure what the hell I've gotten myself into. Kelsea and I are spending the afternoon together, beginning with me picking her up. So we'll see how this goes.

"Ruby!" I hear as I shield my eyes and look out along the field. Kelsea is running toward me, her backpack bouncing as she runs.

"Hey Kels," I greet her, a real smile on my face. She and I haven't had a ton of time with one another, but as Caleb and I have gotten closer, the same has been true for the two of us. "You ready?" I wave to today's coach as she walks beside me.

"I am, it's hot out here." She pushes her hair back from her forehead.

Taking a good look at her, I see her face is beet red, and she's sweated a good deal. "You wanna go take a shower before we go do our thing?"

She looks up at me, nodding. "I feel so gross."

"No problem, your brother's apartment is closer than mine. Is it okay if we go there?"

"How are we going to get in if he's not there?" she questions as we get to my car.

"I have a key," I say the words off-handedly, as we get to my car. He gave me one not long ago, and it had been a turning point in our relationship. Whatever this is between us, is serious.

"He gave you a key?" Her eyes are wide. "Ruby, does that mean you're gonna get married?"

I'm taken aback by her question, but I can understand how she probably came to that conclusion. A kid doesn't understand the way things like this work. "I don't know Kels, maybe one day, but definitely not tomorrow."

"I wouldn't mind it," she announces. "I've always wanted a sister and I'd love it if you were mine."

I'm overcome with more emotion than I want to admit. This little girl with a heart so much like her brother's, has totally worked her way into mine.

"I've always wanted a sister too, Kels, and if I had to choose, you would be it."

She seems happy with the answer as she sings along to the radio. Meanwhile I'm trying to hold my shit together, pleased beyond all belief that she sees me as worthy of Caleb. A part of me always wonders if I will be, because he's had such a hard life, I want to make sure I'm the one he wants to come home to at the end of the day. The one he always wants to confide in, and I want him to know he's the most important person in my life, because I want to be one of the most important in his.

This is definitely a good start.

"ALRIGHT CHICK, WHEN you get done with your shower, we'll head out for some lunch and then we can go get our nails done if you want?" I offer. Getting my nails done is something I truly enjoy, and given the amount of times Kels asks me about it, I'm pretty sure she likes it too.

"Just gonna go grab my clothes." She runs into the room that Caleb calls hers when she spends the night.

Sitting down on the couch, I pull up a girlie show on Netflix I've been watching the last few weeks, before texting Caleb.

> *R: Kels and I are using your apartment so she can take a shower before we go get our nails done. She was really hot when I went to pick her up.*

I expect for it to take a little time for him to text me back, but to my surprise it doesn't. Must be a slow day for him.

> *C: Do whatever you need to, baby. That's why I gave you a key.*

Most days I can't get over the way he talks to me, and today is no exception to that. I haven't seen him in two days and I miss him. Our schedules have been off a little from one another.

> *C: Maybe you can come back when you get done? Not seeing you for two days is not working for me.*

> *R: Funny, hot stuff, it's not working for me either. I miss you.*

Texting isn't the same as hearing his deep voice, not the same as feeling his fingers against my skin, feeling the warmth of his body pressed to mine.

> *C: I miss your face too, Red. Send me a pic?*

The smile that's spread across my face can't be denied. The fluttery feeling in my stomach can't be denied either. I've waited my whole life for a man to make me feel this way, and I'm so happy the man to do it is Caleb Harrison. Holding my phone up, I give him my best smile, along with a wink into the camera. Hitting a few buttons, I send it, and wait for him to get back with me. A few minutes later, I get a response from him. A picture of his smiling face.

I allow a smile back at him, wanting to pinch myself to make sure I'm not dreaming. His brown eyes, the color of bourbon, sparkle as he grins. There's a small dimple in his left cheek, and he's got a five-o'clock shadow coloring his deeply tanned skinned, even though it's only early afternoon. His lips are full, like he's been licking them most of the day, and I can't wait until I put a kiss on them. If anyone had told me when I went into The Café that day, that I'd end up with Caleb, I would have told them they were crazy. Yet, here I am, having the time of my life.

"Ruby, can you braid my hair?" Kelsea asks as she comes into the living room, carrying a brush and a hair tie.

"Sure, let me finish this, and then we'll get it done."

R: Kelsea is done. I'll see you tonight?

We hadn't been planning on seeing one another, but now that I know we're both thinking the same thing, I can't help but want to see him.

C: Be at my apartment when I get off, babe. I go off-shift at 6:30

Looking at the clock, I know Kelsea and I will have plenty of time to get our stuff done together.

"Alright, come over here, and we'll get you fixed up."

Kelsea sits in front of me, crossing her legs. "Can you do a braid in the front?"

"So you don't want all your hair braided? Just some of it?" I verify as I brush her hair.

"I want it the way you had your hair the other day."

I wish I had my curling wand with me, because then I could curl the rest that's not going in the braid, and she could look like me. "We'll get it right." I motion for her to turn around and get to work. Because I do my hair like this all the time, I'm done in a few minutes. "There ya go!"

We grab our stuff and leave Caleb's apartment, setting out for our adventure.

"The Café good for lunch?" I question as we head toward downtown.

"It's where we always go." She nods. "I love their chocolate milkshakes."

"I think after the afternoon you had at practice, you probably deserve a milkshake."

"Caleb always lets me get them too," she admits, a smile on her face. "Mom and Dad don't like for me to have so much sugar, but it's my favorite."

"That's because Caleb and I are the cool couple." I think of Karina and Mason.

Something tells me they aren't as serious as they like to make people think they are. They probably have a damn good time when it's just them, but they try to set a good example for Kelsea.

"You are, you two let me do everything my parents won't let me do."

That's the fun part of not being the parent, but I don't tell her that. Parking at The Café, I turn the car off. "Let's go eat!"

"YOU HOME?" I announce myself as I enter Caleb's apartment. I saw his Jeep outside, but that doesn't mean he's not with Morgan working out. Since our texts earlier, I've wanted nothing more than to see him.

"Yeah." He comes out of his bedroom, towel around his waist, water making rivers along the ripples in his skin. "Just got here."

"I can see that." I lick my lips as I make a feast out of his body.

"You see something you like, Red?" His grin is mischievous. He knows I like his body, knows I love to explore it, and knows exactly what it can do to me.

"Sometimes I just can't believe you're all mine," I inhale deeply as I say the words.

"Believe it, babe, you got me."

For some reason those words affect me in a way that I have to cross the room, fold him into my arms, and hold him close to me. Every day he goes out into the field to protect the people of this town, I worry about him, know that no matter what he's doing, he's living his dream, but when I get to see him at the end of a shift? It's the best feeling, because I know he's okay. I know he's made it, and we're going to have more seconds, minutes, hours, and days together.

"Hey, what's wrong?" He tilts my face up to his, those brown eyes searching mine.

"Nothing." I shake my head, voice thick. "Just really happy to see you today."

The smile he gives me is my favorite kind. It's huge, shows a small dimple in his cheek and works it's way up to his eyes. "I'm happy to see you too. Favorite part of any day I have, Red. You've gotta know that. You've made my life better."

Resting my head against his chest, I close my eyes and breathe in the after shave he still uses. Somehow those words seem like an omen, but I'm not sure if it's good or bad. All I know is I want tonight and every other night with him, and I'll make sure he always knows it.

CHAPTER TWENTY-SIX

Cruise

I LOVE THE smile on Kelsea's face, love even more that I'm the one who put it there. "You excited Kels?" I grin into the rearview as we make the drive to Birmingham.

"So excited, like I knew you knew him." She bounces in her seat. "But I didn't really *know*!"

Him references my college roommate Slater Harlow, known by everyone who watches professional baseball as *Savage*. He's a formidable force on the baseball diamond, having the best season of his career. We're not as close as we once were, because life took us two totally different directions, but we still hang out every once in a while. Typically I like to keep the fact I know him from just about everyone, because I know he values his privacy. Now though? Kels is old enough to go to a major league game, and I'm doing my best to impress Ruby.

"I've known him a long time." I think back to our college days, how both of us had been so damn homesick. Him more than me, since I could at least head home on the weekend. Slater was from Georgia, his parents not well-off at all, and he'd never been able to afford a quick trip home. Hell, he barely went home in the summer, instead choosing to stay on-campus and work odd jobs to make money for the next semester. It was no surprise to me that our senior year he'd opted himself for the draft and gone pro. Within two years, he was the starting right-fielder for the Birmingham Bandits, racking up hits, RBIs, and a ton of fans. Now, it's my pleasure to see my good friend do as well as he is.

"He was your roommate?" Ruby asks as she reaches over and grabs my hand.

I love when she grabs my hand on any drive we make together. Being connected to her makes me calmer than I've ever been. Something about the connection quiets my brain and eases any anxiety I feel. "Yup, up until our senior year, then he opted to join the draft and I got a single room. Which worked out perfect for all that booty I got being a football player." I grin over at Ruby who shakes her head, now used to the way I talk.

"You're so bad, and you're so lucky I'm not jealous anymore over what you did before you met me."

"What does booty mean?" Kelsea asks from the backseat.

"Yeah, babe." Ruby gives me a smart-ass grin. "Why don't you tell her what booty means?"

Fuck my life. "It means spending time with someone you really like." I glance over at Ruby, sticking my tongue out at her for putting me in this position. "Like I spend time with Ruby."

"You mean like Mom and Dad spend time together?"

"Kind of, but whatever you do, don't say anything to them about getting booty. This will be one of our sibling secrets." I reach back, my pinky finger extended to her. "Got it?"

"Got it." She grabs hold of my pinky in hers and we swear on it.

For the rest of the drive, I keep my damn mouth shut about college.

As WE APPROACH the stadium, I follow the signs that go with the parking pass I was given from Slater. I can feel the excitement in the Jeep as we are told to break apart from the pack and follow a much smaller line of cars to a private parking area.

"Are we in the family parking?" Ruby asks, glancing around at the cars surrounding us. They're definitely nicer than my Rubicon, but I refuse to feel like I don't belong.

"I think so." I put it in park, grab my hat and sunglasses, before I hop out. "C'mon, ladies, let's get this show on the road."

Opening the back, I help Kelsea down, and then go around to Ruby's side, doing the same with her.

"Look at you being such a gentleman," Ruby teases, reaching in and grabbing her bag. She's a teacher, for sure. My mom carries the same bag everywhere. I call it a GO bag, because no matter what you might need, it's probably inside that bag. You need a band-aid? They got it. A bottle of water? No problem. A poncho? Definitely in there. A sewing kit? No big deal, it's fucking secured to the side with a magnet. Teachers are better than any Boy Scout I've ever met. When the world ends, I don't need a prepper, give me a damn teacher, any day of the week. Securing it crossbody, she pushes her hair back behind her ears. "We're ready."

"What do you mean, look at me being a gentleman? I'm always polite. You know this." I put my hand out for Kelsea to hold it as we cross the parking lot. I don't want to lose her here, so she's gonna have to be embarrassed by holding her big brother's hand. "C'mon, Cupcake, you got your stuff?"

She holds up the shirt she wants signed and the pink sharpie she wants it signed in. "Got it!"

"Let's go." I hitch my chin to the gate.

Ruby

MY HEART IS so full as I watch the two of them cross the parking lot, Kelsea's hand in his. They're speaking to one another, Caleb leaning down so he can hear her. Quickly, I take my phone out and capture a picture of the two of them, sending it over to Karina, since she's not here to witness this.

As they get to the gate, Kelsea turns around. "C'mon, Ruby!"

I jog to catch up with them. It's a blur as Caleb leads us through some corridors, flashing a badge here and there. Eventually we come to a hallway and standing there is the guy I recognize as *Savage* Harlow. He's almost dressed for the game, wearing a pair of baseball pants, cleats, and a shirt with the arms cut out. It's probably too hot for him to wear the full uniform right now. Kelsea stops in her tracks, letting go of Caleb's hand, turning back to me.

"Kels." He reaches back for her, but she comes to me, hiding behind my leg. I've never seen her do this before, but I recognize it. This is something I did when I was a small child and I was shy to meet someone who meant a lot to me.

"She's a little shy." I run my hand over her hair. "I think she'll be good in a few minutes."

The way she clings to me, makes my heart flutter, my stomach clinch. If Caleb and I ever have a child, is this what it's going to be like? I can see it in the future, but I know I don't want to get ahead of myself.

"It's good to see you, man." Caleb walks up to Slater, giving his hand a shake and pulling him in for a hug.

"You too." Slater slaps him on the shoulder. He glances over at us. "Is that Kelsea? I haven't seen her since she was a baby."

"You knew me as a baby?" That makes her move from behind my leg and causes her to speak up.

"Yeah." He squats down so that he's at eye-level with her. "Last time I saw you, you were about two years old. We used to hang out with you all the time. Your mom and dad would bring you when they came to visit your brother."

She looks up at me. "I think I'm okay, I've known him a long time." She holds out her shirt and her sharpie. "Can you sign this for me?"

Caleb and I share a laugh and a grin over her head. All the shyness that was there before is gone now. She's asking him questions and asked to be taken out onto the field. "Yeah." Slater stands. "We can go toss a ball real quick, if that's okay with your brother."

"Sounds good to me," he answers when everyone looks at him.

As we walk to the field, Slater turns around. "I don't know your name yet and I'm sorry to have been rude, I'm Slater."

"This is my girlfriend, Ruby," Caleb introduces us, putting an arm around my shoulder.

"He's gonna marry her." Ruby giggles before she runs off.

"Is that right?" Slater gives Caleb a look, before he turns around and runs off after her.

"I know she's kidding and pushing what she wants, off onto you," I tell him, letting him know that as much as my heart wants it to happen, I'm putting no pressure on him.

"Slater will take her mind off of it, he doesn't like to talk about relationships," he tells me as we walk to the field. "He and his high school girlfriend couldn't make the long-distance thing work. As far as I know, he's never gotten over it and given having a relationship another shot."

I watch Slater as he throws a ball back and forth between him and Kelsea. Her smile is huge, as is his when they laugh at something one of them say.

"Hopefully one day he'll find what we have." I hook my arms around his waist, holding him tightly.

"That's my hope too." He leans down, kissing me on the forehead.

"ONE MORE OUT!" I look over at Kelsea, who's literally vibrating in the seat between me and Caleb. "Can you believe it? They're going to win your first ever Major League Baseball game. How exciting is this?"

She jumps up and down as the final out is made and fireworks erupt over the stadium. We'd had great seats, given to us by Slater, behind the Bandit's dugout. As we're gathering our stuff to leave, I hear someone yell *Harrison*.

We all turn around and see Slater standing there. He motions for Kelsea to come down, holding out a ball to her. I'm not sure what he says, but it gets him a huge smile, and when she comes back holding the ball, I'm beyond thankful to have experienced this day with the two of them.

"Y'all ready?" he asks after waving to his friend. "It'll be at least a few hours before we get home, and the longer we put it off, the worse it will be."

"Let's go." I grab some of the stuff we bought and we slowly make our way up the stands as the massive group of people begin filing out.

It's been a great day, I realize as we hit the interstate, heading north. The Bandits won by two runs, we got to spend time together, and I got to experience my first baseball game. As I lean back with a huge smile on my face, I don't know that this is the last day everything will be normal for us, and reality is about to make itself known in a big way.

CHAPTER TWENTY-SEVEN

Cruise

THE JULY SUN is beating down on the pavement as I make my drive around the streets that make up Laurel Springs. It's been a boring day, for the most part, but I'm not stupid enough to think it'll last. Lately it's been slow and I've been feeling a lot like the other shoe might drop. This nagging feeling hasn't let go for the last week, but I know eventually either that shoe will drop or I'll get over it.

Rain came through over an hour ago, but it did nothing to cool the day down. It's now a sauna outside. In certain parts there's actually steam coming up off the road. Behind the sun that's moved in, you can see more clouds behind. A dark hazy threat looming in the background, more storms are moving in. The stillness of the day threatens to break wide open when they do.

Because of the heat that's been baking the ground and asphalt for days, most people are inside this afternoon, enjoying the air conditioning and not wanting to have heatstroke. Probably one of the reasons the radio has been quiet for the most part. As I make a turn onto the state highway, I hear dispatch come over the radio.

"Calvert County is requesting assistance. They initiated a traffic stop on a blue Tahoe. When they opened the back, it was full of moonshine. Be advised the suspect shot the officer who pulled him over, and they are traveling at a high rate of speed toward Laurel County. He should be entering in the next few minutes. The officer was pronounced dead on scene. Proceed with extreme caution."

My ears perk up, because I'm the one who's going to cut him off. I'm right where Laurel and Calvert counties intersect. Immediately I feel my adrenaline start to kick in. I grip the steering wheel so hard my knuckles are white. Controlling my breathing is easy, it's something I've conditioned myself to do, but the pounding in my heart? It's a rhythm that doesn't slow as I hit the button and speak to dispatch on the other end of the line.

"Dispatch, I'm where the suspect will enter. Should I deploy spike strips?"

"Negative." I hear Havoc's voice come over the radio. "He's moving too fast for you to get them out. With the road conditions it's risky and he might hit you. He'll be to you in the next two minutes. Take over the pursuit from Calvert County. Make sure that dashboard cam is on and activate that body cam, Cruise. I'll be there as soon as I can."

Doing as my boss has instructed me, I make sure everything is on and recording. My adrenaline pumps harder and I realize I had just been thinking about how boring this day was. Seems like business is about to pick up. I shoot up a little prayer that we all make it out of this as I get ready to take over.

I can hear the sirens before I can see them, but the Tahoe is a blur of blue as it passes in front of me. Like I was instructed to do, I pick up the pursuit. The Calvert County Deputies respectfully stop, and the police package is going through the gears as we pick up speed. Road conditions are hazardous, but I'm used to driving in them; I've been trained on how to handle any situation that presents itself to me. I have no doubt I can handle this one. "Heading east, toward the downtown district," I give the other guys my position, knowing that on this day everyone is spread out around the county. However, they'll all be making their way toward me, now that they know the chase has entered Laurel County.

"Caleb," dispatch comes across. "Be careful, they're trying to get to you. Havoc is closest, but according to GPS he's still ten minutes away."

I know this means I have to take care of whatever happens myself. This is what I've been training for since I started. I don't need anyone to help take up the slack. If I can't handle this, then this shouldn't be my job.

Calmly I relay the directions in which we're moving toward downtown, and I realize soon he's going to be in front of The Café, and there's construction going on down there. He'll be pinned in, but he won't realize it until he's right up on it. I start motioning with my arm, but he doesn't notice, and as we round the corner, there's a sickening thud as he hits the concrete barrier, the front-end of the SUV taking the brunt of the impact. Because of the slick roads, he slid right into it. There's smoke billowing from under the hood, the front crunched in a way that I wonder if the driver's legs are broken. I can see the airbag has been deployed from where I am, but I can also see movement, and I don't want him to get the drop on me. Taking cover behind my own driver's door, I steel my nerves and put some authority in my voice.

"GET OUT OF the car with your hands up!"

The driver's side door is open, and all I want is for them to put their hands up and get out of the car. Or at least hold off until my backup can get here. I don't have time to assess injuries, because I'm hesitant to move forward without the safety of the door protecting me.

"Driver!" I yell again. "Get out of the vehicle and put your hands up!"

There's authority in my voice. I'm doing what I'm trained to do. In my peripheral vision I can see that everyone in The Café is crowded around the plate glass window, looking out at what's going on. For a split second, I let my attention move to the window. There, I see my mom and Kelsea standing there, both with shock written across their faces, fear in their eyes. Desperately I want them to move back, I want Leigh to grab them and take them away from whatever this potential danger might be. This man supposedly has a gun and they're standing like open targets at a shootout. When I get out of this, me and Dad are going to have a discussion with both of them.

"Fuck you!" I hear from the smoking vehicle. The voice is as strong as mine, so I have to assume the driver isn't hurt. He's here to put up a fight, and I have to take whatever fight that may be seriously.

"Driver!" I try again. This time adding, "Come out with your hands up, facing away from me."

It's a split second. Literally five seconds out of an entire lifetime that happens in front of me. He comes from behind the driver's side door, holding his gun pointed on me. It's like a movie flashes through my brain. Meeting Kari for the first time, graduating, winning my first football game at Alabama, meeting Kelsea, watching her take her first steps, say Caleb for the first time, and then my dad. I remember all the things my dad has done for me. In my mind I hear him say I love you, and finally it's Ruby. The way she smiled up at me last night as I sheathed myself inside her. The way her head tilted back as she gave herself over to the feelings we invoke in each other. I never told her I love her, and right now, I might never get the chance to. I have to push all those things out of my head and concentrate on what's happening in front of me right now. Taking control of the situation is of the utmost importance, and I can't have all of the noise. Locking all of it away, I put some bass in my voice this time.

"Put it down," I command.

He doesn't though, he holds what looks to be a glock up, takes aim, and I know the second he decides to fire. It's like I can see across the hood of my vehicle into his eyes. I see there's no other way this can go. He's not going down without a fight, and there's a choice I have to make. It's either him or me. If I want to go home to my family tonight, I have to decide if I'm willing to take this shot. All those people in The Café are in danger, they're counting on me to protect them. The enormity of the situation sends rivulets of sweat down the back of my bullet proof vest. There's not time to second guess my decision because it's then that I hear the crack of the gun firing explode against the stillness of the day.

When he fires, I shift my weight, take aim, and fire too. His shot hits me in the vest, and I'm propelled a few feet backward as I take the impact of the handgun he was in possession of. My shot hits him in the chest, and as he falls, I think it's fatal. I struggle to my feet as I get up, walking over to where he is, my gun still drawn, pain radiating from where I've been hit. I hear the murmurs of patrons, I'm assuming that have come out from the businesses on Main Street. When I get to him, I can see he's not breathing, but I reach down and check his pulse anyway. As I suspected, my shot was fatal. Kicking the gun out of his reach, I finally key the mic.

"Dispatch, be advised, shots fired," I'm panting into the

radio.

"Caleb!" I hear Havoc's voice on the radio. "Are you okay?"

I'm trying to get my breath to answer him, unhooking the vest from around my ribs, inhaling a deep gasp of air. I sink to the asphalt, letting the concrete barrier hold me up, as I try to get my surroundings, try to breathe without it shooting pain through my ribs and as I tilt my head back to the sky, thunder cracks loudly and rain falls in sheets, covering everything.

"Caleb?" This time it's Renegade's voice.

I can't make myself get up, can't make myself move from where I am. Shock is a crazy thing, and I'm so damn tired. It's the adrenaline high coming down, my body trying to absorb the crazy amounts that were flowing through me as the situation unfolded.

"I'm okay, he got me in the vest, but I need an investigator on scene. Suspect is deceased."

I'm in shock as I say the words, not fully able to believe this has just happened. I'm not stupid. I know the risk I take every day, the potential for something like this to happen every time I go on shift. I just honestly didn't think today would be the day. Which I guess no one ever thinks it'll be the day, but I can't help but think about how I was bemoaning the fact it'd been a slow day.

It's a blur as people start pouring out of The Café and back-up finally arrives. My gun is taken away from me, and as per protocol, I'm placed on administrative leave immediately. Morgan is there though, checking me over, making sure the vest did its job. And it's in that moment, I hear a small voice screaming my name.

Kelsea is running from The Café toward me at full speed, Karina is on her heels, and both are crying as they hit me hard, each taking me in their arms.

I allow myself to bury my head in my mom's neck, allow my baby sister to hold me around the legs, and as they pull me back behind the side wall of The Café, away from prying eyes I let it go. I cry, I cry like I haven't cried since I was pulled over by Ace and I had to face my dad with all the shit I'd done as a teenager. Huge sobs wrack my body and out of nowhere, I feel strong arms wrap around us, and I know Dad is there. He's holding us all as I cry like a baby in my mom's arms.

"I'm sorry," I choke out. "So damn sorry."

His voice is near my ear, and I hear every word he says. "Don't you be sorry, Caleb. You saved a lot of people today, including your mom and sister. Never apologize for doing your job."

But I know me, and I know it's going to take me a while to be okay with this. And I know something else too – I'm fucked up, and I have no idea how to process any of this.

Ruby

"WHAT HAPPENED TODAY?" My voice is shrill to my own ears, but I've heard rumors all day. I hadn't been anywhere near The Café when the incident happened with Caleb, so I've had to hear it second hand each time. Right now, all I want is to be with the man I love and make sure he's okay. I tried to be polite and knock on his door, but when he wouldn't answer, I used the key he gave me and let myself in. What I'd found scared me.

Caleb sitting on the couch, nursing a beer, still wearing his clothes from this afternoon, some of them still partially wet.

"He pointed a gun at me," he says the words blankly, without emotion, and that's what's bothering me more than anything. The lack of emotion. I'm pretty sure he's still in shock, but I don't know how to help him, not sure how I can make this better for him. Part of me wants to call Morgan, the other part of me is scared to leave Caleb alone long enough for me to do that.

"He was going to kill me." He swallows hard. "All I could think about was you and my family. What would happen with you all if I wasn't here anymore. Would you find someone to take my place? Would Kelsea remember me in ten years? How would Dad take it? I mean so much shit went through my head. It was like a highlight reel of my life, like someone was playing it at my funeral. Every bit of it was so surreal, Ruby Red. Every bit of it. It was like an out of body experience that I couldn't get away from. A dream I couldn't wake up from."

"What can I do to help you, Caleb?" I grab his cheeks, forcing him to face me. "What do you need from me?"

"I'm so fucked up right now." He gets up from the couch, quickly going to the kitchen and grabbing another beer. "I don't know what I need. All I know is I fucking killed a man, Ruby. I killed a man. You want me touching you? Do you want to go to bed with a man who ended another life? Can you honestly say you can live with me knowing I did that? Because I'm not sure I can live with myself right now."

"You killed a criminal who had warrants out of five counties and an attempted murder charge, along with the fact he killed another deputy today. You saved what could have been a mass killing situation, you're a hero, Caleb."

"A hero?" I see tears pool in his eyes. "I don't feel like a damn hero right now."

"You're in shock, you have to give yourself time to work through this, to recover. You've got to give yourself a break. No one says you have to digest this whole situation tonight, right now."

He takes another drink of his beer, and I'm at a loss on how to help him. I'm not sure what I can do to break through the bullshit he seems to be stuck on. He's looking at this the wrong way.

"How's that going to help his family recover?" His voice is hoarse as he asks me this question. I can tell it bothers him, and to be honest it bothers me too, but I can't let him stay locked in his head like this. It isn't healthy.

"How do we even know he had a family?" I point out. Not much has been released about the man Caleb took down today.

"Well then that just makes it all better, doesn't it?" He gives me a look that so smartass I'd like to smack him across the face. This isn't the man I know, the man I've fallen in love with. I've never told him, but I do love him. Love everything about him.

"You don't have to be so mean, Caleb."

The look on his face isn't one I've ever seen before, and suddenly I'm scared. More scared and worried than I had been this afternoon. I wonder what it's going to take to make him believe he's not a monster. Am I strong enough to pull him out of this? Will my love be enough to make him see? Right now I'm doubting it, but I can't let him know that. I can't let him know that I'm scared. Right now I have to be the strong one for him, because he's always been the strong one for me.

"Sweetheart, this is the real Caleb, he's just been on his best behavior so he can fuck the shit out of you. Surprise and sorry about your luck."

And that's when I know that not only is my heart broken, but his is too, and I have zero idea how to fix it or make it right. I refuse to believe this is him, and tonight, I also refuse to let him wallow in his pity alone. He wants to drink himself silly? Then I'll drink right along with him. Kicking my shoes off, I stalk over to the fridge and grab my own beer.

"You're not doing this alone, Caleb."

"You're cute if you think you're gonna stop me."

"Try me, because maybe I've been on my best behavior too. You push me, and I'll push back. You might not like it, but you're not going to be alone tonight."

"Fuck it." He takes a drink from his bottle. "Do whatever you think you have to, but this changes nothing."

"That's where you're wrong. This afternoon, it changed everything."

"Good that you found out now, Ruby."

It doesn't escape me that he doesn't call me Ruby Red, but that's okay. I'll get my name back, just like I'll get him back. With patience and love.

CHAPTER TWENTY-EIGHT

Ruby

I'M SITTING IN my car watching Morgan and Caleb eat through The Café window. This is what I've been reduced to. It's been a week since the shooting, and so far, Caleb's refused to see me. I went to see him the other night, and it was a bad scene.

"What are you doing here?" Caleb opens his door, arms crossed over his chest. "I figured me not answering any of your calls let you know I'm not up to talking to anyone right now. Including you."

Not gonna lie, this hurts. Seeing him like this hurts, hearing him talk to me the way he is hurts. But I won't give up on him. I promised Kelsea months ago that I would be here if he needed me, that I could handle whatever was thrown at me.

"You need me," I talk against the tightness in my throat.

"I need to be left the fuck alone. You. Mom. Dad. You all need to leave me the fuck alone."

"We won't," I shake my head standing my ground. "We won't leave you alone to deal with this by yourself."

"Fine, then if you won't leave, I will."

I watch helplessly as he puts his shoes on, grabs his wallet, and storms out. Once I'm there by myself, I clean up, making myself busy until I realize he's not coming back. Finally I take myself to his bed, tuck his pillow under my chin, and cry it all out.

When I wake up alone the next morning, I know he hasn't been back, and I know he won't until I'm gone. It's sobering, and it's not the best feeling in the world. But he won't push me away that easily.

That fear of rejection is still here, but I've finally decided that I don't care. He's sent every one of my calls to voicemail. Any text I've sent has gone unanswered, and I'm beyond frustrated.

I can't understand why he's pushing me away, when even sitting here like I am, staring at him from a distance, I can see he needs me. He and Morgan drove separately; I see both their vehicles. I plan on confronting him when he leaves – I'm beyond sick of being ignored.

Some may say I'm crazy, and maybe that's a fact, but I know this man. I know him better than I know myself, and he needs me, I need him, and I've got to get him to see reason. Before we have nothing else to fight for.

Morgan gets up, throwing some money on the counter, before he walks out to his vehicle and leaves. He's in his EMT uniform, so he must either be reporting for duty, or he's got to be somewhere. Caleb is slower, and I can't help but think maybe that's a little help from the big guy upstairs, maybe he's helping me get this man I care for so much alone.

As I see Caleb start to come outside, I get out of my car and go over to his driver's side door, waiting patiently until he can see me.

"Red?"

The nickname slips from his lips, I can tell because it looks like he wants to put it back where it came from. But I don't let him. "Yeah, it's me. Ya know, the person who's been by your side for the past few months. Ruby Red?"

A wall is erected between the two of us. He switches off his emotions, holding himself rigid as he looks at me. "We have nothing to talk about."

"We have *everything* to talk about, starting with why you won't see me, why you won't talk to me, and what the fuck's going on inside your head right now."

"Nothing you want to get involved in."

"How do you know, Caleb? You won't tell me, you won't talk to me. I have literally zero idea what's going on there, and it's all because you've decided I can't handle it."

"You can't," he yells. "Because I can't."

"Don't decide what I can and can't do. I don't appreciate it."

He fumes, I can tell by the way his face is red, the way his hands clench into fists at his sides. "I can't live with myself, Ruby, how can I expect you to live with me?"

"What you need to do is realize this is when you need me, not when you need to push me away. Please Caleb," I beg. I break down and beg, something I promised myself I wouldn't do. "I don't want to see you hurt like this, please just let me be there for you."

"So people can talk about you behind your back? I know people are talking. Mom and Kelsea are upset about it. I don't want you to be upset about it too. What if we had kids, Ruby? How would they handle it?" His voice is hoarse. "How would they be able to separate their dad from the man I was?"

"Easy! The same way you do. What the fuck is going on here?"

"I don't know." He puts his hands up to his forehead. "All I know is I can't stand for you to look at me with that fucking pity in your eyes. It reminds me too much of how people looked at me when they realized I didn't have a mom. I don't want to be that poor, pitiful guy, twice in my life."

"You aren't, you idiot, and if you'd get your head out of your ass, you would see that."

I'm losing the battle, I can tell. He's retreating and there's nothing I can do to bring him back. The Caleb I know isn't there right now; he's somewhere untouchable, and all I can hope for is that we can bring him back.

"I'll wait for you," I tell him. "Wait until you can figure out what's going on in your head, wait until you see it's all clear."

"Don't." He holds up his hand, like he wants to run his thumb along my lip, the way he always used to. "Don't wait for me."

"Why can't you touch me?" The tears pool and fall. I miss it, miss his touch, the easy way he had to be touching me all the time. I crave it, want it badly, can't understand why he's punishing both of us.

"Because I can't touch you with this blood on my hands. Red, you're everything good and pure. I'll fuck you up too."

"You're not fucked up," I argue. "You're in shock over what you did, and you're trying to process it. Stop pushing me away and let me help you."

I reach out to grab his arm and he pulls it away, pushing me when I get too close. "Don't push me away."

"Don't make me hurt you." His voice is deep, dark, and full of something I've never heard before.

"You're already hurting me." I pull my arms around my waist. "I gave it all to you, Caleb, everything. The good, the bad, and the ugly. And you only want to give me the good, how is that fair?"

"Life isn't fair, Ruby, and it's better you learn that now, rather than five years from now when we're married and you hate me enough to divorce me."

"Where is this shit even coming from in your head?"

"I've seen it."

"And you've also seen your parents have a great relationship. Don't lump me in with people who can't handle it. Do you not remember who I was the first night I met your dad? The person I was the night you almost didn't get that guy cuffed." I wipe the tears out of my eyes, wipe them off my face. "I understand that you're drifting right now. You don't have a job you can go to, you're worried people are going to label you something you aren't. I get that, but don't you give up on me."

"How can I not give up on you, when I've already given up on myself."

That's when he gets in his Jeep, leaving me there crying. Letting me watch the taillights in the darkness of the night as he drives out of my life. As I look at the people watching me, I feel like a freakshow. Like everyone knows something I don't.

He'll come back, he has to, because what we have is too good to throw away. He'll see he's a hero, he'll believe it, and then he'll realize just how much he needs me.

That's what I keep telling myself as I walk to my car, compose myself, and drive away.

Cruise

IT'S HARD TO explain to everyone who keeps asking what exactly is going on in my head. There are so many thoughts and emotions I have swimming through the noise. It reminds me how I felt when my friend died in high school, and I'm trying desperately not to let myself turn down that destructive path again. I'm feeling guilt for taking another man's life. Pride for making sure my community is safe. Denial in what I did could have been prevented, and partially dirty at the blood on my hands.

I don't want to corrupt Ruby or anyone else with what I've done, but it's hard to live with. Knowing I ended another man's life is inherently shocking, and while I wait for the internal review, I'm increasingly worried they're going to say I had another option.

That's what's driving me right now. The fear that I did have another option.

The fear that I made the wrong decision.

The fear that I'm one of those cops who didn't think about the consequences before he committed an action that can't be reversed.

Until I know where I stand on what I've done, I can't come to Ruby clean, I can't be at peace with my decision, and I sure as fuck can't be expected to go on with my day-to-day like nothing happened.

Because it did. A man is dead. I shot him.

And I still have no idea whether it was justifiable or not.

My career and life lay in the balance of what the internal investigators find. They hold my entire life in their hands, and I'm nervous as fuck that they won't see it the way I did.

If they don't, my life and career as I know it is over, and I definitely won't be the man that Ruby thought I was. That's possibly the hardest part I'll ever have to come to terms with. So right now, it's easier to think I'm a fucker, rather than letting her know I care way more than I should.

CHAPTER TWENTY-NINE

Cruise

"HOW'D YOU GET in here?"

My dad is waiting on me, probably ready to rip me a new one, just like Ruby did. I'm so not in the mood for it tonight.

"You don't need to know how I got in here." He gets up from where he's sitting on my couch. "Instead, what we need to do is talk about how we're going to get you to where you need to be."

"What the fuck is that supposed to mean? This is me."

"This isn't you, we both know that. I didn't raise you to be a fuck face. You haven't been answering my calls, your mom's, Kelsea's, or come to find out Ruby's, so let's talk about this Caleb. What the fuck is going on?"

"Nothing." I grind my teeth together, not wanting to do this with him.

"We've done this once before son, and we won't do it again. Do you remember when your friend died? Remember when you pushed everyone away? How'd that work out for you?"

"How does having a murderer for a son work out for you?" I fire back at him. "Because I'm on administrative leave for committing murder."

"No." He shakes his head. "You aren't. You're on administrative leave for using deadly force related to your job. They are two different things, Caleb. Two very different things."

"They don't feel like different things," I argue as the door opens behind me.

I turn around, seeing Morgan standing there. His inked arms folded over his chest. His eyes meet my dad's. "Figured you might need some help and wanted to offer it in case you did."

"So what? You two gonna gang up on me, confront me like Ruby just did? Let me cut you to the bone with the venom I'm gonna spew? We all know I'm a fucker when backed into a corner. I strike first, ask questions later. You wanna confront me? You better be ready to take it."

Dad comes to stand in front of me. "You've been like this since you were a kid. Always trying to strike first, always trying to deliver that blow before it's dealt to you, but I swear to you, that's not what's happening here. Let me explain."

"There's nothing to explain," I yell. "I shot a man and it's fucked me up."

"It's not the first thing that's ever fucked you up, Caleb," Dad starts. "You wanna go back to the beginning? Lay this shit down at my feet. Blame me. I'm the one who started it. I've told you before I shoulda given you away and not kept you for my own selfish reasons. I kept you, even when I deployed to a war I wasn't sure I was going to come back from. I wasn't a perfect parent, I put you through shit you're probably still trying to deal with today. You wanna *start* at the beginning? Blame me. Let's get this all out. If you ain't gonna listen to me, then fuckin' cut me down, and when you're done, I'll tell you what you need to know. I've been here, I've done this. Maybe not as a member of the MTF, but I've killed to live. When you're faced with the decision, you make it. I'm a big man." He sits down on my couch and spreads his arms wide. "I can take it. Whatever you want to dish out. I can take."

He points at his chest. "Give it to me, don't give it the women you love."

"I never told her I love her." My throat gets tight. "That was the one thing that kept rolling through my head when that guy pointed that gun at me," I admit. "I never told her I love her."

"And if you keep pushing her away–" Morgan's voice is gentle at my back "–you're never going to be able to. Now I know what your dad's gonna tell you. Shut the fuck up and listen. Then you'll get a chance to make this shit right with Ruby, and this fucker won't win. Just give him a chance."

I look between the two of them.

"If you still feel the need to let loose when I'm done, I'm here," Dad says, his words strained. "I'm always here. Just give me five minutes."

"Okay," I agree. "What is it you need to tell me?"

"The deputies in Calvert County are familiar with him, they've dealt with him on numerous occasions. He's been threatening suicide by cop for the last two months, but they've been able to deescalate the situation every time it's arisen. We didn't have that background info, man. None of us knew it, and all you knew was a man was pointing a gun at you. You did what you're trained to do, you did what any of us would have done. If it hadn't happened when it did, it would have happened later. He would have kept putting himself into situations that escalated to where no one had a choice. He left Calvert County knowing what he was doing."

The admission hits me straight in the chest. It does make it easier, but it doesn't fully erase all of my guilt. "At least I know I was never going to have a choice, but it still doesn't change the fact I killed a man."

"No, you weren't, and it doesn't," Dad agrees. "He was

going to force someone to do it, and you were that person. If you hadn't of, who knows what he would have done to force someone. There were all those innocent people at The Café, including your mother and sister. Would you have been happier if he pulled his gun on one of them? Or God forgive, shot one of them?"

I swallow roughly, not wanting to comprehend what he's asking me. "No, God no. I couldn't live with myself if I didn't protect them."

"Regardless of if you want to hear it or not, you saved lives. You saved a lot of lives, and you'll get medal for it."

"I don't feel like I deserve a medal."

"You will." Morgan claps his hand on my back. "When the shock wears off and it can all sink in, you'll realize that what you did was heroic. You'll realize that not many people would have acted as quickly as you did, and in acting that quickly you were a hero. No one blames you man, we just want to see you get better. We want to see you with Ruby, and happy."

Ruby. Her name affects me unlike anything else ever has. "She hates me."

"She doesn't hate you," Dad and Morgan say at the same time.

"She's a good woman," Dad keeps on. "She'll forgive you, but that doesn't mean you won't have to work for it."

I'll have to get her trust back, because right now I've walked all over it without even thinking about how this affected her.

"For God's sakes," Morgan chuckles. "Tell her you love her. All of us have known how you feel about her for at least the past five months, let her in on the secret."

I tilt my head back, my emotions getting the better of me.

"Before I leave…" Dad reaches beside him on the couch. "Here's your gun and badge back. You've been cleared. Havoc said to give you a few more days off work, but if you want it, your spot is still available. Look–" he puts his hands on my face, forcing me to meet his eyes. "I know this shit's hard. It's never easy, but it's important. The work we do is important, and you'll never know how proud I am that you chose to follow in my footsteps, but if it's not for you Caleb, there's no shame in getting out. I'm not gonna love you any less. You're my firstborn, my only son. Having you turned me into the person I am today, and you're always gonna be my best friend, no matter what you do."

Now I'm really trying to keep the emotions from getting to me. "I just want to make you proud, and I felt like what I did wasn't honorable. Maybe I could have done something else, ended it peacefully."

"You. Could. Not. Have. You did everything right, son."

I sniffle slightly because this has been weighing so heavily on my heart. "Then I'll call Havoc and let him know I'll be back the first of next week. There's some things I have to do. Like get Ruby back."

"Hey," I yell at Dad as he turns to leave. He stops, cocking his head to the side. "Thank you."

"No problem. I love you, son."

"Love you too." I'm finding those words mean so much more now than they ever did.

"You got this?" Morgan asks as we watch Dad leave. "You know what you're gonna do and shit?"

"Yeah, thanks for being here, I…" my voice trails as I try to think of some way to repay him for what he's helped give me.

"Don't even say it, man." We clasp hands, hugging each other. "If anyone gets it, it's me. Now go get your girl back."

As they leave my apartment, I breathe for the first time since this whole situation went down. Damn it feels good to inhale and exhale without the weight of the world on your chest.

I'VE LET MYSELF have a little breakdown, allowed myself to purge all the emotions that have been so close to the surface since the day of the shooting, and I've come to a few realizations. I need Ruby to live my life, more than I ever imagined. She kind of makes my world go round.

And if there's one thing I have to do, it's show her how much she means to me. The first order of business to accomplish that is to go get something that means a lot to both of us and show up on her doorstep. There's nothing more romantic than that. Right?

When I get there and she lets me in without a word, just steps aside and lets me enter, I know I have one chance and I better not fucking blow this. If I do, I'll always wonder what would have happened if I wasn't such a dumbass.

CHAPTER THIRTY

Ruby

I'M LYING ON my couch, re-watching some TV show I've seen a million times, trying to figure out how to get through to Caleb when the doorbell rings. At first I ignore it, not wanting to disturb my brooding, but then I hear his voice.

"Red?" It's unsure and soft as he knocks on the door this time. "I know I don't deserve for you to let me in, but I'm asking you to. Please?"

For a moment I think about ignoring him, I think about letting him sit out there and sweat. Give him the same type of reaction he's given me, but I realize quickly one of us has to be the bigger person. That person is me, because I know he's hurting and I know he's dealt with the situation he's been thrust into the best way he knows how.

Opening the door, I stand there with my arms crossed. Until I see what he's carrying in his hands.

The ugliest looking cupcakes I've ever seen in my life.

"I finally realized why he made them, even though they looked like shit," he gives me a slight smile. "It's the thought that counts, and the selflessness that he knew I'd hate them because of what they looked like. He did it because he loved me, and he wanted to try and make me happy."

Tears are already pouring from my eyes, as I step back and

let Caleb in.

A little while later, we've moved to the bedroom. We're laying with my head on his chest, and while it feels good to be wrapped up in his arms, I'm feeling anger. He did fuck up, it did hurt, and I'm not over it yet. We lay with one another, comforting each other against whatever it is that's bothering us. It's a familiar place to be, but now it's been slightly tainted by the way he's acted.

"I know I've broken your trust, Ruby, because I didn't let you be there for me, but I want to prove to you I'm worthy of it now."

I hear what Caleb is saying, and while I'm willing to give him a free pass on what happened after the shooting, it doesn't mean that I'm not still upset with him. It hurts, to know that he didn't trust me, and yeah in a way, my trust is broken now too. "Caleb..." I let the word fall off because I don't know how to explain, don't know what I can say to change it.

"No, I get it. I hurt you when I didn't need to. Instead of coming to you for help, I pushed you away, and then I gave you mixed signals. I fucked up, I fucked up in a big way."

The frustration and anger seeps over. I fold my arms across my chest, fix him with a stare, and let him have it. "I told you I'd be here for you. I'm glad you're here now and I want to help you. What I don't want is for you to just think that when things get hard, you can be a fuck face, say you're sorry, make me cupcakes, and all will be forgiven. That's not how this is going to work, babe. I need to know if I put my trust in you again, I won't regret it."

I've said my peace, and he nods, accepting it.

"C'mere." He motions for me to lay on him. "Let me prove you can trust me."

"How?" I'm suspicious as I look down at him, wondering if

he's playing some sort of game. I'm not sure my heart can take it if he is. These last few days have been difficult, at best.

"Give me your hands." He holds his to me, palms up.

For a split second I think about it, but then I place mine in his.

"Brace against me," he instructs.

And that's when I feel him lift me up, propping me with his hands and feet in the air. "Caleb you know I'm scared of heights." The fear is making my heart pound, even though I'm literally inches away from him.

"I know, Ruby Red, but trust me to make sure you don't fall. Let go and have fun, enjoy the feeling in your stomach and the excitement in your throat."

"More like I'm about to puke on you," I ground out between clenched teeth. I'm scared, shaking, not trusting him to take care of me, not trusting him not to let me fall.

"Relax," he instructs, his dark eyes boring into mine. "Relax and trust me, Red. Please, just trust me."

There's hysterical fear in my body right now, most of it is unfounded. Even if he does drop me, I'm only going to fall off the bed, but the fear is real. It's there. It's a war within myself as I try to determine if I'm going to forgive him. If I'm going to trust him. If anyone had asked me before the incident, I would have said with zero hesitation that Caleb was mine, I was his, and we were going to be together. I thought he believed in me, believed in us, but he threw all of that into my face, and didn't give a shit.

Another part of me argues that he'd been through a traumatic experience, and none of us ever know how we're going to react when that happens. Maybe he was doing the best he could with what he had, emotionally, and maybe what I'm here to do is be the person who supports him no matter what. Who stands behind him and is strong when he doesn't believe he can be. Who picks him up when he falls down or forgets what he has. Looking inside myself, I wonder if holding the grudge is worth missing out on everything we've shared together. I've given many things to this man that I've never given anyone else, and I'm not about to throw it all away, because times got a little rough.

Decision made, I close my eyes, relax, and trust him. I feel like I'm flying as he props me up on him, holding me with his palms against mine. "I trust you," I whisper.

He holds me aloft for a few seconds, then rolls me over in his arms. "Thank you." He holds me tight, wrapping his arms around me, burying his face in my hair. "I'm so fuckin' sorry, Ruby. So sorry that I couldn't get out of my own head." His voice is hoarse as he finally...fucking finally spills his guts.

"I felt like shit, ya know? Like there was some way I could have prevented what happened, if I would have done something differently." His voice is deep as he talks. "It was my first kill." There's tears in his eyes. "All the other guys on the team, they have that military experience, but all I did was ROTC in college. I didn't go to war, I didn't know what it was like to end a human life. It's a lot to take in, Red, a lot to forgive yourself for. I couldn't look at myself in the mirror. How could I think you or Kels, or Mom and Dad could look at me?"

"Who got to you?" I ask softly, holding him against me, running my hands up and down his back.

"Morgan. He said some things that make a lot of sense. Dad too. They found out that the guy had threatened suicide by cop before. There was no way he was being taken without a fight. I literally had no choice."

I breathe deeply, so happy that he's forgiven himself. Elated that he's overcome this speed bump that's been hindering us for the past few weeks. At the same time, it scares me even more. There will be a next time, there always is. Will he push me away? Will he let me help? "Promise me," I whisper digging my nails into his shirt, holding him tightly against my body.

"What? What promise do you need?"

"I need you to promise that next time you won't shut me out. Next time you show me, next time you let me see the ugly, the vulnerable. And there will be a next time, Caleb, in your line of work, we both know that. You can show me the anger too, but not to push me away, to let it out. I can take whatever you have to throw at me. I'm not letting you go, and I don't run away that easily."

His brown eyes cloud, when he puts a hand to my face, cupping my cheek. I turn into the caress, kissing his palm. "I forgot that some people do stick around when things get tough."

"Most people do, and you can count on me to always be one. Love doesn't mean you're around when everything's perfect. Love means you see the ugly, you comfort the hurt, and you fix the broken. Love isn't always easy and it's not always beautiful, but that's what makes it worth it."

"I don't deserve you, Red. As much as you lost your trust in me, I flat out didn't trust you."

I fight back the tears that are threatening to fall. "I forgive you, and that's all that matters."

He moves his hands around to the nape of my neck, pushing our foreheads together. "The whole time, the only thing running through my head was *I never told Ruby I love her*, even after eight months together, I never told you. I wanna tell you now, I don't want you to ever doubt it."

My face is breaking apart in one of the biggest smiles I've ever had. "I love you, Ruby Red, you're my everything."

"You're my everything too, don't ever forget that."

And as we lie there with one another, I let all the tears fall, let all the hurt go, and look forward to what the future holds for us.

CHAPTER THIRTY-ONE

Ruby

September

BACK WHEN I bought this dress so many months ago, I had assumed I would wear it for Valentine's Day, but because of Caleb's schedule we were never able to make a special date work. He never did take me to that dinner, but we've had so many other special moments that I truly can't complain. Tonight, however, I'm thrilled to be wearing this dress to watch him get an award for bravery.

"You look absolutely gorgeous." He comes up behind me in the mirror as I'm applying a layer of lipstick.

"You don't look so bad yourself." I turn around in his arms, helping to straighten his dress uniform.

I don't think Caleb has ever looked as hot as he does right now. There's something about him being so buttoned-up that I'm loving. "It's cutting off my circulation." He pulls at the fabric around his neck.

"You're fine." I slap his hands away. "Are you nervous?"

"Not really," he says with a shake of his head. "Nerves was playing for the college football championship. This is more anxious than anything. What if someone thinks I don't deserve this award?"

"Then they'll have to deal with me." She gives me a grin.

"Nobody's gonna talk shit about the man I love."

"Don't I know it? I think you've become my most vocal supporter, even more vocal than Mom and Kels."

The blush covers her cheeks and neck. It's the one I love. The one that says she's embarrassed, but not really. "I'm sorry."

"Don't be." I lean in, kissing her. "I appreciate you looking out for me. I love that you will do whatever it takes to defend me. You're one of a kind, Ruby Red."

Her eyes glaze over and immediately a frown comes to my face. "What's wrong?"

"There was a time last month when I wasn't sure if you'd ever call me Ruby Red again, hell I wasn't sure if you'd actually even see me again."

"I was stupid," I assure her. "There was so much shit rolling around in my head, that I couldn't figure out what was real and what was noise. It took talking to family, friends, and the work appointed therapist, but I'm good now. I'm over whatever it was holding me back. You're never going to get rid of me."

"Good." She grins. "There's no way I'd ever want to."

"Now, we've gotta get this show on the road, if we're going to make it in time."

Ruby

PROUD DOESN'T EVEN begin to describe how I'm feeling as I watch Caleb accept his award from Holden. There's not a dry eye at our table between me, my mom, Karina, and Kelsea. I guess they were smart to sit most of the women together.

I watch as he's interviewed by the local news station, and then the newspaper before he comes back over to join us. "You did so good up there," I whisper, leaning in to kiss his neck. "I love you."

"Love you too, Red."

I'm still not used to him saying the words to me, but every time he says them they seem more real. As a few more officers line up to receive their awards, Caleb puts his arm around my shoulders and leans back, enjoying the rest of the ceremony.

"We're hosting a little get together," Holden says as the group stands together after the ceremony is complete. "If anyone wants to come hang out with us."

Caleb and I look at one another, I don't know what his plans are, but judging by the look in his eyes, he doesn't want to hang out with his friends from work.

"Nah, we got plans," he answers. "Thanks, though."

Cruise

"WHERE ARE WE going?" Ruby asks as she sits in the passenger seat of my Jeep.

"You'll see," I deflect the question, hoping that she won't notice where we're headed. Which direction I went in, when I got on the interstate and just how long we've been driving and talking.

Luckily for me, she doesn't, until we pull up to the gate. "Caleb, isn't this where they practice?"

"Yeah," I answer as we look at Alabama's summer practice field. I still have some connections from when I played here, and for some just the mention of my name can get me exactly what I want. "It's where I practiced too."

"What are we doing here?" She gets out when I come around to her side of the Jeep, opening her door.

"Little fantasy I've always had." I shrug. "And you in that dress tonight, is giving me so many ideas."

"Fantasy?"

"Yeah." I let a smile play at the corners of my lips. "There was this thing all the seniors did, but I never got to do, because I didn't have a girlfriend at the time, or really any girl I trusted to bring out here."

"What kind of thing?" She raises an eyebrow in my direction.

I hold her had as we walk toward the locker rooms, using a key that was given to me to enter. Above the lockers, there are names, along with seats to sit on. I glance around, memories coming back to me as I think about the four years I spent here. The good times, the tough times, the times I wanted to give up. It hits me square in the chest that those four years aren't any different than these last five on the MTF. Life will always be trying to knock you down in some way or another, it's up to you if you want to keep standing tall or not.

When my gaze lands on what was my locker, I tilt my head toward it. "Every senior player brought their girlfriend out here to christen their locker for luck, before the season started."

She giggles as she looks at me like I've lost my mind. "Are you serious?"

"Dead."

"But this isn't your locker anymore."

"Nope, looks like we'll be giving Walker, whoever that is, a free round of good luck for his season."

She bites that full bottom lip. "Why is this such a thing for you?"

I pull her into me. "I think I've proven to you just how much I like sex that's risky, and back then, this was as risky as it got. Had I known you back then? We would have been here the first day of spring practice."

It looks like she's thinking about it, wondering if I'm telling her the truth or not. "Trust me, we would have done it more than once."

"More than once?"

"Oh yeah." I run my hand along the slice of skin that's visible at her mid-section. "Any chance we would have gotten. I would have shown you the stamina a running back has."

"Well then, when you throw down a challenge like that?" She takes her top off, throwing it in my direction. "How can I say no?"

I watch as she steps out of her skirt before I grab her around the waist, pulling her up against me, carrying her over, before I tilt her chin to look at me. "Easy, Ruby Red. You can never say no to me, just like I can't say no to you."

When I dip my head, running my tongue along the flesh that's exposed over the top of her bra, all I hear is her whispered, "Yes."

"See? Never say no…"

CHAPTER THIRTY-TWO

Ruby

"WHERE ARE YOU taking me?" I watch as Caleb drives through the streets of downtown. This fall night is cool as rain falls from the sky. It's not sheets like the day he shot the armed man, but a steady drumming against the roof of the Jeep.

"You'll see." His deep voice has a secretive lilt to it, one that I've come to know well in the year we've been together. He's not great at keeping secrets, but when he does, they're the best kind.

As he turns in front of The Café, I grin. No matter what's happened inside the building or in front of it, this is still one of our favorite places to go, to be. On any given night, we can walk inside and find any number of friends or family inside. It's darkish in there tonight, but I figure maybe the electricity is flickering because of the rain storm we're in. Earlier in the day, the school had lost power.

He snags a parking spot near the door. "Don't touch the door, I'll come around for you. I don't want you get wet."

Since the first night I met him, he's been a gentleman. I mean, don't get me wrong, he can be pretty demanding too, but no one has ever taken care of me like Caleb does. He comes around to my side of the Jeep, holding his jacket over our heads as we make a dash for the front door.

As we enter, I realize there's something off about what we've walked in to. Typically The Café is almost so loud you have to speak with some bass to be heard, and the tables are usually jam-packed. Taking a look around tonight, I notice the only people here are our friends and family. People who have come to mean a lot to us in the year we've been together. People we've made memories with.

My parents and brother, Caleb's parents, and Kelsea sit in one booth. Behind them Morgan, Brooks, and Trinity look at us, small smiles on their faces. In all the other booths I see members of the Moonshine Task Force and their families, as well as a few of the teachers I'm friends with and roommates from college. I have no idea how they all came to be here tonight, or why they even are, but I do have an idea that Caleb is probably behind it.

"What's going on?" I whisper to Caleb as everyone watches us walk to the middle of the room. We're the center of attention, and it makes me a little self-conscious, but I also want to know what's going on.

"Nothing." He shakes his head, as he leads me to the table.

It's almost like everyone is holding their breath as they watch us, and it makes me nervous. But I trust Caleb, with everything I have. We've been through a lot together. There's no one I trust more than him, and no one I want to do life with more than him.

"You remember this table?" he asks quietly when we get to the middle of the room. It's the one I sat at while I listened to that awful date of mine make disparaging remarks about me.

Glancing around, I'm hit with a flashback of the first night we met. Giving him a huge smile, I nod. "I do."

Cruise

"MORGAN AND I were sitting right there–" he points to where his parents and mine sit. "–when Leigh came over to us and told us the couple sitting right here–" he touches the Formica top with his finger "–weren't having a good night. That the girl seemed scared out of her mind, and the guy was creeping even Leigh out. I kinda thought maybe Leigh was overreacting, because that's kind of what she does, but then I listened."

"Hey!" Leigh yells. Whatever else she says is muffled as Holden pulls her to him, covering her mouth up with the palm of his hand. I laugh, thankful as hell I did listen.

"I remember." She puts her arms around my waist, tilting her head as she looks up at me. "He really was creepy," she says loud enough for everyone to hear. "I was eating our appetizer like I hadn't eaten it weeks, just trying to choke it down to get out of the situation. At one point, he looked at me, and told me at least I could swallow."

She makes a face, looking around at all the people who have gathered. There's a sound in the room as everyone gets offended for her, at least the people old enough to realize what he'd meant.

"Then the jerk made a comment about knowing where she lived because he'd picked her up, and how he was going to invite himself in." I pick up the story. "At that point, I knew I had to step in."

She giggles. "I remember him pulling up a chair, and when I glanced over I was in shock. I'd never seen a guy as gorgeous as you, hot stuff."

"That's right, eat your heart out." I give a wink as I look around. Moving my hands up from her waist, I cup her jawline. "But I'd honestly never seen anyone as beautiful as you. And it

219

pissed me off that this guy was scaring you and didn't realize what he had sitting there right in front of him. I knew pretty quickly that I wanted you in my life."

"You did?" she asks softly, almost as if she doesn't believe I knew almost immediately, and I can tell why she wonders. It took me forever to tell her my feelings. But that was more me than it ever was her.

"I did." I lean down kissing her lightly on the lips. "Then the months of amazingness came, and I wondered what I'd done to deserve it, waited for the bad thing – whatever it was going to be – to happen. Because, babe, with me, there's always something right around the corner."

I hear sniffles in the room, can see tears in Ruby's eyes, and I know she's thinking back to the summer. How I pushed her away, how I was a fucking asshole, just trying to cope with the bullshit that was handed to me. "But you didn't leave me, Ruby Red. You kept fighting for me, for us. It wasn't long after that, I knew you were the one."

"It took that long?" She pinches my arm as everyone laughs through their tears.

"I knew it before then, but it took me longer to admit it. Sometimes, I'm slow. You know this."

She leans in, kissing my jawline. "Doesn't matter, Caleb, I love you just the way you are."

My heart pounds in my chest so loudly I'm surprised she and everyone around, doesn't hear it. "You do love me. Anyone who didn't, wouldn't have been able to put up with me for those weeks while I did everything I could to push you away." I swallow roughly. "They wouldn't have stayed, they wouldn't have listened to the shit I spewed and still kept coming back for more."

"Caleb…"

"No." I put my finger up to her lips. "Let me finish. You're the strongest woman I know besides my mom, it takes a strong woman to love me. For all my goodness, I have a lot of faults. For all my strengths, baby, I have a ton of weaknesses. But with you beside me, they don't cripple me. Not like they used to. I've learned that instead of pushing you away, I need to lean on you. That when I'm not strong, you are. When I'm faced with a mountain of self-doubt, you're right there beside me when we scale it, go over it, and conquer that bitch."

She laughs, as does everyone else. It makes me feel like I'm doing a good job, and I'm not fucking this completely up.

"You love me, you love my sister, and that means more to me than anything in this world. I waited a long time for her, as you've come to know." I grin. "But I've waited even longer for you, Ruby Red. I didn't know it, didn't realize it, but everyday we're together I'm reminded of what my life could be like without you. I smile so much now, I laugh, I get this fluttery feeling in my stomach and chest when I see you."

"I get it too," she whispers, standing up on tiptoe to kiss the dimple in my cheek. "Every time I see that strut you have, the swagger, the attitude. Every damn time."

"You're beautiful, and you're too good for me, but I don't want to ever let you go, don't think I ever can let you go." I lean my forehead into hers, closing my eyes as I breathe deeply.

It takes a lot of courage to bare yourself in front of your friends and family, in front of the woman you want to spend the rest of your life with. But I'll do it anytime I need to for the woman whose forehead touches mine. Taking a big inhale, I remove my forehead from hers, reach into my pocket for the ring, and take a knee in front of her.

The whole place loses it, as does she. There's already tears streaming down her face, and fuck it, I'm feeling choked up too.

This is the culmination of a lifetime of not feeling like I'm good enough, and I'm about to ask this woman if I truly am good enough for her. There's a chance she could say no. I don't think she will, but there's always a fucking chance. I push that thought out of my head and forge on with what I want, more than anything.

"Ruby Red, will you do me the absolute privilege of letting me take care of you the rest of your life? You can take care of me too." I bite my lip, trying to hold back the emotion. It's threatening though, threatening to break free and show everyone just how much this woman means to me. "We can do this thing you've taught me – ya know? Take care of each other. We can wake up together every day, go to sleep together most nights – when Havoc doesn't have me working night shift."

The guys laugh, and so does she.

"But more than anything, I'll have a partner. We can eat junk food, watch stupid TV, walk in the rain, and do everything either of us have ever wanted to. Bonus is we don't have to do it alone."

She leans down, caressing my face. "You're never gonna be alone again, hot stuff."

"Do life with me? Be my best friend? Be the amazing mom to my kids I know you'll be? Marry me?"

"Yes!" she screams loudly as she launches herself at me, knocking me to my back on the floor.

I close my arms around her, holding her tightly to me, whispering so many words, I don't even know what they are. She's straddling my waist, kissing my neck, mouth, every piece of skin she can get to. I'm kissing her too, giving her everything she's giving me. Eventually as everyone surrounds us, they pick us up, and I put the ring on her finger.

Eventually I feel someone tugging at my waist. I look down

and see Kels. "Yeah?"

She reaches up, hugging me tight. I pick her up, so that I can hear her above all the noise. Ruby comes to us. With a huge smile on Kels face, she says what I'm sure she's wanted to say a long time. "Told you both you were gonna get married, and now she really is going to be my sister!"

A while later, Dad pulls me aside. "How does it feel?"

I look up at him, because he's still a little taller than me. "Just like you said it would. It feels good to be wanted."

"You'll never know what it's like to be alone again." He hugs me tightly.

And I realize he's right. What my mom did to me, didn't define me. It never has, and with Ruby Red by my side, I'm never going to feel like the kid who wasn't good enough again.

As I walk over to her, scooping her up in my arms, twirling her around, Leigh brings out the food she's prepared. I realize this is the beginning of my journey. It's not the end, not the middle.

This is where Caleb Harrison beats the odds and becomes the man he's always been meant to be.

EPILOGUE

Cruise

Five Years Later

"MOLLY'S ASLEEP." I press my wife up against the door to our bedroom, spreading open-mouth kisses along her neck as we grind against one another. Pulling back, I push my hands up her tank top, palming her breasts, moaning as I feel her nipples peak against her bra. "I paid Kelsea her stupid-ass babysitting fee, she's gone. We're alone." I can hear the annoyance in my voice. It's been an on-going argument between the two of us, how I'd watched her for free as a kid, and now she charges us.

We've been out with friends and family, had a DD, and both of us have had a little too much to drink. Her with the margaritas she likes to indulge in with the ladies, and me with the whiskey Morgan and I were shooting straight with my dad.

"God, I want you." She rakes her nails across my neck, down my back, and fists my shirt in her hands.

I want her too. Molly is three now, born within the first two years of us getting married, and we've finally got this parenting thing down. But for the last few years, we've been winging it, quickies while she's napping, weekend fuck fests when we can both get the time off and grandparents are willing to take her, but all of it is planned. There's really no spontaneity anymore, except tonight. This right here, is the most spontaneous we've been since we brought Molly home from the hospital. It's not planned, set aside time to be with one another. It's this crazy passionate moment where she's been teasing my cock all night, and as soon as the bedroom door had shut, I couldn't wait to get my mouth and hands on her, cock inside her.

"Fuck, I want you too," I moan as I finish pushing the tank top up and over her head. My hands are clumsy as I pull down the lace cups of her bra, those tight nipples calling to me, making my mouth water as I lean my head down and take first one, then the other deep, twirling my tongue around them. When I lean back to admire my handiwork, I see the evidence of the moisture of my mouth there, bringing my thumbs up to worry the nubs into even harder points.

"Damn it, I ache for you." She's pushing her core hard against my cock.

I haven't been this drunk in a long time, and all I know is I want to fuck. It's the only thing I want to do when I get this far gone. "I ache for you too." I hold her against the door with one hand, while with the other I tear at my belt, push my boxers down, and free my engorged dick. "Shit, that feels better." I lick the palm of my hand, bringing it in between her thighs, where the only thing covering her is a short skirt, and some skimpy as fuck lace panties. My girl knew what she wanted tonight when she got dressed.

"Really, Red? Lace bra and panties? Were you horny? Did you want to tempt me? Is that why you couldn't keep your hands off me under the table tonight?"

Her head falls back against the door, a loud bang, that I pray to God doesn't wake up our daughter. "Yeah." She thrusts against my fingers. "I need you, hot stuff, need you so bad."

When I push inside her, throwing my head back, because

every time with her is always like the first time, she gasps loudly.

"Babe, do you have a condom?"

What the fuck? "No, we're married. What the hell Ruby?"

"I'm late in getting my birth control renewed. You know, with us having two more-than-full-time-jobs, a child, life. I don't have an appointment until the end of next month."

But that doesn't stop her from grinding on my length. "You keep doing that, and there's no chance in hell I'll be able to pull out," I groan loudly, wrapping my forearms around her thighs, as I walk us over to the bed, throwing her down as I climb on top of her, and really give my hips room to work.

"Feels so good." She claws at my shirt, fisting it as she pulls it off my body, running her hands along my chest, tweaking my nipples how I like it.

"Fuck, Red." I'm trying to keep it together here, but she's not making things easy. She's thrusting against me, and I'm pushing into her, the bed is hitting against the wall, and neither one of us are caring about the noise we're making. That's when I feel it, the tingle in my lower back. Separating from a kiss that's out of control, I pant. "Gotta stop, babe, we need to stop. I'm gonna come." I try to prevent my dick from pushing inside her, try to pull away. I give it a valiant effort, but at the last second, she thrusts up. "Gotta come." And right as I feel my cock pulse, she encloses me with her wet heat. "Fuck," I groan out for more reasons that one, as she trembles around my body, holding me tightly.

Long minutes later, we're still lying connected, each panting as we try to get our breath back. "I tried," I breathe into her neck. "I love you, so I tried."

"I know." Her breath tickles the skin of my ear as she giggles in that way tipsy people do. "I don't think the timing was right anyway. I've only been without birth control for a week or so, it's probably still in my system. We're good, hot stuff. Either way, I love you for trying."

Ruby

A Few Weeks Later

"BEFORE I GIVE you the prescription. is there any chance you could be pregnant?" My OB/GYN asks as I sit in her office, having already done all the other examinations I need to get my birth control refilled.

"No," I answer, but then that super-hot night where Caleb and I didn't use anything comes to the forefront of my mind. "Wait, yes. There was one time, a week after my birth control ran out, but I figured it'd still be in my system, and it was only once," I shrug. "Although I haven't had a period since then, and I have been feeling a little off the past few days, I just figured it was stress."

"Once is all it takes," she laughs. "Let me go ahead and take some blood. We'll run the test, call, and let you know."

Sitting in the chair, waiting to have my blood drawn, is the most nerve-wracking experience ever. Molly had been planned; we'd gone into it with the decision we wanted a baby, had bought a house in preparation of her coming, not too far from either one of our parents' and had done it by the book. This is giving me anxiety. This, if it turns out to be positive, has not been planned. As I get up from the chair, I'm a little dizzy, causing me to sit back down for a minute while they wrap my arm with gauze. "I haven't eaten today," I explain when they look at me funny.

When I leave, I head straight for The Café, where Caleb and I are meeting for a rare lunch date. As I walk in and look around for my husband, I'm struck with how hot he looks sitting in the booth, Molly sitting on his lap, him holding his phone, so they can watch something. He's got his chin resting on her head, and they're engrossed in whatever it is. Fuck he's hot when he's being such a good dad. As I get closer, his head lifts, and the smile that spreads across his face makes my heart pound faster. Getting up out of the booth, he carefully sets Molly down, before meeting me and wrapping his arms around me.

"Hey, Red, what's with the arm?" I kiss him softly before we snuggle into the booth together, sitting next to one another. "By the way, I already ordered for you."

That's the good thing about having a husband that knows you so well. He knows what you like, when you're freaking out, and when something is going on. The waitress comes, dropping off a water for me with lemon. I offer her a smile, before I turn to my husband.

"They had to do blood work."

Immediately, those brown eyes of his are worried. "Something wrong?"

Looking around, to make sure none of our families are here, I lean in. "I had to take a pregnancy test. Ya know, because of that night?"

"Shit, it was once, I mean that doesn't happen, right?"

"Karina said it happened for her and your dad." I push my hand through my hair. "It wouldn't be an awful thing, I've been thinking about it." I hook my arm into his elbow. "Granted it wasn't planned like Molly, but if it happens, it happens."

EIGHT MONTHS LATER as I'm holding my son, Levi, in my arms waiting for my in-laws and Molly to come meet him, I glance up at my husband and smile.

"Are you happy, Red?" He leans down, pushing the blanket back from Levi's face.

"Very! Tired, but happy."

When the door opens and they walk in, Molly slowly makes her way over, before I reach out with my hand, smiling at her. She smiles back at me, the same smile her dad has. "Come meet your little brother," I encourage her, glancing at her "Big Sister" shirt.

Caleb stands next to his dad, the two of them patting each other on the back. Mason folds his arms over his chest. "What did y'all end up naming him?"

"Levi Mason Harrison," he says the words like they're no big deal, but when we get to his middle name, Mason and Karina gasp, and I can feel the emotion in the room.

My husband looks at his dad. "A strong name for my son that matches the strongest man I know."

As I watch them embrace and hand Levi over to Kelsea, I reach down to my phone and take a picture.

Two men, thrown away by one woman, who overcame every obstacle to be the amazing people they are today. If that's not a testament to love, I don't know what is.

In this moment, Caleb and Mason Harrison, they set the bar for this baby held in his aunt's arms, and they show Kelsea who real men are. And the one on the left who wears the ring I put on his finger? He shows me loyalty, compassion, and the love of a great man every day.

If anyone asked me to describe him?

Caleb Harrison. Good man, wonderful father, and the greatest love of my life.

The End

Go here for a bonus Cruise scene!
bookl.ink/CruiseDLScene

The MVP Duet featuring Slater "Savage" Harlow is next!

On the DL – July 20th
MVP – August 3rd

SNEAK PEEK OF
ON THE DL

PROLOGUE

Savage

March

MY GAZE IS intensely focused, watching as the pitcher on the mound of dirt checks the runner on first base, and then throws a fast ball towards home plate. Me and him? We've faced each other twenty times, and I'm batting about fifty percent. He's one of the few in the league that's stumped me.

When he rears back to throw again, I take my practice swing, imagining the bat connects with the leather covered baseball, that it goes over the fence, and I've defeated one of my foes. Instead, my teammate strikes out to the annoyance of every fan behind me.

"Batting third, Center Fielder, Slater "Savage" Harlowe!"

The roar of the crowd is deafening. I'm a fan favorite, and have been since I was called up from the minors. Even in spring training, people come to see me. It's not cocky when it's the truth, and I'm the real fuckin' deal.

When I get to the batter's box, my eyes connect with his. Every single person I face when my feet plant in the dirt, I stare down. There's no way in hell I want any of them to know they intimidate me. The first pitch is a ball, second is a strike, and the third one is a fuck up on his part. It's huge as it comes to me, in what seems to be slow motion. As I situate my body to send this ball over the fence, I plant my foot down and turn into the swing. As I do, my cleat catches on something, chances are, I'll never know what.

Instead of feeling the vibration of the bat making contact with the ball, I hear a loud popping and feel an explosion of pain in my right knee. It's a kind of pain I've never felt before. Which is saying something, I've played injured more often than I care to admit. I fall to the ground, holding my knee as the bat drops, and the crowd silences.

The trainer runs out, making me release my leg. "Let me see, Slater, let me get a good look at it."

I'm rolled to my back, as I feel them manipulating my limb, I open my eyes wide, looking up at the cloudless sky. I'm gulping deep breathes of air, trying to calm the pounding of my heart, the pain radiating through my entire body. The day has been picture-perfect, until this moment and when I hear the trainer's words.

"Slater, I think you have a torn ACL, we're going to transport you to the hospital to get your checked out."

Just like that, the picture-perfect day, and my second MVP season in a row, is over.

CHAPTER ONE

Malone

May

ROLLING OVER IN my childhood bed, I reach over, grabbing my phone off the nightstand. Three months ago I was one of the most sought-after entertainment journalists in the world. My phone was never quiet, I always had at least thirty messages at a time.

Until the great fuck over.

I call it the great fuck over, because there was a concentrated plan by three people at the company I worked for, who'd conspired to get me fired. Spoiler alert – they succeeded.

Judging by the empty cell phone I have, I'm not sure I'll ever have a job again, at least one in the field I love so much.

"Malone! Time to get up!" My Mom yells from the kitchen.

Oh yeah, did I mention I've had to move back home? As in with my parents. Back to Willow's Gap, Georgia. A small town that holds too many memories? The last few months have been hard, but the last two days? They've been the absolute worst. Every turn of this town reminds me of something I'd rather forget.

"I'm up, I'll be down in a few," I yell back to her.

She's trying to keep me from being depressed, by making sure I get up and do something every day. While I understand her intentions, I would really appreciate a few days to lick my wounds. I'm mourning the loss of life I know it. All the cool stuff I got to do, when I lived in Los Angeles.

Now I'm not sure I'll ever be able to do any of that stuff again.

"YOU'VE GOTTA GET out there," Mom is saying as I sit at the kitchen table, eating a piece of toast with her homemade strawberry jelly on it. "At least get some applications in. With the summer season coming up, people will be hiring, and beggars can't be choosers," she reminds with the raise of an eyebrow.

She's saying it without really saying it. I have bills to pay, and if I don't get off my ass, I'll be stuck not only living with my parents but having my car repo'd and my credit completely trashed.

"I'm going to," I sigh, taking a drink of my coffee. "Today I'm going to."

"Del's is hiring," she hands me a piece of bacon.

I most definitely won't be working at Del's Diner. Too many memories. From the greatest to the worst ever. "I'll look into it," I tell her, just to pacify this situation. "I'm gonna head down-town and see what's going on."

"I love you, Malone. I just want you to not let this break you. Not like last time."

And here we go. "Mom, I lost the love of my life last time I broke. This is a job. Not the person I was going to spend the rest of my days with." Somehow, it still hurts talking about it. Even though I was a teenager the last time I left small-town Georgia.

"He's back in town, ya know?"

"I'd have to be living under a rock to not know that," I take a snapping bite of the bacon. It had been national news when Slater tore his ACL, and for a few weeks, no one had left him alone. Even though I've tended to be able to ignore stories about him since we broke up, this one I'd read. A part of me wonders who's taking care of him. Probably some chick with fake tits and lip fillers.

"He's at his momma's," she continues. "Going to physical therapy when he has to, the family is driving him around."

"Good to know he's still got them," I take a drink of my coffee, staring off into space. "His girlfriend probably stayed behind in Birmingham."

She snorts. "Malone girl, you got a lot to learn. For most of your life you've made a lot of assumptions, and I think having to come home and face the truth, is gonna be the best thing that's ever happened to you."

I have nothing else to say, so I set my cup down. "Guess I should get moving on finding a job. See ya later, Mom," I lean down, kissing her on the cheek. "Be back later."

As I step out onto the front porch, I take a deep breath, and hope that not everyone in this town has the same opinion of me she does.

Savage

"WANT YOUR USUAL?" Stephanie, the morning waitress at Del's asks as I have a seat in the booth I've proclaimed as my own. She and my Mom are friends, they went to school together, and while my parents were married. Stephanie started a job here, that she's never quite given up. The people of this town though, we love her to death.

"Hell yes, I'm starving," I rub my stomach with the palm of my hand.

"You're always starving," she gives me a grin.

"Because I always come in here after going to physical therapy. They work me hard," I remind her.

Sinking into the booth, I put my leg up, sighing as it's finally allowed time to rest. The PT I'm going through is hard, but it's what I'll have to do if I want to be able to play professional baseball again.

"You want me to double your order?"

"Why not?" I shrug. It's an omelet and I'm definitely losing more calories than I'm putting back in. I've lost ten pounds since the injury, and I can't afford to lose much more. "Add some bacon and sausage to it."

"Will do," she sets a coffee and a water in front of me.

Glancing around the room, I nod at the group of older men sitting at a table not too far away from me, before I grab my phone and start checking emails. Even though my season is done, for the most part, I still have appearances I'm hoping to be able to make in a few months, endorsement deals, and paid sponsorships that have to be posted on social media. My agent has promised to keep me in the forefront of fans minds, and I know he will.

Logging onto Instagram, I see that I've been tagged in a multitude of get well posts. It's happened every day since I went down in spring training. Most everyone told me I needed to rehab in Birmingham with team doctors, surrounded by my teammates, but the truth is I needed a break. I know myself and being with the team, while not being able to play, would have driven me insane.

"Here ya go," Stephanie pushes a plate of food in front of me, along with a bottle of hot sauce.

"You know what I like," I give her a smile before I liberally dose the omelet, and move to take a bite.

"She's back, ya know?" Stephanie says right as the fork is situated at my mouth.

"Who's back?"

"Your girl. She rolled into a town a few days ago."

I force myself to put the bite of food into my mouth and chew, before taking a drink of my coffee. "Don't have a girl."

Stephanie laughs. "Sure ya do, and look alive, she's walking in right now."

Over my egg white omelet and the cup of coffee I'm holding in my hand, I see the girl, now woman, who broke my heart all those years ago.

Malone Fulcher. No one's come close, lived up to, or taken her place in my heart since that summer night we both drove away from Williow's Gap and never looked back. As our eyes meet, a film strip of memories replays in my head, and I wonder if this small town is big enough for the both of us.

Thank you so much for reading "Cruise"! If this was your first book of the Moonshine Task Force, I encourage you to look the other's up. "Renegade" is a personal favorite, but this one holds a really special place in my heart! I'm sure Caleb's book will as well!

If there was a part you loved of "Cruise", please don't hesitate to leave a review and let other readers know!

Also, if you do leave a review, please email me with the link so that I can say a personal 'thank you'!!! They mean a lot, and I want to let you know I appreciate you taking the time out of your day!

Email Me
laramie@laramiebriscoe.com

Also, if you find an error, know that it has slipped through no less than four sets of eyes, and it is a mistake. Please let me know, if you find one, and if I agree it's an error. It will be changed. Thank you!

Report an error
laramie@laramiebriscoe.com

CONNECT WITH LARAMIE

Website:
www.laramiebriscoe.net

Facebook:
facebook.com/AuthorLaramieBriscoe

Twitter:
twitter.com/LaramieBriscoe

Pinterest:
pinterest.com/laramiebriscoe

Instagram:
instagram.com/laramie_briscoe

Substance B:
substance-b.com/LaramieBriscoe.html

Mailing List:
sitel.ink/LBList

Email:
Laramie@laramiebriscoe.com

CHAPTER ONE

Tatum

I JERK MY head upright as the roar of a motorcycle breaks through the otherwise peaceful Bowling Green, Kentucky morning. The book on my phone's reading app is forgotten as I put a hand to my chest and cut my gaze directly across from Cash's Customs, the body shop specializing in foreign makes and models I work at. Walker's Wheels, which specializes in domestic vehicles and motorcycles, is my dad's shop, and the man leaving the parking lot is the one who pissed me off a year ago. In all honesty, he's still pissing me off. I glare at his leather-jacket covered back as he rides down the street. Pissed off because he ruined my concentration, I try not to think about how the guttural sound of the engine mimics the way he moaned when he came. Remembering our interlude in the garage of the Heaven Hill Clubhouse does nothing but make me angry – angry that things aren't different than they are right now.

"It's been a year Tatum, you ever gonna talk to him again?"

My eyes roll by themselves as I shift my weight to one hip. Leaning back against the counter with my other, I shoot a glare at my boss. Cash Montgomery has been fair to me, but this question? Makes me purse my lips and roll my eyes heavenward, letting out a huge sigh to go along with it.

"You think I should just because he's your brother?"

He shakes his head, running a hand over his scruffy jaw. "I'm just a guy who knows that guys screw up, and I'm wondering if maybe you aren't overreacting."

"Overreacting?" I spit the word out like it's on fire. "You have no idea what went down with us last January. Boss, friend, and his brother, or not, you should probably shut the fuck up."

It was still embarrassing, the way we'd treated each other. I almost wish he'd left me on the side of the road. For weeks after, I'd cried, trying to figure out where the fuck we'd messed up. How had we gone from this crazy attraction that suffocated a room when we were in it together to me having sex with another guy? I know that part was my fault, and I feel guilty. I wish I could take it back. That part of my personality is a bitch – ya know the one where I have to hurt anyone who hurts me worse? Truthfully, I think I learned my lesson this time.

The words Remy spoke to me still ring in my ears. *Are you proud of yourself?* Even today, they cause goosebumps on my arms, and I rub my hands up and down the flesh to warm it. I hate the way we left things; I would change it if I could. But I can't be hurt again by him, and I don't think I can stand to hurt him, either. No matter how much I've had to harden my heart to him, I know it's the right thing to do. We can't seem to be mature around each other – we get stupid. Not speaking to him is my way to keep my head about me. I know the minute I give in, it'll be like it always was with us. He'll give me that sexy smirk he doesn't give anyone else, be his quiet, brooding self, and I'll be doe-eyed again, wanting to know all the secrets he keeps. Nobody knows how difficult this has been for me. We were good friends. I want to talk to him, I want his opinion on things, and I sure as fuck don't want to have to avoid him at every club get together. We were building something, even if others didn't know it, even if I was the only one willing to put my heart out there. Remington Sawyer has always been a loner – quiet, closed off, and happy to spend time on his own. I wanted to change that, be the person he could be his true self with, but we never got the chance.

"I'm gonna take lunch if that's okay with you."

Cash gives me a grin, and for a moment I'm reminded hardcore of Remy. In looks, they don't favor each other, having different fathers. In mannerisms and smiles, they could be twins. "You're gonna do it whether I say it's okay or not, girl. Go ahead, I need to run by the bakery and pick up something from Harper anyway. Just stick a note on the door saying when we'll be back."

"Will do, see you in about an hour."

I watch as he leaves, then stick a note on the door, giving the lock a turn. When I hear the click, I go to the back of the building and let myself out. Quickly I arm the alarm for the garage and get to my car, cranking up the heat and checking out the gray sky. The clouds are low today, a low-ceiling I've heard it called. Later on in the day, they're calling for rain, and given how cold it is, it might turn into something more.

It's reminiscent of the day last year when Remy and I stopped speaking to one another. I have no desire to relive that day, and stupid me never realized it'd be such a turning point in my life.

Remington Sawyer. I shake my head as I think of the teenager I met when I wasn't even a teenager myself and the man he's become. Even now, I get chills when I think about him. He's an addiction I can't quite kick, one I'm not sure I want to. As much as I want to feel his hand in mine, get more kisses, and generally have him around, the stubborn part of my personality won't allow it. Especially not when he's the one who created the issue by telling me I'm too young for him, thinking I don't know my own mind.

What a fucking joke. I've known my own mind since I was old enough to know what love and sex are. My parents, Liam and Denise Walker, aren't shy when it comes to showing how much they care for each other. I've grown up with a very healthy respect for marriage and sexuality, and I've wanted that with Remy since I realized the thumping of my heart when he's around meant I like him in a way that's not going anywhere anytime soon.

I threw myself at him. Let him take the first orgasm I'd never given to myself at a club party, and then given him the same pleasure before he pushed me away. Talking some shit about him being too old for me and he respected me too much to take my virginity.

"Oh, my virginity." I curl my nose up as I make a left-hand turn at the end of Louisville Road heading for the strip of fast food restaurants, hoping that at least one of them didn't have a line for lunch rush.

Thinking back to the night I gave my virginity to someone else, just to get rid of the obstacle, still causes a pain so deep it makes my chest hurt. Rubbing my hand against my breastbone, I wonder when that pain will go away. Because what happened that night set into motion this face-off between the two of us, and it looks like neither one is willing to give in anytime soon.

And that sucks, because before all of this happened, he'd been one of my best friends, and fuck if I don't miss him. But I have enough friends. Tatum Walker wants a love like her parents, like my brother and sister have with their significant others, like every other member of the Heaven Hill MC has, and

I'm not going to settle until I get it. Never again will I settle. Settling hurts, and I've had enough of that to last a lifetime.

Remy

"IT'S COLD OUT here today," I comment as I enter my sister-in-law's bakery in the Bowling Green downtown district. It's quiet this time of day; most people want sweets in the morning, not so much after lunch, so I have the place to myself.

"You here, Harper?" I yell out, when I don't see her manning the front counter.

"I'm here." She laughs, coming from behind the wall that separates the front area from the private area. She's fixing her hair, and I have to wonder what I've interrupted when my brother comes out from behind her, wiping his mouth of her lipstick.

"Shit, y'all. I'm sorry."

"No, it's okay." Cash gives me a shit-eating grin. "Wrong place, wrong time."

They look at one another, giggling again, and I feel the kick in my chest. That damn loneliness. God, I want what they have so badly. The fact that my brother has been able to find it after the childhood we had gives me so much fucking hope. My problem is that the woman I want it with still won't talk to me. Three hundred and sixty-six days now, to be exact, since Tatum Walker has looked at, let alone spoken, to me.

Oh sure, she's said things when we're in a group together, but it's never directed at me. Never pertaining to anything I talk about or ask. It's as if I'm an invisible entity to her, and I wonder what I'll have to do to get her to see me again. Being invisible to her hurts, taking me back to my childhood when I was invisible to everyone except Cash and Harper. They were the only two people who truly cared about me.

Both of them come out from behind the counter, having a seat at the table nearest me. Taking the hint, I sit down too, waiting for them to speak.

"What brings you by here?"

"Harper, do I have to have a reason to come visit my sister-in-law?"

"Not usually, but you've seemed down the past few weeks. I'm worried about you, kid."

At twenty-seven, I'm not a kid anymore, but everyone still thinks of me as the small boy who toted around an inhaler like a backpack. Still, I can't be rude, not to the two people who've always supported me.

"Just got a lot of shit on my mind."

Cash leans forward on his biceps, letting the table take his weight. "Hey man, you know you can always talk to me, no matter how old you get. I'm always going to be here for you. Nothing changes that, you know?"

"I know, and I appreciate it, but it's shit I don't wanna talk about, to be honest."

"Shit having to do with a certain employee of mine who just told me to shut the fuck up when I asked if she was ever going to speak to you again?"

"Why the fuck did she do that?" I flick a piece of paper off the table. "I swear to God she does stuff just to piss me off."

"No, she does stuff to get a rise out of you," Harper argues.

"What does it even matter when she won't speak to me? I can be yelling in her face, and she won't speak to me, doesn't even act like I'm looking at her."

I hold my hands palms up in a *what the fuck* gesture before I put them back on the table. "I'm at a loss."

Harper turns her chair so that she's looking at me head-on.

"Have you ever wondered if she doesn't talk to you because you're so loud about it? Loud isn't the Remy any of us know. You've never been that type of guy, but I get it. You're frustrated. You want things to go back to the way they were. She's always been one of your best friends. But what happens if you go about it in a way that's not a show? Send her a note? Make a small gesture, one that she'll know is from you."

"I tried texting her."

"Jesus Christ," Harper moans, rolling her eyes. "Texting is so impersonal. Write her a damn note. Use a pen and a piece of motherfucking notebook paper, and let her see you took a minute out of your day to do it. Women want to know you can make time for them, that in the middle of the craziness of everything you've got going on, you're thinking about them. Which is why your brother is here today and almost got lucky in the back."

"Cockblocker." Cash coughs into his hand. I shoot him a glare, trying to remind him we're talking about me here.

"I think about her all the time," I admit softly. The hole she's left in my life is big, one that no one else is ever going to be able to fill.

"Then show her. Don't tell her, *show* her."

The idea has its merits, and I understand what Harper is trying to say, but I wonder if I'm too late.

"What if she doesn't want me anymore?"

Cash chuckles darkly, rapping his nails on the table. "Trust me, she does. The way she watches you across the street every day, she wants you and the relationship you two can have. The guys who try to give her their numbers, that she doesn't take? She's waiting on you bro. Now man up and do something about it."

For the first time in a year, I have a plan.

I'm going to win Tatum Walker back, I'm going to show her what she means to me, and I'm not going to stop until I have her in my arms.

No matter how long that takes.

Made in the USA
Monee, IL
27 January 2020